# KUSAMAKURA *AND* BUNCHŌ

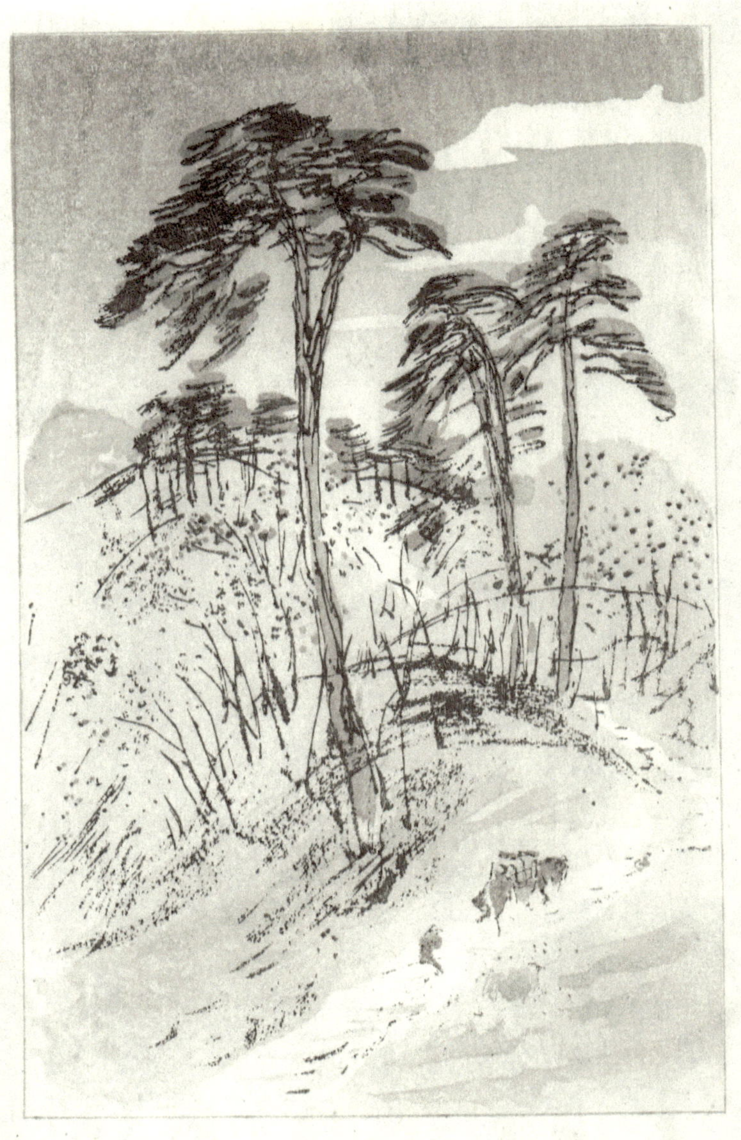

# KUSAMAKURA
## AND
# BUNCHŌ


*By*

SŌSEKI NATSUME

*Translated by*

UMEJI SASAKI

*Illustrated by*

HYAKUSUI HIRAFUKU



ZEA BOOKS

LINCOLN, NEBRASKA

2025

*Kusamakura* (草枕) was first published in Japanese in 1905 and *Bunchō* (文鳥) in 1909.

This English edition was first published in Tokyo by Iwanami-Shoten (Kanda, 1927) and was printed by The Toppan Printing Co., Ltd, Honjo, Tokyo.

Grateful acknowledgement is made to the University of Chicago Library for the loan of their copy, and to the Office of Interlibrary Loan in the University of Nebraska–Lincoln Libraries.

Notes and Appendix in this volume were prepared by Paul Royster.



ISBN 978-1-60962-349-4 ebook
ISBN 978-1-60962-350-0 paperback

# PREFACE

The graceful branches of a zelkowa-tree spread protectingly over the tomb-stone of Sōseki at Zōshigaya cemetery. A century-old crow perched on the highest branch of the tree when I visited the grave yard on the afternoon of the 9th of December, 1923. Very few people visit the grave now. Many do not know or care where his remains lie in peace, and it is well that it is so, for he writes, —

> "O that I were born a violet,
> It is so very tiny!"

"Caw, caw," said the bird, as he came down to a lower branch as though he wanted to talk to me. "What do you want of me, my feathered friend?" I asked him as I looked up towards the bird. "Return!" he seemed to say. "Yes," I answered, "I shall be going home right away." "No!" said the bird as he shook his head. "Dost thou then mean that we have to *return* something at least to the West as we have already borrowed too much from her?" I asked. The bird nodded 'yes'. Then ruffling up his black feathers and fluttering his wings, he flew slowly away across the cemetery to join his companions in the woods beyond.

That evening I took up my pen to translate Sōseki's "Kusamakura," (literally, Grass Pillow or Pillow of Grass), the best known of his works. It took me just three years to finish the translation. Happily would I sit at my desk in the evening to resume the translation after a day's work of teaching was done. As I drew near to the end of the book, I felt rather sad, as one feels when he bids adieu to his friend who is going away to a distant land. Well this might be, for it had been, so to speak, my meat and drink those three years.

What "Beneath the Stars," the English title I have chosen for "Kusamakura," claims to be or wishes to tell is only to be found out by the reader himself, so I shall say nothing about it. I am humble enough to know that mine is not the best translation, and earnestly hope that there will appear some better ones in the future. However, I shall be happy and content if the humble position of a pioneer along the line is accorded me.

Bunchō (Java Sparrow) added in way of an appendix will, I hope, interest some of my readers, for it graphically tells of the daily life of the great novelist at his Waseda home.

Encouragements, either oral or written, have been given me by my friends since I began the work, and my sincere gratitude is due to them. Mrs. Natsume has helped me in more ways than one, and I am very grateful to her. Prof. E. W. Clement has again assisted me so kindly in correcting my manuscripts, and I can send the book out to the general public with much confidence. My thanks are also due to Mr. S. Iwanami of the Iwanami

Publishing House who has very generously consented to publish my translation of "Kusamakura". Those helps and encouragements have enabled me to finish the work and send it forth in respectable book form.

A pale crescent moon hung dim in the western sky when we visited and lingered about the tomb of Japan's Literary Star at Zōshigaya, late in the afternoon of the ninth of December, 1926. What did it suggest? Let posterity tell.

Umeji Sasaki.

January, 5, 1927.

# NATSUME KINNOSUKE SŌSEKI

"A boy born on the day of ko-shin (coin and monkey) will be either a great man or a great robber," so goes a popular belief, "And in order to prevent him from being a great thief, the boy must have the letter kin 金 somewhere in the composition of his name."

The fifth of January (the day of coin and monkey) 1867, was the day on which our future literary star first saw the light of day. In a week, his name was entered by the clerk of the district office as Natsume Kinnosuke, which he bore till his death, Sōseki being the *nom de plume* of the novelist.

A fortnight had hardly passed when the baby-boy was sent out to nurse to a bric-a-brac dealer in Yotsuya whose wife was a sister of the maid-servant who had served long in the Natsume family. "O! Kin-Chan, my dear little thing!" cried the startled sister, who happening one evening to pass the main street of Yotsuya where the poor tradesman had deposited on a stall his old wares to sell, caught sight of her little brother snugly cradled in a bamboo basket, his two little black eyes shooting up to the piping cold December sky. With tears of compassion and love, she snatched the baby from the old couple and carried him away to her home at Kikui-cho, Ushigome.

Soon afterward, however, the child was restored to the foster-parents under whose care the boy lived till three. At the delicate age of four, Kinnosuke was adopted by a certain Mr. Shiobara of Shitaya Ward, who feeling grateful for the happy years of his apprenticeship in the Natsume family had expressed his wish to take the infant to his home and bring him up as best he could. Smallpox was then raging throughout the city and many a child fell victim to the dreadful epidemic. The foster-parents getting very much scared, had their child vaccinated as a preventive against the disease, but the inoculation proved futile, and the little boy had genuine pox, marks of which he carried on and about his nose until he died. The foster-parents were very indulgent to the boy, whose will was always their will. In all things the boy had his own way and in three years he was an incurably spoilt child.

The seventh birthday found him again at his own home in Kikuicho where he behaved as freely and wildly as though he belonged to nobody. The first chapter of *Botchan* well describes how wild, rude, rough and self-willed our little Kin was. The boy was his own king: there was no authority whatever over him; he was an abandoned case to his parents, and his brothers and sisters had not the least control over the unruly little scapegrace. The godown was the only fold in which the enraged father often confined the black sheep of the family.

Though mischievous to the core, the boy was very clever and resourceful. He would not apologize to his father even when he did wrong and was imprisoned in the godown. He would cry out that he wanted to go to the lavatory, and if they refused to open the door, he would soil the floor and everything else. At first the people were deceived and the little rogue went free.

Moreover, he was idle; he never studied, but played all the time. The mother growing very impatient and anxious about her little son, one day took him alone to the godown upstairs and pleaded with him holding out the dagger-point before him. She told him that he and she must die if he would not mend his ways; that she would first kill him and then follow him. The boy had never tasted such bitter medicine before, but it proved good to the stiff-necked boy, and he began to turn over a new leaf.

A decade we have to pass over before we find him hard at work to prepare for the entrance examinations to the University Preparatory Course, afterwards the First National College. These ten years were a series of experiences in the *wilderness* where the young man wandered from one place to another with companions as wild as he. Once Chinese classics became a passion with him and he devoured book after book, thus storing up all the knowledge the language is capable of; this proved to be of infinite value to him in his future literary career.

A man's character increases its strength during a period of obscurity and apparent rest just as land acquires new vigor from lying fallow. This time of his life is to be termed the "Fallow Period." With the return of spring, 1884, our hero fully prepared and equipped sat with others for the entrance examination to the First National

College and was admitted. In July, 1893, he was graduated from the English Literature Department of the University; the new *bungakushi* (B. A.) full of hope and ambition came proudly out of the *Red Gate* into the cold world, all indifferent to him and to his prospects.

It was in August of the same year that Sōseki was first introduced to Sōen, the prior of Engakuji, Kamakura. Esoteric Buddhism had aroused the curiosity of the young scholar: this curiosity deepened into strong desire to inquire into the mysteries of the philosophic religion. For a year or so, he was an earnest votary studying and meditating upon the doctrine of Zen at the temple. The experiences he had during this period are described in his *Mon* (Gate). The secret of the cult is to unite oneself to the universe; this can be accomplished only when one commits oneself to the dictate of Heaven by giving up one's own ego. This thought current pervades all his novels. The "meditation" at Engakuji was an invaluable help to him in his after life both as teacher and man of letters, and the teacher's position in the Peers' School was what Mr. Natsume eagerly tried to obtain at the time. He all but succeeded, but for some reason he was not to go there. It is said that he had had a new morning suit made to order fully anticipating the position as secure, and the writer is not inquisitive enough to inquire into the fate of the doomed clothes. Some of the readers may be curious to ask why he tried the Peers' School above others. I'll tell you. True, he always declared that he disliked an Englishman, but he was a gentleman of pure English type, careful in dress with an inch of a snow-white linen handkerchief peeping out of his breast-pocket. Being a man of decidedly classic stamp, he had greater sympathy with Classicism than with Romanticism and it was quite natural that he wished to enter the society of nobles. Afterward he repented of this mistake and thoroughly became a friend of plebeians. His novel describing the life of a poor miner (Kofu) amply proves this.

Soseki taught at the Higher Normal School, and at the expiration of a year he was down in Shikoku teaching English at Matsuyama Middle School, in the year 1895. The experiences pleasant and otherwise he had had down there were interwoven in the famous novel *Botchan.* This abrupt resignation from the Normal School, a comparatively good position, is suspected to have been caused by a love-affair, the issue of which was unfavourable to the young dandy.

In April, 1896, he was professor of English at the Fifth High School, Kumomoto, and in September of the same year he married Miss Kyōko Nakane who survives her husband.

Mrs. Natsume is a woman of strong character, firm in her belief. She was too often too strong in her convictions to be guided by her intellectual husband. Quarrels they had very often, in which the man of letters was compelled to resort to his superior physical power in order to subjugate his fair antagonist. A minute account of the family turmoils, and what hard times Mrs. Natsume had with her *mad* husband during their married life is given by herself in recent numbers of the Kaizō.

The frank statement of the widow may have shocked some of my young unmarried folks who honestly believed that such a great man as Sōseki could never treat his wife so cruelly, yet they will too soon learn that a good honest blow of the husband is much more acceptable to the wife than a cold-blooded indifferent kiss. Dr. Nitobe in his Bushidō tells us that an Occidental husband kisses his wife in public, but beats her in private, while a Japanese husband acts just contrariwise. A clergyman one day called upon the elderly Bishop Harris and proudly told him that he and his wife had been married thirty years and never had a "row." "It must have been a dull life indeed!" said the bishop. And I sincerely wonder whether the so called *ill treatment* of her husband may not have been a "honey-moon" treatment. It may sound a little bit paradoxical, but he loved her too well not to beat her. Mrs. Natsume gave her husband seven children: two boys and five girls. Fruitfulness was the miraculous issue of their quarrels.

Six miles away from the old town of Kumamoto there lies a small village snugly nestled among the mountains. It bears the name Otemizu where a hot spring has bubbled up from eternity, known as Nagoi Hot Spring in "Kusamakura", although its real name is Yunoura. It was owned by an old gentleman, a retired *samurai* of Kumamoto clan. Sōseki, then a young professor of English at the Fifth High School, spent one summer vacation at the Hot Spring. He was charmed by a beautiful maiden, the old man's daughter known as O-Nami-San in "Beneath the Stars." Enslaved by this-enchantress, the young professor repeated his visit time and again.

"One thousand miles is only one mile to an accepted lover;

To one disappointed a thousand miles are so many miles." Thus sings a popular ballad.

Sōseki was, however, too true a teacher and philosopher to be carried away by the ruling passion and fall a victim to it. He idealized his love in gems of expression in his famous work "Kusamakura". There carnal love was transformed into Platonic love—the love of soul for soul.

In February, 1905, the first instalment of "We are a Cat" took the reading public by storm. Everybody read it: a patrician bought it; a plebeian borrowed it from the circulating library; a student devoured the contents of the novel under his desk, his text books laid aside, and the dull lecture of his teacher passing innocently over his head. Swift's Gulliver's Travels may have suggested to Sōseki the conception of such an unparalleled production, or more probably the old Tom-cat which the Natsumes had kept so long in the family may have furnished the novelist with the unique title, for this domestic animal had been the constant companion of his idle days at his home, Kikui-chō. Every movement of the cat was an object of interest to the young man by whose keen eyes nothing passed unobserved. His mewings, purrings, pawings and ear-twitchings grew intelligible to him, and he believed that mute as it is, the cat is just as intelligent as man or perhaps more.

In the prose satire by the *good hater,* the hero travels through several countries of dwarfs where he notices many a sham among the societies he visits and makes it the target of his venomous arrow — pen. In our Sōseki's work, the hero (the cat) seldom goes out of his home, but always finds himself beside his master Prof. Kushami, whose guests, male or female, he observes with his keen penetrating eyes. An emperor or a king uses the first person plural "We" in referring to himself, and our cat does the same in his remarks as if he were an emperor or a king. Some of the critics seem inclined to believe that Sōseki got hints from Sterne's Tristram Shandy in getting up his satiric novel; others say that he borrowed much from Swift's work in preparing his "Cat", but all these critical speculations are curious rather than essential. Soseki, always among the most original of writers, is nowhere more thoroughly himself than in his charming romance "We are a Cat". Whether we read it, as children do, for the story, or as students of social science, for the social allusions, or as men of the world, for the satire and philosophy, we can not but acknowledge it as one of the most wonderful and unique books of the world's literature.

The publication of this prose satire made his fame and fortune secure. Thereafter his productions were a succession of triumphs. In 1907, he resigned his lectureship at both university and college, and became a member of the editorial staff of the Tokyo Asahi. No man can serve two masters. Being a conscientious man, Sōseki could no longer remain in the place whence his sympathy had already gone. Now that his fame as a literary prodigy had been established, his writings, whatsoever they might be, were eagerly sought for. The cathedral-like study at Minami-chō, Waseda, became the rendezvous of journalists, publishers and students. Many waited impatiently for Thursday to come, as it was his at home day, when admirers and devotees of his gathered around him as the fountain-head at which they could quaff the water of inspiration to their hearts' content.

The second and third volumes of "We are a Cat" were received by the reading public as enthusiastically as the first volume, but the 13th of September, 1908, was an evil day on which the old cat who had made his master Kushami famous died. A post card announcing the death and burial of the poor animal startled his friends and well-wishers and made them mourn over his death very deeply. Here is the translation of the card: —

Sept., 14, 1908.

Dear Mr. N,

The cat upon whom you had lavished your favours had long been ill; every possible means had been used in order to make him well, but all in vain. This morning we found him dead on the old unused oven stored away in the corner of the back-shed. As to the burial, our 'rikisha-man is to attend to it. An orange box will serve as his coffin and the back-yard is where his remains will be interred. You need not come and attend the funeral, as his master is busy writing "Sanshirō."

Yours in haste,
Natsume Kinnosuke.

In the course of eight years, he produced a number of great works such as Gubijinsō, Bungakuron, Sanshiro, Mon, Higansugimade, Kōjin, Kokoro, Michikusa and Meian, the last of which was never finished, as he was taken seriously ill on November 23 and died on the 9th of December, 1915. It is worthy of note that Dickens died with a novel partially written, *Edwin Drood,* as did also Thackeray, who left *Denis Duval* unfinished.

Love and the entire possession of it has been the leading theme of his novels hitherto, but in "Kokoro" we find greater love unfolded which at last culminates in the hero's self-destruction. Here he confesses love is crime; his conscience is smitten with remorse that he has killed his pure innocent friend by taking possession of the young woman whom his friend loved. He tries every means to pacify his conscience; his daily visit to the grave of his friend serves only to deepen his sorrow; he resorts to his books for consolation, but they turn their cold backs upon him; meditation and contemplation will call back the memory of his departed friend. His purgatory proves too severe and too heavy for him to bear, until at last he seeks the expiation of his sins by committing suicide. Reviewing thus, we can distinctly trace the slow, but steady growth of his soul and mentality — from carnal love attended with sensual desire to greater love ending in self-sacrifice on the altar of friendship. Love is great, greater still is friendship.

Sōseki was a man of nice taste; decency or propriety was the motto of his life. He was very particular to wear neat linen. One of his pupils resembles his master in this particular point: his hair is parted according to the latest fashion; he wears a high double collar; even in the street car he seldom takes a seat lest his trousers should lose their crease. This gentleman imitates his teacher in every detail of his toilet.

Friendly as he was to his pupils, Soseki never allowed them to become too familiar with him. He firmly believed there must be a certain boundary line between teacher and pupil, which neither of them can trespass on with impunity. It was while he was giving a series of lectures in the university, that Prof. Natsume noticed one student who sat and listened with *his left hand in his pocket.* Day after day the student did the same, never mending his manners. Offended at the rude behavior of the young man, Prof. Natsume left his desk and coming up to the seat where the impudent rascal was, told him to behave better while listening to his lecture. The poor student blushed, hung his head, but never said a word. The bell rang and the lecturer was about to leave the class-room, when the student came up and told his teacher in a whisper that his left hand had been amputated. Resourceful as he was, Mr. Natsume was very much grieved and stood mute a full quarter of an hour, compassionately looking at the sad face of the poor student.

The artist had spared no labour and skill in painting a portrait of Oliver Cromwell but he considerately left out the mole on his face. On seeing this, the great dictator was much displeased and the poor artist had to work it over again with the *mole.* Would it have displeased our man of letters if an artist had done the same in making his portrait? His eldest son growing very mischievous and naughty would call out "Abata" (pock-marked face) whenever he saw his father. "This little rogue seems to think it a compliment to his dad," he said as he patted the boy on the head.

One day while riding in the street car in London, he was very much worried by the old lady who sat opposite; she grinned as she looked at his face and then at his neighbour's, and our hero was happy to find that his neighbour's face was disfigured by smallpox much worse than his own. Once as he was turning the corner of a street in East London, he caught sight of a small ugly creature full of pock-marks on his face. He paused in sympathy to see him better, but on closer examination discovered it was his own visage reflected from the looking-glass in the shop. Our dandy seemed to believe that he would have been more successful in his love-affairs but for the pock-marks on and about his nose. I greatly doubt it.

Many seem to think it a great honour to be granted a doctor's degree (hakase), while some regard it a disgrace to their true merit. The former belong to the class of people who wish to live in the hearts of the present generation, but the latter are those who desire to live in the hearts of future generations by going through the ordeal of Time. Sōseki's rejection of the degree *Bungakuhakase* conferred by the Department of Education sent a pulse wave of sensation throughout the length and breadth of the Empire. Some criticized his act very severely, regarding it a kind of self-propaganda, while others commended it very highly saying it was a noble inspiring deed. All these anti and pro criticisms passed over the head of this great literary figure like a ripple caused by a passing gale on the surface of the great ocean whose bosom ever remains calm and placid.

> O that I were born a violet,
> A modest little flower.

Gold, rank, fame will not satisfy one; they are trash to him who knows how transitory life is. He would rather be a modest humble violet that blows by the roadside. Sōseki has written over three thousand haiku, and what makes his style catchy and epigrammatic is his *haikai* sentiment that lies at the bottom of all his writings. The haikai, or haiku, the seventeen syllable verse, is the shortest form of Japanese poetry. It can be likened to a little hermitage (iori) four and a half mats in size with one round hole in the mud wall through which the contented poet looks out into the broad universe. Rain finds easy access through the roof to the straw seat of the inmate who sits quietly with an old tub to receive the dripping drops. At night he can look up to the starry heavens without going out of his hut. Imagination is a chimney swallow; you may think her sooty, but no! her wings are glossy black, and black is the colour that never tires our eye-sight. The imagination of the haikai-poet creeps out of the little light hole of his hut. Once out, she spreads her wings and the whole heaven is hers. From morning to night, she can not touch the bounds of her liberty.

No reader of Soseki can fail to notice that he owes much to English literature in depicting his characters, especially in the analytical and psychological part of his delineations. It is too plain a fact to require elaborate treatment here.

Chinese classics
Esoteric Buddhism
Haikai poetry
English literature

These are four great tributaries with myriad nameless streamlets that constitute our mighty river, Sōseki. It flows on and on like the River Nile through sterile land giving fertility and comfort as it goes.

"Men may come,
Men may go,
But I go on forever."

The favourite food of Bashō, the haikai poet, was beans and peas, and our Sōseki's was peanuts, which he took profusely as he went on writing. Bashō died of stomach and bowel trouble, and so it was with our man of letters. Illness softens one's heart. Helplessness caused by indisposition made our self-willed literary man rely, body and soul, upon his faithful wife who nursed him day and night anticipating every wish and whim of her sick husband. He breathed his last at the age of fifty, surrounded by an anxious group of his friends on the 9th of December, 1915.

Mr. Baldwin, prime minister of Great Britain, was one of the pall-bearers at the funeral of the late Thomas

Hardy whose remains were interred in the Poet's corner, Westminster Abbey. The press was severe upon King George, who did not attend the service.

Sōseki has been dead these thirteen years and his fame is rising as the years roll by, while the memory of his contemporaries is being buried deep in the dust of oblivion and forgetfulness. The house where Shakespeare was born at Stratford-on-Avon is a national treasure preserved and maintained by the national coffer of England. The small study of our literary star at Minami-chō, Waseda, is well kept up by the sympathetic care of Mrs. Natsume; the books, the curios and everything else are arranged as neatly and carefully as they were in his life time, but mice and rats with their prodigious hosts of descendants are driving their chariots of devastation along the ceiling of the room, and in the course of several years more it will have been turned into their foul nest. Who knows?

The Japanese are a strange people who have created lords of the warriors and statesmen who have made the national debt greater and heavier, but a Shakespeare, a Milton and a Tennyson have all passed away unnoticed. Japan, thou art poor, I know, but thou willingly payeth five *sen* for a mouse, dead or alive, when the black death is threatening the lives of thy people. The germ of the pest is indeed dreadful, but still more terrible is the germ of ingratitude. Canst thou not spare an atom of thy stupendous annual expenditure to save the relic of thy great literary genius from the sharp teeth of those *revengeful* rats? I repeat it, madam, Wouldst thou not like to bequeath it as a rich legacy unto thy posterity?

A bush-warbler, uguisu, has come to my little garden this morning and is singing sweetly as she migrates from branch to branch of the plum-tree. I softly open the shoji an inch and waft her my welcome, but she is gone like a sprite!

Umeji Sasaki.

March 28, 1928.

## ILLUSTRATIONS

Facing title page and on pages 23, 77, 93, 105, 143, 149, 185, and 198.

# KUSAMAKURA

Beneath the Stars

# KUSAMAKURA

## I

THUS he mused as he went up the mountain-path:—

"Let Wisdom be your guide and you will become harsh and rigid; let Emotion be your boat and you will drift away; let Will have her own way and you will be like a snail in her narrow shell. The world in which we live is a hard world after all.

"The harder the world weighs upon you, the easier the place where you seek to go. The Muses will give you poetry or painting only when you have found out the truth, 'No better place there is than where you are.'

"The world where we live was made by neither gods nor demons. Your honest neighbours who are busily getting about on your right, your left and opposite you have founded it. If you begin to find it unendurable to live in the world you yourselves have created there will be no other place to go to. Even if there be, it will be the one peopled by beings unlike us. It will be a country of elves, where it will be still harder to live.

"Seeing we could not go away from this world so hard to stay in, the only thing for us to do would be to try to make where we are a little better and a little more comfortable during our short pilgrimage on earth. Then and there the appearance of an inspired poet or a painter with his divine message is awaited as impatiently as a shower by the parched land. Why is a poet, or a painter, or a sculptor, or a musician honoured? Does not he try to make this world of ours sunshiny and our hearts free from so many sordid cares?

"Poetry or painting is that which represents before our eyes a world of bliss independent of this world, so full of troubles and sorrows. Music and sculpture do the same. In other words, you need not paint it either in words or in colours. Your poem or a picture will have been completed if you could but see that vision of the blessed world. Even if you could not put down your beautiful conceptions upon paper, the tintinnabulation of Muse's silver bells will be still audible. Bright colours with no imagination will give you only a poor picture, while imagination with no colours will paint a beautiful one on your mental canvas. Viewed from this new stand-point, the world will assume entirely a different aspect from what it actually is. The world reflected upon the lenses of your spiritual camera then will be the one purified and refreshed by Lebanon's balmy dew. Although a poet may sing no song, or a painter paint no picture, yet he finds joy in the world full of sins and sorrows. He can set himself free from the yoke of evil passions and can go in and out the world of saints. He can build up a new heaven and earth, where selfishness or covetousness will have no sway. No rich man's son, no prince with his ten thousand chariots, nor a popular man lionised by society could be happier than he.

"At twenty, I found life worth living. At twenty-five, I came to know that light and shade are to be likened to the smooth and rough sides of paper, and where the sun shines there comes shadow at his heels. With thirty years' experience, my thought runs along this channel,—

'When your joy is full, your sadness deepens: the greater the pleasure, the bitterer the sorrow. You could no more separate them than you could separate your soul from your body. You and your world will perish in the attempt. Gold is important, but your sleep will be as much disturbed as your wealth increases. Love is sweet, but too soon it will lose its keenness and you will be looking back with a longing eye to the days when love was a locked casket. Cabinet ministers are honoured and respected, but they have to support the feet of tens of millions upon their shoulders with the great burden of state on their backs. A mere glance will never gratify you when dainties are laid before your eyes. A few bites will tempt you to greater appetite. When indulged, you will suffer.'"

My drifting thought reached this point, when my right foot was caught by an ugly stone full of corners. I thrust out my left foot in order to keep up my balance; thus recovering my stability, I found in the next moment my hips well posted upon a solid rock about three feet in diameter. My paint-box hanging from my shoulder danced out from under my arm. No further incident deterred my progress.

I sprang up to my feet again and looked around, when my eye caught towards the left a high mountain whose shape was like a bucket turned upside down. From bottom to top, the mountain was covered with trees either cedars or cypresses. The green leaves of the trees made it look very dark. The mountain cherries with their pink blossoms peeping out from amongst the branches broke the monotony. The haze trailed its fleecy train over all; it was so thick and deep that no line could be drawn between the ever-greens and the blossoms. A little this side, I saw a bald-headed mountain, so conspicuous that all other mountains were thrown into the background. A giant with his enormously big axe must have hewn its perpendicular side so sharp and driven it deep, deep down into the bottom of the mountain gorge. On its crown, stood a pine-tree whose branches were so graceful as to let you peep into the blue sky. Some two hundred yards away, the road seemed to come to an end, but a peasant in a red blanket was seen moving higher up the path and assured me that I could come out there if I kept up my steady pace. The road was very rugged.

Only a little time and labour would be needed to level the earth. But there are on the ground stones which you can not smooth away, although you can smooth the earth. You can break the stones to pieces, but those adamantine rocks defy your power. They stand out erect and calm; they seem to say, "We will not make way for you." If they will not yield, we shall have to jump over or go round them. It was, however, no easy job to walk along the places where there was no rock, for each side of the pass was high with its centre all hollow. You may justly imagine that it was altogether like a triangle scooped out with its vertex running through the centre. It was not a road, but rather a river bed I was walking along. Being in no special hurry, I walked leisurely along and at last came to the "Seven Turnings."

All at once I was startled by a skylark's notes coming from beneath my feet. I looked down into the valley, but he was nowhere to be seen. He did not show me his shadow even, although he sent forth volumes of his sweet melody. So busy and constant is his strain that you might imagine that ten thousand square miles of the ethereal world were being disturbed by so many fleas. There is no pause in his breathless music. He does not seem quite satisfied unless he sings on, sings away and sings out a mild spring day. Singing he goes up higher and ever higher until he dies away among the clouds. When he has reached the zenith, he will get into the clouds and be floating along the banks. By and by his form disappears and his voice alone remains in the sky.

The corner of the rock made an acute angle. A blind shampooer would have fallen head over heels. Hazardously turning to the right, I gave a side glance down below. The *natane* flowers tossing their tiny yellow heads in the breeze stretched as far as the eye could reach. The larks will, I thought, come down and go up from the golden plains; by and by those descending and ascending will meet in mid-air like warriors' spears engaged in single combat. Lastly, I thought, they will be singing ever louder even while coming down and going up, or when they meet in mid-air in the letter X.

Spring makes you sleepy. The cat forgets to catch rats. Man forgets his debts. It is a fountain of sweet wine, and those who have drunk at the fount often forget even the existence of their souls. Your drowsiness is cured only when your sleepy eyes have caught a distant view of *nanohana,* and the wholesouled music of the skylark awakens you to the sense that you have a soul. The bird never sings with his lips, but with his whole soul. Of the voices coming out from the fulness of the souls' activities, his is the strongest and excels all. O how sweet! O how happy! Thus by musing, thus by getting happy, your poem is wrought.

This ecstasy called forth in my memory Shelley's beautiful "Ode to a Skylark." I recited the few passages I had learned: I hummed,

> We look before and after
>   And pine for what is not:
> Our sincerest laughter
>   With some pain is fraught;
> Our sweetest songs are those
>   that tell of saddest thought.

Happy is a poet, yet he cannot sing half so joyously as the lark. The winged songster just pours out his melodies boldly, unreservedly, rapturously.

Not only in Occidental, but also in Oriental poetry do we often meet with such an expression as "a lakeful of tears." It seems then that a man grows sad and weeps so much simply because he is a poet, while an ordinary man is spared with a spoonful of tears. Perhaps it is that a poet suffers much more than, and is twice as nervous and care-worn as, the common set of people. He may have joy he alone can enjoy, and he may have sorrow which defies measurement. If so, it may be much safer not to be a poet at all.

For some time the road was even and smooth with a copsewood on my right, and the endless expanse of *nanohana* on my left. A dandelion would often peep out from between my sandalled feet. Its saw-shaped slender leaves protectingly holding a yellow jewel in their midst, courageously stood up on the road-side. Too eager to enjoy *nanohana* to satiety, I frequently trod upon the modest flower. Feeling very bad for the outrageous act, I looked back, but lo! and behold! the yellow gem of a flower was sparkling as brightly as before. It looked so very innocent. Again I took up the line of thought.

"Melancholy is perhaps a characteristic trait of a poet, yet while he is listening to the lark's song of hope, sorrow finds no room in his heart to creep into. The *nanohana* make him dance with joy. The dandelion also preaches the gospel of happiness, and the cherry-blossoms, too. Well, they have been left far behind. Everything he hears and sees charms him when he finds himself thus among the scenes of nature in her mountain home. It is an unmixed joy spoiled by no speck of sorrow. The only drawback is that he has got tired and hungry, yet he has nothing nice to appease his hunger.

"And how is it that he is free from pain while looking at this natural scenery? Simply because he sees it as a picture, or reads it as a volume of poetry. Now that it is a picture or a poem, he is not tempted to get it gratis and open it up into cultivation, or make money by building a railway there. This landscape—it neither gratifies our appetite a bit nor adds a single penny to our salary—this landscape charms us only as landscape, hence no pain, no anxiety. And there lies the greatness of nature. Is it not she that purifies our emotions instantaneously and turns our whole being into one divine poem?

"Love may be sweet; filial piety, noble; loyalty and patriotism may well be exalted to heaven; yet the instant you appear on the stage to act, the whirlwind of selfishness gets hold of you and your eyes are no longer open to things sweet, noble and pure. Then Poetry will hide her bashful face from you forever!

"In order to avoid this, you will have to place yourself in the elevated position of a free third person. Then theatre-going or novel-reading becomes a joy. While your attention is entirely occupied with the performances on the stage, or with the development of a plot in a novel, you forget every personal interest and you are a poet.

"Humanity is, however, the theme of an ordinary drama or a novel. The *dramatis personae* get excited, sad, angry, make a fuss, or sob and cry. Sympathy gets hold of the spectators, who soon begin to be excited, get sad, angry; make a fuss, or sob and cry. True, selfishness enters not your heart so long as you are a mere on-looker, but other emotions will begin to be far more active. That I dislike.

"Grief, anger, merry-making and weeping seem to be indispensable to man. Thirty years' actual experience has made me sick of them. The repetition of similar experiences by going to the theatre or reading a novel would certainly mean my nervous bankruptcy. The poetry I wish to have is not such as stimulates the human emotions, but delivers me from the earthly bondage and lets me enjoy the companionship of saints even for a while. No matter how excellent a play may be in its workmanship, it always dwells upon human feelings. Few novels are above right and wrong. Perhaps it is their characteristic that they cannot step out of this world of love, sorrow, intrigue and what not. Especially Occidental poetry seems to build its foundation upon human affections; even the best of Western poets are not entirely free from this general tendency. Sympathy, charity, righteousness, and liberty—the articles which attract many customers at the bazaar of human society—are their favourite themes. No matter how high they may soar in imagination, their feet will still be on earth where everybody is busy over his countingbook. Shelley may well have wept over the song of a lark.

"Fortunately some pieces of Oriental poetry are free from this earthliness.

> Chrysanthemums by the east fence invite my
> scissors;
> Fondly towards Nan-Shan turn my eyes.

"Short as it is, the couplet presents before our eyes a man quite unconscious of the existence of the material world, close and foul. It does not seem that his neighbour's pretty daughter is peeping through his fence, nor has he an intimate friend in the office at Nan-Shan. It takes us up to a region where we can freely inhale the breath of Heaven and be far above the loss and gain of the world.

> Alone I sit in the bamboo thicket,
>   My harp twangs: I sing aloud;
> No caller disturbs my sylvan solitude,
>   The moon repeats her nightly visit.

"The quatrain with two dozen words is itself a creation, the virtue of which far excels that of "Hototogisu" or "Konjikiyasha." It is the medicinal virtue of a refreshing sleep after one has got tired of steamship, railway, right, duty, morality, and decorous ceremony, etc., etc.

"If the twentieth century needs sleep, it no less needs supermundane poetic sentiment. Unfortunately those who write poems and those who enjoy them are all dazzled by the brightness of Occidental poetry. Very few are simple enough to float a boat of unworldliness on the brimming river and row upstream, like that famous fisherman to the "Grotto of Peaches" where peace, innocence, longevity reign. Not being a poet by profession, I have no intention to preach the gospel of innocence incarnated by Tao-yuan-ming and Wang-wei, yet to me this poetic exaltation seems far more precious than the excitement we get from a ball or a theatrical entertainment. Great as it is, I cannot grow so happy over "Faust" or "Hamlet." My tramping thus alone with my paint-box and three-legged stool along the mountain path on a spring day is because I wish to saturate myself in the poetical atmosphere enjoyed by these Chinese poets. People may call it my eccentricity, yet I shall be amply repaid if I can obtain that poetic enthusiasm directly from the hand of nature and be a loiterer even for a short time in a universe above human passions.

"Being a member of human society, however, I may be unable to sojourn in that dreamland as long as I wish, and even Yuan-ming, we can reasonably imagine, was not looking at Nan-Shan all the year round; Wang-wei was not so fanciful as to sleep in his bamboo-grove with a thousand mosquitoes attacking him. In all probability, only one or two bunches of chrysanthemums were enough for Yuanming's flower-vase and the rest went to the flower-vender's, and the green-grocer frequently visited Wang-wei's bamboo-grove to buy the shoots in their season. I am no exception to the rule. It is true that I am very fond of larks and *nanohana,* but I am not yet such a visionary as to lay my head upon the grassy pillow and go to sleep beneath the stars. In such a secluded place far from human habitations, I often meet with men—men with skirts tucked up high; with heads and cheeks unceremoniously done up with towels briskly walking by, or sometimes my dreamy eyes are startled by the flashes coming from the red petticoats of country damsels who hurry by with a "Good day, gen'leman!" or often horses' longer faces greet me with their familiar neighs. Surrounded by myriad cypresses, and breathing in and out the air at several hundred feet above sea-level, I can hardly get away from the smell which emanates from human bodies. Moreover, the Hot Springs of Nagoi are where I am to put up this evening after having covered that hill yonder.

"The view-point determines what a thing is. Leonardo Da Vinci once said to his pupils, "Don't you hear that bell? It is one bell, but you can hear any sound you wish." Viewed from different angles, a man or a woman will take as many different shapes as you will. As this trip was first planned to cut off every human tie binding me to society and to give full liberty to my rambling propensity, I shall try to observe men accordingly, and then they will appear quite different from what they did when I was living in a small humble cottage on a crowded back street. Even if I failed to accomplish this, I might be able to enjoy that soft sensation which we get from *No* dances. True, humanity governs *No,* too, and we shall be unable to see the "Seven Cavaliers' Flight" or the "River Sumida" without being moved to tears. However, emotion does not play so great a part in *No* as art does. The former occupies only three-tenths, the latter seven-tenths. Our gratitude to *No* is not because it can delineate or depict for us human emotions true to life; but by putting so many costumes called art upon human feelings, it leads us into the primitive world whose manners and customs are no longer ours.

"Let me compare the events and people I shall meet during the rest of my journey with a plot of *No* and the actions of its actors. It may not be possible for me to lay aside all human conventionalism, yet as it is originally a poetic trip and I may not have another opportunity of being such a wanderer, I expect to make it as much like *No* as I possibly can. Nan-Shan, the bamboo-grove, the skylark and *nanokana* may not well harmonize with the persons I meet in my journey; but if possible, I shall try to approach and observe them from the same angle. Basho, the *haikai* poet, once stayed overnight at an obscure inn among the mountains. He heard the cattle making water at his pillow side. It strongly appealed to his poetic sense and he composed a poem. I, too, will try to imagine the people I shall meet—peasants, townspeople, the clerks of the village office, and old folks, male and female—as so many figures painted out by nature herself on her broad canvas. Unlike painted figures, they will naturally behave as freely, whimsically or eccentrically as they will, yet I shall not be like an ordinary novel writer and try to dig deep down into the psychological phenomena, or examine the complicated details of human affairs. If I do so, I shall be just as prosaic as he. I do not care how much people get about. I might just think of them as so many painted figures who are moving about. No matter how freely and wilfully they may get about, they can never step off of a plane surface. Complications, collisions and differences of interests arise from our supposing them to step off of the plane surface and act cubically. The more complicated a thing is, the farther is it from being æsthetic. Taking a bird's eye view of the people I may meet from now on, I shall try to prevent human passions from acting like lightning flashes upon one another. However closely they may watch for a chance, they will find no unguarded point on my side. In short, I shall be like a man who, standing before a moving picture, observes the figures therein getting about to and fro. The distance of a yard or so will give me a nicer and safer view of the whole panorama. In other words, no personal interests coming into play, I shall be able to observe their actions entirely from an aesthetical point of view, and be a fair judge of what is good or otherwise."

In the meanwhile, the sky had been busy gathering rain; a suspicious bank of clouds which had been hanging above my head began to break, and soon there was spread a sea of clouds all around me. Patter! patter! came the gentle feet of spring rain. The *nanokana* had been left far behind, and I was walking along between the mountains. How far apart they were from each other I could not tell, for the misty rain had covered all with its grey sheet. Sometimes a gust of wind would sweep off the high clouds and disclose a dark mountain head on my right. The mountain range might be lying just beyond the valley. On my immediate left, there stood a lofty hill with its broad skirts. Trees like pines would often put out their faces from amongst the drizzling drops of rain only to hide them again. Did the rain move, or did the trees? Was it a dream that moved both? I was just like a man in a fairy land.

The road was now wide and smooth, and it was rather easy walking, but not being equipped for rain, I hurried on. Drops began to drip from the brim of my hat, when my ear caught some dozen yards ahead the jingling sound of a bell, and the rain, the black conjurer, produced out of his magical cloak a pack-horse man.

"Do I have to walk much further to an inn?"

"Yes, half a mile. You have got pretty wet, sir."

Thinking half a mile was rather hard to cover, I looked back, but the driver had already melted away like a moving picture into the rain.

The rain drops which had been as fine as rice-bran now grew very big, and each long line of them was being driven about by a wind that had just sprung up. I was wet all through, from my coat down to my underwear. The temperature of my body made it lukewarm. Feeling very uncomfortable, I walked briskly on with my hat pulled over my eyes.

A boundless inky world with myriad silver shafts of driving rain was where I, all wet, was plodding steadily along. Had it not been my own poor figure, but somebody else's, it would have made an agreeable poem or a picture. Completely forgetting oneself as one is and taking purely an objective view of oneself, one can then be a figure in a picture and can beautifully harmonize with the natural objects painted there. But the instant he begins to be troubled by rain or sore feet, he is no longer a hero in a poem or a figure in a Picture, but a detestable worldling you meet any time on 'Change. Such a worldling is blind to a peerless landscape with fleecy clouds and smoky rain; blossoms falling like snow-flakes or sweet melodies of singing birds, will not appeal to his sordid imagination. How beautiful it is to be a solitary loiterer among the mountains refreshed by the soft vernal rain is a mystery to such a man. At first I walked with my hat pulled down; next I walked with my eyes fixed on my feet; finally I walked cautiously on shrugging my shoulders. The rain, after giving a gentle shake to the surrounding trees, closed upon the poor wanderer from all sides. I had ridden my hobby a little too far, it seemed.

## II

A loud halloo brought nobody out. I looked in from beneath the low eaves, but the partition shōji all black with soot hid the inside from me. Some half a dozen pair of sandals which were hung from the eaves were swinging so sad and forlorn that the three cake boxes placed underneath seemed to sympathize with them in their common loneliness: a few coppers were lying loose.

Another hallo and the hens that sat swelling like so many stout matrons on the stone mill in a corner of the earthen floor were startled and cried in great alarm. Just over the threshold, all wet and partly discoloured by the rain stood an oven with a black kettle on it, challenging you to tell whether it was of clay or of silver. The fire in the oven had not yet gone out.

Still no response. I went in uninvited and seated myself on the stool. Down came the hens fluttering their wings from the mill, up they flew on the matted floor and might have run into the inner apartment but for the closed shoji. The alarmed cock cackled loudly; his family, taking up the note, cried "cutt, cutt, cutt" all in unison. They seemed to think me a dog or a fox. A tobacco tray as large as a one *sho* dry measure stood on the stool so quiet and peaceful that it seemed not concerned at all with how fast the day might wane. A blue smoke from the incense coiled like a snake in the tray was tediously rising. It had begun to clear up.

Five minutes had hardly passed before a foot-step was heard within, and the sooty shōji softly opened showing an old dame out. I was quite sure that somebody would come out. There was fire in the oven: coppers were lying loose on the cake-boxes, and a cloud of smoke was peacefully curling up from the incense. Everything told that the house had not been deserted. What struck me as very different from city life, however, was that no anxiety seemed to enter the mind of the shop-keeper who left her shop at the mercy of an intruder. Nor was it a twentieth century way for me to sit on the stool and wait patiently until somebody should come out. Such a supermundane scene could be met with only in fairyland. Moreover, the physiognomy of the old dame appealed to my fancy and charmed me immensely.

Some three years ago, I remember I saw "Takasago" on the stage of Hōshō, a leading *No* actor. I thought it was a beautiful living picture. An old grandsire with a broom over his shoulder had come and hardly walked five or six steps along the railed passage way leading to the stage before he turned gently round. His eyes met his old lady's and the image the scene presented is still vivid and fresh in my memory. My seat commanded the front view of the old dame, and the instant I felt the beauty of her facial expression the picture was complete in my mental camera. The face of the tea-house matron and that of the old dame I had described were so much alike that I wondered if the latter had come to life again.

"Pardon, Ma'am; I took the liberty of coming in."

"You are welcome, sir; excuse me that I did not know."

"We have had a very heavy rain."

"Yes, very heavy. You must have had a hard time of it walking through the rain. Oh, you have got quite wet. A cheerful fire, and you'll be comfortable in a minute."

"Please feed the fire in the oven a little and I'll dry my clothes and warm myself over it. A little rest has made me rather cold."

"Yes, sir, the fire shall be bright in no time, but let me first give you a cup of tea."

As she rose, she drove out the hens with two hisses. "Co, co, co, co" cried the feathered couple and ran out into the street over the old discoloured *tatami* and the cake-boxes. The cock was impolite enough to soil the cake by discharging something dirty as he ran.

"Tea, please," and a round tray with a tea cup on it was placed before me. As I sipped I noticed through the dark gray fluid three plum flowers painted and baked on the bottom with so much natural ease.

"Help yourself, please," said the hostess, and some of the *gomaneji* and *mijimbo** the fowls had walked over was placed before me. I looked over the cakes to see if there were not dirty spots on them, but the excrement had been left harmless in the box.

The old woman, girdling up her long sleeves with a

---

* cakes of the roughest kind.

silk cord, crouched before the oven to feed the fire, her short sleeveless jacket giving a sense of neatness all about her. Taking my sketch-book out of my pocket, I began to draw her profile, addressing her thus, —

"I like this quietness, ma'am."

"Indeed? It's a lonely place among the mountains."

"Do nightingales sing here?"

"Yes, sir. No day passes without my hearing them sing, 'Hohō, hokekyō, Teru, Teru, Teru.' They are found here even in midsummer."

"I wish I could hear them. I miss them very much."

"Very sorry, sir, but the rain has scared them all away."

In the meantime, the fire in the oven began to make a crackling sound, sending its red tongue out a foot.

"Come, sir; make yourself warm over the fire. You must be cold." The blue smoke which had been caught and crushed by the eaves was still lingering about them in a faint trail.

"I have got very comfortable, ma'am. Your kindness has brought me to life again."

"Thank Heaven! It has cleared up. Don't you see the Fairy's Rock over there?"

The mountain breeze which got impatient at the lingering cloudiness of the spring sky swept away with his enormous brush all the mist that had enveloped the mountains beyond, and to my view was disclosed far away in the direction the old woman pointed the Fairy's Rock, a towering column roughly hewn.

First I looked at the Rock in the distance, then at the old woman; then with my eyes half on one and half on the other I looked at both. The faces of old women kept in my brain as a painter are those of the old dame in the "Takasago," and of the mountain sibyl painted by Rosetsu. When I saw the picture, I felt that the woman idealized by the old master was horrible and should be placed either among the maples in autumn, or under the cold moon in winter. At the special *No* entertainment given by Hōshō, my prejudice was pleasantly dispelled, and I learned that such a sweet expression might exist in an old woman. The masque worn by the actor must have been cast by a master hand. Pity that I did not ask the name of the maker. Thus expressed, old age looks very calm, sweet and noble. A gold screen, spring breeze, or a cherryblossom would be set off to advantage by having such a figure in the foreground. The old woman with her sleeveless jacket on, who, straightening her bent body, shading her eyes with her hand, was pointing at the Fairy's Rock far away, harmonized a great deal better than the Rock itself in the spring's mountain path. I was busy taking a sketch of the old dame. A moment more and the picture in my portfolio would have been complete, when down came the spell, and her posture had changed.

Having nothing else to do, I began to dry my book over the fire and thus addressed her, —

"Ma'am, you look very healthy."

"Yes, my dear traveller, I am. Thank Heaven, I do my own needlework, spin hemp and pound dumpling flour myself."

It would make a fine picture, thought I, if she were

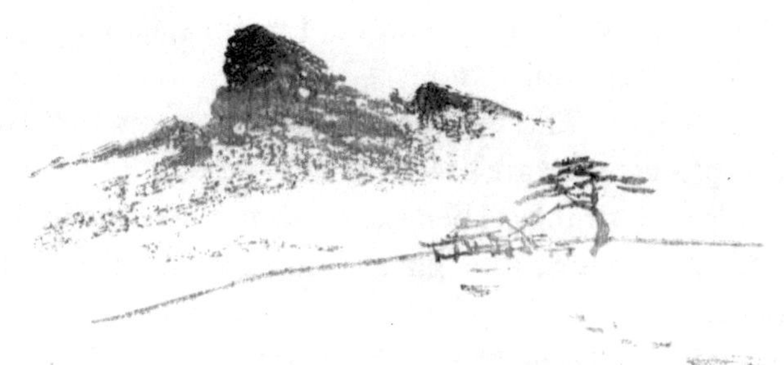

grinding her handmill, but thinking it would never do to ask a favour of her, I asked another thing of the old woman. "Less than a *ri* from here to Nagoi, is it not?"

"Yes, sir, less than a *ri,* twenty-eight *chō,* they say. Are you here for a bath-cure?"

"Yes, and if it is not crowded, I might spend a couple of weeks, but I don't know, —"

"Please do. The War keeps so many away from the Hot springs; they are practically closed up."

"It's very strange. Then they may not take me in."

"O yes, they will be glad to take you if you ask for board."

"Only one tavern there, if I remember right?"

"Yes, ask for Shioda-San, and anybody will tell you. He is the wealthiest person in the village, and nobody can tell whether his is a hot-spring hotel or the private residence of a gentleman retired from active life."

"Then he does not care for a customer?"

"Have you never been here before, my dear traveller?"

"Yes, but it was long, long ago."

Here the conversation came to a pause. I opened my portfolio and was quietly drawing the hens, when a sound of jingling bells borne by a gentle breeze reached my ears. The sound gradually developed itself into a certain tune and produced in my head a melody which led me into dream-land where I had such a delicious sensation as we get from a sweet slumber into which we are lulled by the peaceful sound coming from our neighbour's hand-mill. I stopped drawing the fowls and put down at the margin of the page, —

O Spring Breeze!
Thou waftest to Inen's* ears the jingle of
horses' bells.

Since I began climbing the pass, I had met no less than six horses, all of which had belly protectors and had jingling bells around their necks. One should have thought them belonging to another world.

Soon the soft monotony of the dreamy path in the latter part of spring is broken by the cheerful ditty of a pack-horse man. There is sadness all over the song, but at its bottom you will have noticed an I-don't-care-a-bit tone. A song, if painted, would be such, I thought.

A song goes up the Suzuka pass,
It comes from a pack-horse man;
The spring rain is soft and dreamy.

I put this down obliquely on the page, but found the poem was not mine.

"There comes another," said she half to herself.

There being no other road than this, travellers in going back and forth seem to make acquaintance of the tea-house keeper. Those drivers I had met on my way here must have gone up and down the pass, each pictured in the mind of the old woman, who repeats, "There he comes." Spring may come and spring may go, but the lonely path remains the same all the time. The tea-house keeper in her village so small that you can hardly get

---

* Inen or Izen, one of Bashō's pupils, was a tramp poet whose favourite bed was the way-side grass.

about without disturbing the flower-petals on the ground, has counted the jingling sounds of pack-horses' bells and has thus grown old. Her gray hair tells the tale.

The pack-horse man sings;
She dyes not her grey hair;
The spring is departing.

I put this down on the next page, but thinking it did not express even half of the feeling I had at the time, I meditated and meditated until the end of my pencil became the focus of concentration. "Grey hair" must not be left out in the composition, thought I; "longevity of evergreen bamboo" must be put in somewhere; "a pack-horse man's ditty" must give the poem seasoning; and the traditional rules of the ki* should not be neglected: and the whole must be compressed into a neat seventeen syllable verse. Thus I was laying word-bricks one after another, often doing and oftener undoing, when I was startled by a loud whoa, and a hoarse voice addressing the old shop-keeper, "Hello, good-day." It came from a real pack-horse driver.

"Oh, Gen-San, is it you? Are you going again to the castle-town?"

"Yes; and I shall be glad to do purchasing for you if you have anything to buy down there."

---

* The ki (season) is a rule or limitation observed by the old school of *haikai* poetry, which you will have to keep in mind in composing a *haiku*. For instance, when you wish to write a poem on a plum blossom, you must do so expressing the sentiment of spring, for it blooms only then.

"Thank you, Gen-San, will you please get me a charm of Reigan-Temple from my girl if you pass Kaji-machi?"

"Yes, certainly, will one do? O-Aki-San is a happy girl to have married well, is she not, auntie?"

"Heaven be praised! They seem to be free from a hand-to-mouth life. I should think she is fortunate."

"O yes, she is, my good woman. Comparison makes it plain; think of the young lady of Nagoi."

"I am so sorry; she is such a beauty. Is she any better nowadays?"

"No, she is not."

"Too bad," she sighed.

"Indeed it is," said Gen-San, stroking his patient animal on the nose.

The rain-drops fresh from the deep sky had lodged on the luxuriant foliage and blossoms of a wild cherry tree by the tea-house. A mischievous mountain breeze saw and seized those ethereal sojourners by the foot, and they thus losing their balance fell pell-mell upon the head of the horse, who greatly startled began to toss his long mane.

"Whoa!" scolded the driver, and together with the sound of tinkling bells it aroused me from my profound meditation.

The old woman says,—

"I remember it well, Gen-San. The young lady in her bridal toilet still comes and goes like a phantom before my eye. A charming bride in a long-sleeved gown beautifully embroidered on the skirts; her hair dressed in big *shimadamage,* and on horse-back."

"Well, yes, ma'am. It was not by boat, but as you say by horse, and here she stopped and rested."

"Yes, when her pony halted beneath that cherry-tree, the blossoms fell like so many snow-flakes on her *shimada,* making it spotted."

My sketch-book was again open. The scene would have made a picture or a poem. My imagination soon conjured up the graceful figure of the bride and the surroundings in which she played the principal part. My face was beaming with happy satisfaction and I wrote on the page just opened, —

> The season of cherry-blossoms,
> A flower bride on her spirited
> horse passes along the pass;
> The pass feels great honour.

Curious to say, although her dress, hair, pony, and the blossoms came out so vividly in my mind's eye, yet the bride's face would not come. "This face?" "No!" "That one?" "No!" I thought and thought a good while until at last Ophelia's face painted by Millais made its appearance, and without much ado went and wore the bride's *shimada-mage.* "This will not do," I cried. Down came the mental picture, and the dress, hair, horse and flowers were all gone in a twinkling of time from my imaginary stage, but Ophelia, wringing her hands and being borne away by the current, would not go, but haunted me, a dim spectre whom I tried in vain to brush away as I do smoke with my palm broom. I was possessed by a somewhat similar mysterious sensation as when one sees a comet that trails its long tail in the firmament.

"Good"bye, aunt, I must be going," said Gen-San.

"Welcome awaits you on your return. Unfortunately it is wet, and the Seven Turnings will be pretty hard to cover."

"Yes, ma'am, it'll be a little bit harder," said the driver and with this, he left the shop, followed by his horse. Jingle! jingle! went the merry bells.

"Is he a man from Nagoi?"

"Yes, he is Gembei of Nagoi."

"Did he once go down the pass carrying a bride on his horse?"

"Yes, sir. It was he who, taking hold of the bridle, led through the pass a black steed on which sat the young lady of Shioda in her bridal dress as she proceeded to the castle-town to be married. Years roll by so quickly and five years have already passed."

Happy is he who grieves over his grey hair only when he looks into the glass. The old woman who never knew how fast years had rolled by before she counted them five on her fingers rather belongs to a fairies' community than to human society. Thus I answered, —

"What a beautiful bride she must have been! I wish I had been here to see her."

"Well, you can see her now. When you put up at the Hotel in the Hot Springs this evening, she will probably come out to greet you."

"Do you mean to say, my old lady, she is now at her parents' homestead? I wish she would be in her long-sleeved gown richly embroidered and in her charming *shimada."*

"Ask, and I dare say she will oblige you."

I was not so credulous as to believe what the old woman told me, but she was seriousness itself. Dry and monotonous my supermundane trip would be, I thought, unless some such things did happen. The old shopkeeper went on talking: —

"The young lady of Shioda and the maiden of Nagara very much resemble each other, my dear traveler."

"Faces?"

"No, sir, their life stories."

"And who was the Nagara Maiden?"

"Well, sir, long ago there lived a beautiful girl called Nagara Maiden, who was the daughter to the wealthiest in the village."

"Yes."

"Two young men made love to her at one time."

"Indeed!"

"'Shall I give my hand to Sasada-lad or to Sasabe-lad?' She thought and thought day and night until at last she found the solution in suicide.

Akizukeba
  Obanaga uyeni
Oku tsuyuno
  Kenubekumowaha
Omohoyurukamo.

Autumn comes with its cool breath;
  Dew finds its lodging on arundo leaves;
My life is, I feel, short as the dew.

"The poor girl left the poem to tell her sad fate.

"Next morning her corpse was found in the pool by a fisher-man out fishing on the stream."

It was an entirely unexpected treat for me to come to such an old-fashioned mountain hamlet and to hear from such an old woman such a classical romance in such classic language.

"Five *cho* down from here stands by the roadside a stone pagoda dedicated to the memory of the Nagara lass, and it will do you good to visit the tomb as you go along."

I made up my mind to go and see it. The old woman continued, —

"The young lady of Nagoi had also two from whom to choose. One was a young man whom she had met while she was at school in Kyōto; the other was the wealthiest in the castle-town."

"Well, which did the lady give her hand to, I wonder?"

"Personally she wished to get married to the young man of Kyōto, but there may have been various reasons, and her parents made arrangements to give her away to the millionaire against her will."

"Then she was happily spared from throwing herself into the pool, ma'am."

"Well—; her wealthy husband, you may imagine, was kindness itself to his young bride as he was charmed by her peerless beauty, but it being a forced marriage on the part of the young lady their nuptial bed was not so sweet, and his relations began to entertain great anxiety about their future. Evil never comes alone; the War broke out;

the bank he served failed, and the young wife returned to her home at Nagoi. People criticize her severely, saying she is hard-hearted, ungenerous, ungrateful. She was such a shy, sweet soul before she married, but recently it seems she has got quite wild in her manners, causing great anxiety to those around her. So says Gembei each time he comes."

"Enough, enough, no more, thank you," I seemed to say to myself. Further information would break the romance to pieces. I entered the land of fairies with no slight difficulty and I should be a fool if I returned the feather garment to the charming tempter who urged and begged. I did not come up the steep pass of Seven Turnings to reach here only to be drawn back to the sordid world below. My wandering thus away from home would amount to nothing. Gossip is good to a certain extent; beyond it, it becomes stale and from it emanates a wordly smell which getting through the pores of the skin will make the body heavy with filth.

"One straight line of road clear up to Nagoi, my dear old woman?" I asked and placing a ten *sen* silver piece on the stool, I stepped out of the shop.

"Nearer by six *cho,* sir, if you go down to the right from the stone pagoda. It is a pretty bad road, but a young gentleman prefers it. O this tip, thank you; you are generous to a fault. Fare you well!"

## III

I felt rather strange last night.

The hotel was reached about eight; the curtain of night had already dropped upon the house, the garden and everything else. I could hardly tell the east from the west. After being led through a maze-like corridor with many turnings, I was at last shown into a small room about six mats in size. A great change seemed to have taken place since I was here last. After supper, I had a hot bath and was sipping tea in the room, when a little maiden came in and asked if she might make my bed for the night.

The damsel who had welcomed me at the door of the hotel was the waitress at my supper, the guide to the bath-room, and it was she who made my bed. The girl was, it seemed, the only handmaid kept in the establishment. This was strange enough. Moreover, her words were few, and there was no rustic shabbiness about her. Doing up her red sash innocently, the maiden with an old-fashioned paper lantern in her hand led me through so many flights of a corridor or staircase up and down, round and round. It was the same sash and the same lantern that went before as I descended many a step down to the bath-room. I felt as though I were a figure in the picture moving hither and thither on the canvas.

At supper table, the maid told me that, as there were few visitors then, the other rooms were all closed except the one used by the family and she was sorry they had to put me in the room. At bed time, she went away, politely bidding me "Good-night, gentleman!" As her steps through the long winding corridor gradually died away, away down below, I wondered if I were not left alone in a haunted house.

Such an experience I had had only once before. I remember it was long ago that, starting from Tateyama I went through Boshu and Katsusa up to Chōshi all along the sea-coast. One night I put up at a *certain place;* any other words would be too good. It was so wretched and miserable a place that the names of the place and the house have all gone out of my mind. I doubt if it could possibly be called an inn at all. Two women were the only inmates of the high-roofed house. On my asking if they would take me in for the night, the older one said, "Yes, sir," and the younger inviting me in led the way. Many a large apartment long deserted had been passed before I was shown into the innermost upstairs room. A thicket of long-leaved bamboo standing dull beneath the eaves got life from an evening breeze which had just sprung up and brushed me on the head and shoulder as I passed with three strides from the hall into the chamber. Dilapidation had already begun its work of destruction upon the verandah floor. On my remark that the bamboo sprouts would shoot out from the decayed floor and the whole room would be turned to a rank bamboo forest next year, the maid said nothing, but smiled a bitter smile and went away, leaving me all alone in the loneliness.

I was kept awake all through the night by the rustling sound of the bamboo leaves. I opened the *shōji* to the grass-covered garden lit by a bright summer moon.

The garden reached far into a broad meadow, neither fence nor boundary of any sort obstructing the view. Just beyond the grass-plot, there came the great ocean dashing its white-crested surf against the rocks, as if disputing man's sovereignty over land. Not a wink of sleep visited me till dawn. Patience was a prescribed dose to take in a comfortless mosquito net, and I thought I should be a splendid theme for the "London Charivari."

Lying on my back, I accidentally turned my eyes up towards the lintel, over which hung a tablet in a vermilion-lacquered frame. "Bamboo-shadows sweep the steps; no dirt arises" were the characters distinctly read even in bed. The signature Daitetsu was also easy to follow. I am no connoisseur of calligraphy, yet the scripts written by the High Priest Kōsen of the Ōbaku sect are ever a joy to me. Ingen, Sokuhi and Mokuan are each good in his own sphere, yet Kōsen is best in classic simplicity and natural elegance. Nobody who saw those seven characters would doubt they had been written by a master-hand. How characteristic of the priest's were the touches and the strokes of the letters! The sign "Daitetsu" however told me that it was not he. Perhaps there lived long ago a priest of the same name in that sect, but the paper was so fresh and new; it must have been prepared yesterday or the day before.

Giving a side glance on the alcove wall, I caught the picture of a solitary crane painted by Jyakuchū. No sooner had I got to the room than my professional eye observed it to be a splendid piece of workmanship. Most of his paintings are in bright colours, giving elaborate minuteness even to the smallest detail. No thought of the world, however, seemed to disturb his mind when he took up his paint brush and drew the bird with a touch or two. One straight line was the leg; an egg-shaped circle was the body innocently resting upon it. Nothing could be more simple and pleasing than this. A careless 'I don't-care-a-bit' air pervaded all his system even to the tip of his long beak. The ornamental shelves beside the alcove were dispensed with and the part was turned into an ordinary closet in which the weird sisters might be hidden well covered.

Soon I was in dreamland; I dreamed,—the Nagara maiden in her bridal dress mounted on a black beauty is going over the pass. All at once, Sasada Lad and Sasabe Lad spring out of their hiding places and begin to persecute her from either side. The bride all of a sudden turns into Ophelia, who, singing in her plaintive voice, is being borne away on a willow branch by the current. Thinking I am in duty-bound to save her from drowning, I follow her along the river-bank of Mukōjima. The love-stricken girl, showing no sign of distress, laughs, sings and goes down the stream, not caring a bit what her fate will be. I, with a pole on my shoulder, cry out with all my might, "Young maiden, ahoy!"

Cold perspiration in the arm pit awoke me from the delirious slumber. It was an incongruous mixture of prose and poetry. In the time of the Sung Dynasty, there lived a Zen priest named Tai-hui who said; "After I see Light, I can almost think and do as I will, but I am very much worried over the evil passions that put out their ugly heads in my dreams," and he is said to have fought long against the enemy. I can easily sympathize with the priest. I have pledged to devote my life and all to the Muses, and shame to me if I could dream no better dreams; painting or poetry would cry out "O fie!" against such an ugly dreamer: Turning on my bed, I saw several tree branches in the broad light of the midnight moon casting their graceful shadows aslant upon the paper sliding doors. It was a spring night, so clear and so transparent.

It might have been mere fancy that I heard somebody singing in a low plaintive voice. The song in dreamland might have found its way to this world of ours, or that of this world might have gone astray to fairy-land in delirium. I listened and listened. I was quite sure that somebody was singing. True, it was a still, small voice; it was, so to speak, a breath of life wafted through a sleepy spring night. Strange to say, not only the music, but also the words of the song—how, you will ask, could you catch the words so far away from your pillow?—Well, ... but the words came as distinct and plain as could be.

"Autumn comes with its cool breath;
Dew sparkles on arundo leaves;
Its life counts but a few moments,
I am just like to the dew."

The voice seemed to be repeating the very words of the song of Nagara Maiden.

At first the voice was heard towards the veranda. Fainter and fainter it grew until it died away far in the distance. That which stops all of a sudden gives us a sense of suddenness accompanied by little compassion. The bond of love is snapped and those who hear the sound are satisfied that it is so. The thing that grows fainter and ever fainter without marking its periods imperceptibly dwindles away into nothingness; it leads us into the sense of helpless loneliness, with which Time ticks away from second to moment. The plaintive air I heard was a chain of sad melancholy notes ever lengthening and never ending. It was like a bed-ridden husband who awaits Death to come and snatch him away; it was like a flickering candle before a gust of wind. The song was, so to speak, an epitome of the sadness of the world's spring.

I had been listening to it in my bed. As the voice grew fainter in the distance I became all attention, my ear trying to catch the faintest sound. I was aware that it was a great tempter, yet I loved it and would run after it until my body had decayed, all save the ear. The instant I felt it would no longer reach my ear, no matter how impatient I might grow, I was out of bed, and the *shōji* softly opened. It was an instantaneous act of impulse. My legs below the knees I found were bathed in the broad light of the moon, which cast on my night-gown shadow pictures of the tree-branches shivering in the night breeze.

Nothing uncommon was observable when I opened the *shōji* to see where the voice had gone. I looked to the place whence it seemed to proceed and—what do you think I saw but a ghost? The tree against which it leaned was full of flowers very much like those of an aronia. It was a shadow dim in the distance stealthily wading through the broad sea of moon-light. Before I could form any definite idea as to what it was, the silhouette turned its steps to the right treading upon the shadows of flowers as it went. The angle of the wing in which my room stood shivered, and the tall female figure flashed out of sight.

I was in the light bath-gown the hotel gave me. I stood there motionless holding the *shōji*. I was as deadly as a statue. In a few moments I was myself again. I never knew before that the spring in a mountain hamlet was so cold and chilly. Thinking it would never do to be so long out in the cold, I slipped into the bed-hole whence I had crept out. I began to meditate. I took out my watch from under the pillow-case and it was ten minutes past one. Putting it back where it had been, I took up the line of thought. "It cannot be a ghost; it must surely be a woman. It may be the daughter of the hotel yet it is indecency itself for the divorced young woman to be out, in the dead of night, out in the garden leading to the wild hills yonder." However hard I might try, sleep would not come, and the watch under my pillow seemed to talk to me. I was never before bothered by the ticks of a time-piece yet it turned that night to be a hard taskmaster, who said, "Come, think. Thinking is what you have to do to-night. Don't go to sleep. Sleep is death." The admonition was imperious. I was sorely perplexed.

Terror just as it stands bare and naked will make poetry; horror as it is objectively viewed will give you a painting. It is the same with disappointed love; it becomes a good subject for an artist or a man of letters only when its pain is forgotten and only its self-sacrificing devotion and its sweet agonies are remembered. To go a step further, as he calmly reflects and takes a purely objective view of the whole scene in which the tormented love tries to extricate herself from the quicksand of agony, he can turn it into a piece of art or literature. There is in the world one who fabricating love which does not exist at all tries to fret and indulge in the pleasing sorrow therein. The man of the world calls him a fool or a maniac. However, one who building himself a house of misery fondly dwells in it may be justly compared to a man who painting an imaginary mimic landscape tries to find brimming enjoyment in a Lilliputian tub. Each equally finds an aesthetic platform on which he can stand. Therefore, many an artist (not regarded as a man of the world) is more foolish and insane than a matter-of-fact man of the world. We set out on a journey on foot. From morning till night, we do nothing but complain of the privations and grievances we meet as we drag our weary sandalled feet. Once we begin to tell others about the experiences of our travel, there is nothing unpleasant and ugly, but all is nice and agreeable; even those complaints are now a source of inexhaustible pleasantness and we talk on and on in great triumph. By this, we do not mean to deceive others or ourselves. We simply are men of the world while we journey from day to day, but so soon as we talk about the journey we have had we are poets, hence the inconsistency. If so, an artist is he who, cutting off the corner called common sense from the square world, tries to live in the world with three sides only.

Be it nature, or be it things human, the artist will find innumerable peerless gems and priceless diamonds in places so foul and filthy that popular minds think them horrible and unapproachable. People call it beatification, but it is not so. These brilliant jewels of exquisite beauty have existed on earth ever since the creation, but you find them not because of the beam in your eyes. Those beautiful flower-petals, falling like so many snow-flakes, fall in vain, because so many sordid cares of the world keep you away from them, and Honour, Disgrace, Loss and Gain are imperious in their demands, saying, "Don't look far beyond; stick to us and you are safe! "Thus we saw no beauty in the railway train before Turner painted it for us, or we found no delight in a ghost until Ōkyo gave it in his immortal picture.

The shadow I saw just now will no doubt give ample poetic mood to anybody who sees or hears it. A solitary mountain hamlet, a hot spring; spring eve, flower-shadows; the silvery moon, a low plaintive air; a dim moonlit night, a ghostly figure—each is a fine subject for an artist to work on. These were exhibited before my eyes, and they should have satisfied my poetic instinct but for my petty reason, which, making unnecessary inquiries and criticisms, spoiled the whole structure of poetry the Muses had built for me. My profession to be 'above the world' would amount to nothing if such were the case. I should be ashamed to make out to the public that

I am a poet or a painter, if not better educated. Salvator Rosa, an Italian painter, once became so furiously anxious to study the life of a bandit; he braved so many dangers and at last succeeded in getting into the company of banditti. I wandered away from home, a sketch-book in my pocket. It would be a great pity if I were not ready to do as he.

How, you will ask, can we get back to the poetic atmosphere whence we wandered away? The solution is rather simple. Placing your feeling a few paces away from you, view it calmly, examine it critically as if it concerned you not at all. A poet has a duty of cutting open his corpse in order to ascertain the cause by which death was brought about and make it known to the general public. Various are the ways of doing it, but the simplest and most convenient is to turn everything you see or hear into a seventeen syllable poem. It is the shortest form of poetry and is serviceable at any time. At the lavatory, at the water-closet, or in the car, it can easily be composed. When I say it is very simple to learn, I mean you can be a poet with the least possible effort. To be a poet is a sort of spiritual illumination, and it must not be despised, even if the way is so easy and accessible to anybody. The simpler it is, the more virtuous it becomes and the more highly should it be valued. Suppose you get angry; try to turn it into a seventeen syllable verse. The instant you begin to think how you can do it, you are no longer an angry man. Anger and poesy are not good friends; you can never be an angry man and a poet at the same time. You get sad and tears begin to flow down your cheeks; you try to turn them into a poem. So soon as you get well started, you are no longer a sad man; by the time you have made them into one compact exquisite verse, they will have left you and you will be happy to think that Pity could have moved you to tears.

It was the belief I had long cherished and I thought I would put it into practice that night. My bed was where I began to reflect upon that affair from all angles. I was preparedness itself and had my sketch-book ready at my pillow side in order to put down all the verses I might be blessed with lest I should forget.

A woman mad in love came;
  She shook the aronia flowers decked with dew.

I put this down as the first fruit and recited it to myself; I thought it rather dull, but not so intolerably bad. Next I entered this: —

On a dimly lit spring eve,
  The flowers cast a shadow upon the ground;
It was disturbed by that of a woman.

I was not satisfied with that, for I found that two subjects overlapped each other in one composition, yet I let it stand as my first object was to get calm and thus obtain peace of mind.

Reynard the Fox assumed the shape of woman;
  The night was ghastly dim.

I could not help smiling at this, for it turned out to be a regular comic poem.

Inspiration was at my service, and I put down all the verses as they came flowing from my brain: —

1. She calls down midnight stars;
   She wears them on her hair, as ornaments.

2. Maiden, beware of the night clouds of spring;
   Thy washed hair is just dry.

3. This is the night of spring;
   Sweet maiden, sing, surely thou canst sing.

4. O moon, bright moon!
   Thou hast tempted out the spirit of Aronia.

5. Listen, there she singeth!
   Listen, again she singeth;
   The spring moon walketh or she.

6. Spring in his chariot rides post-haste;
   The night is deep with a solitary woman in the midst.

The versification acted like a charm upon my nerves and I was in Dream-land before I knew it.

"Subconsciousness" may be an appropriate term to express such a dreamy state. Nobody knows of self in his sound sleep. While wide awake, every one knows there is the physical world all around him. There is, however, between the two states a border land lying like a thread. It can be justly called the "Vision-land." Awake? It is a little too dim. Sleep? It is a little too lively. Put *sleep* and *awake* in one flower vase; stir them up with all your might with a poetic paint-tube, and there you have it. Gradually and carefully blending nature's tints up to the border line of dreamland, you throw your paint-brush away and thrust the actual world into the land of fairies with trailing haze all over. With the aid of Morpheus, you cut off, level and smooth away all the corners—rough stubborn places. After having turned it into a soft ghostly land, you send a little pulse-wave into it. As smoke creeping over the earth can never leave it however much it wishes, so my soul can never leave the body, its shell, but lingers and still lingers. It can be likened to a snail who tries ever so hard to get away from his home but can never do it. At last unable to keep it up as an individual soul, it transforms itself into transparent volatile ether. It sticks to your hands and feet; it fills your nostrils and eyes, until you can no more get rid of it than a fly of a spider's web.

I was thus sauntering along the border land, half dormant and half awake, when the sliding door at the entrance softly opened and the shadow of a woman stood there like an apparition. I was not surprised, I was not afraid, I simply looked at it with a feeling of relief. It would be, however, wrong to use the words "looked at," though, for the phantom woman had come sliding into my closed eye-lids without asking me leave. She came stealthily into the room like a fairy walking on the waves. The *tatami* seemed to feel no weight, hence no creak, no rustle. Dimness was pardonable as it was seen through the closed eye-lids, but it was a woman graceful as a Swan-Maiden. Her perfect pretty neck, her snow white complexion, her jet-black luxuriant hair. Think of a vignette picture now in vogue which you see through a dim light, and there you have it.

The phantom stops before the wardrobe, it opens. The snow-white arm leaves its sleeve and flashes into the darkness. The closet closes. The matted sea sends it back to the harbour, the entrance. The sliding door shuts behind. I was deep in dream-land where slumber sealed up my spirit. You died as man; the suspense before you are turned into an ox or a horse was the state I was in.

I do not know how long I had been sleeping midway between a man and a beast. I heard a woman laughing aloud quite close to my ear and I awoke. The curtain of night had already been cut down and the world was one broad day-light. The mild sun of spring shone upon the bamboo-lattice of the bay window casting a black shadow far beyond. "Wonderful" seemed to have lost its hiding place; "Mystery" had fled back to eternity and had probably crossed over to the other side of the Stygian River.

I was down at the bath-room in my nightgown. The water came up to my chin; five minutes had passed. I was too lazy to wash or to come out. I wondered how I had been led into that wonder-land the night before. I was greatly dissatisfied to find myself again in the world of broad day light, so different and prosaic from that which I had been in during the night.

I was out of the tub. Too lazy to wipe my body thoroughly, I let it go wet and dripping. I opened the door from inside, and whom do you think my eye rested upon but *her?* "Good morning, gentleman. I hope you had a nice sleep last night?" My opening the door and the greeting came almost simultaneously. I did not expect that anybody was there, and the greeting was so sudden and unexpected that I was utterly at a loss what answer to make, when she added,—

"Well, sir, can I help you to put this on?" So saying, she went round and gently put a soft *kimono* on my back. "Thank you" was all I could manage to say. I turned round; she retreated a few steps.

It has been customary from of old for a novelist to describe the heroine of his work very minutely and elaborately. Enumerate the epithets in languages, East and West, ancient and modern, which he has used in order to depict a beautiful woman, and you will be surprised to find that they will take up as much room as Buddha's Sacred-Books (Daizōkyō). Here stands a woman just three paces from me, her body slightly twisted. She looks and smiles complacently at the surprise and bewilderment I am in. Pick out from amongst the inexhaustible store of epithets appropriate ones to describe the woman in question and they will be legion. Still in my thirty years' experience never did I meet with such a facial expression before. Art critics tell us that the ideal for which the Greek sculptor strove was *grace,* which I presume means the pose in which man's vital power ready to burst is watching its opportunity to act. If out, what will be the issue? Wind? Cloud? Thunder? Lightning? Nobody can tell. There your imagination catches sweet music reverberating, ever rising and falling, each note giving profound significance.

Immortality will record it in gold letters on her marble pillar. Majesty, dignity, on earth are hidden behind this brimming potentiality, which, once brought to action, will come out as one, two and three. Each of the numbers has no doubt some special power, yet since they are known numbers, they will reveal dirty spots or defects hitherto unknown, and it will be impossible for them to go back to their original perfection. Therefore, anything that expresses itself in some form or other is sure to suggest disgust to the one who sees it. The Deva carved by Unkei, the sculptor; or the cartoons painted by Hokusai all failed in this one single point. Expression or non-expression is, it seems, the vital question which determines the destiny of a painter. Either of these two great principles has from of old governed the painters in depicting their beauties.

The expression of this woman was a puzzle to me. Her lips were sealed in one straight line showing composure. Her eyes were alert watching an unguarded point in the beholder. Hers was a classical face, a little broader towards the bottom; it was pleasingly calm and serene. Her forehead was, however, small and fussy, it was the forehead of a popular type, so-called *Fuji-bitai* (conical). Moreover, her eye-brows knit together were nervously moving as when you put a few drops of mint upon them. Her nose was nearly perfect, it was neither sharp to frivolity nor round to dullness. Painted, it would make a beautful picture. The features had each its peculiar characteristic trait and they came crowding into my eyes for criticism. No wonder that I was taken aback.

Rest is the all-pervading nature of the Great Earth. Some part of it goes down and the the rest feels the shock. If you recall it contrary to its original principle, it tries to regain its former stability. Now that it has lost its balance and is controlled by inertia it is kept in motion against its will. Despair engraves its image upon it, and it will go on and on to exhaustion. If there be any such thing, that will exactly explain the expression of the woman who stood before me.

In her contemptuous looks, there lurks a wish to depend on others for protection. At the bottom of her haughtiness which puts everybody to naught, one can never fail to find chaste decency. If she be ambitious and chooses to use her natural charms to the best advantage, a hundred lads will come at her beck and kneel and weep and die at her very feet. And yet under that arrogant guise, one will have discovered a mild womanly sympathy like living water bubbling out of the fountainhead, the heart. There is no unity in her expression. It can be justly likened to the house where Light and Darkness make a home, often coming to blows. The lack of unity in her countenance is the proof that she has none within. No peace in her heart tells plainly that the world in which she got about was a disturbed one. Misfortune gets hold of her and she struggles to come out of it victorious. She must surely be, I thought, an unfortunate woman.

"Thank you," I repeated with a bow.

"Don't mention it, please. Your room is swept clean. Go and see, sir. By-by, till later." No sooner had she said this than she turned round, twisted her waist a little and swept down the long hall, a veritable butterfly. Her hair done up in fan-shape fashion revealed a pretty snow-white neck from beneath the back hair. The black satin of her *obi* must have patterns of peonies on the other side.

## IV

Vacantly did I return to my room. It had indeed been swept clean and nice. Feeling a bit anxious, I opened the wardrobe to make sure. There was a small hand-chest on the floor, and a sash-holder of *yūzen* crape was dangling from the partition shelf. It was easily conjectured that somebody had got in stealthily and hastened away with her dress. The upper half of the holder was not to be seen, for an irritatingly gay gown buried it deep in its folds. Part of the shelf was occupied by two piles of books, whose top-most places were respectively given to Orategama by Hakuin and Isemonogatari. The vision I saw last night might not have been a mere illusion.

I was seated on the cushion before I knew it. On the ebony desk, the sketch-book with a pencil between the leaves was carefully placed just as it had been left. Wishing to see in the morning what sort of verses I had put down in the sleepy hours of midnight, I took it up and was turning over the pages when my eyes rested upon the verse: —

"Dew drops sojourned on aronia flowers;<br>A crow at dawn shook them off."

This I found just below the one I had written: —

"Dew drops sojourned on aronia flowers;
A woman mad in love shook them off."

It had been hastily done in pencil, and was very hard to follow. It was a handwriting a little too strong for a female, yet a little too weak for a masculine hand.

Another surprise as I went on reading: —

"It was a dim lit night;
Was it the shadow of a blossom or of a woman?"

I found it altered as follows: —

"It was a dim lighted night;
The shadow of a blossom was overlapped by that of a woman."

Again beneath the following: —

"Reynard the fox disguised himself into a beautiful woman;
The moon was ghastly dim."

I found

"The moon was ghastly dim;
The young lord assumed the form of a beautiful woman."

Did the unknown versifier mean to imitate my style, or try to touch up my verses, or did he mean it as an exchange of literary compliments, or was it a fool's foolery, or did he mean to fool me? "Let me see," said I and fell into reflection.

"By-by till later" were her parting words, and sure she would be here to serve at my morning meal, and then I should be able to find out something definite from her. Consulting my watch, I found it was past eleven. What a heavy sleeper I was! It would be better for my stomach to have nothing to eat till noon.

Opening the *shōji* on my right, I looked out to see if there was any trail left where the apparition had stood the night before, but the aronia tree which I had rightly guessed was there all alone on the spot. The garden was much smaller than I had expected; some half a dozen moss-covered stepping stones scattered here and there invited one to come down barefooted and have a delightful walk over them. The edge of a hill-range on the left had been cut into a precipitous cliff, on which stood a brown pine whose graceful branches coming out from amongst the huge rocks reached out its arms far over the garden. A small thicket of underwood made the background of the aronia-tree. Further on, and a great forest of bamboos whose colossal limbs soared high was basking in the spring sun. On the right, the view was obstructed by the roof of the house, yet judging from the physical features of the land, the grounds must be sloping down, down to the baths.

The mountain sloped down to form a hill; the hill reached towards an open field about three blocks wide: the field running toward the sea hid itself in the waters. Thirty miles further on, rising to the surface of the water again, it formed itself into the Isle of Maya twelve miles in circumference. These are the natural features of

Nagoi. The Hot springs are a compound cut deep into the side of the hill, and the landscape gardener exhausted his skill in taking the greater part of the beautiful precipice into the garden he laid out. Look at the establishment in front, and it is a two-story building, but if you see it from behind it is just a one-storied house. Hang down your legs from the verandah, and your soles will feel the pleasant coolness of the lichens below. No wonder that I was led through so many a stair-case up and down, round and round the night before, thinking it a strange maze-like house.

On opening the window on the left, my eye rested upon the circular basin nature had carved in a rock about thirty-six square feet. Spring water finding its way into the hollow formed itself into a mirror in which the wild cherry found its beautiful image reflected. The corners of the rock were fantastically hemmed with some half a dozen bushes of dwarf-bamboo. Over beyond, there was a thorn-hedge. The path running up the side of a steep hill from the sea below now and then had pedestrians whose murmurs would reach my ears. Across the foot-path, orange trees had been planted in the incline that goes down towards the south. At the extremity of the valley, there was a large bamboo forest which glowed white in the sun. I never knew before that bamboo leaves shine white when seen at a distance. Above the forest, the hill was covered with pine-trees between whose brown trunks was seen a flight of stone steps leading up-probably to a Buddhist temple.

A railing ran all along the square building of the hotel with a court inside. On coming out to the verandah by the *karakami* at the entrance, my eye was arrested across the court by a front room upstairs in the direction where the sea must be rolling. I was much interested to know that the room was on the same level as mine whose balustrade I was leaning upon. Way down in the subterranean room stood the bath-tank, and I had to go down three flights of stairs before I could have a bath. To be exact, my room was on the third floor and not on the second. It was a large establishment, yet the opposite front room upstairs and my room on the right along the railing seemed to be the only chambers occupied, save the sitting room for the family, and the kitchen. Every other guest-room which could have any claim to the honour had been closed up. It seemed that I was the only boarder in the hotel. The closed shutters were never opened to admit daylight. Once opened, they were left day and night to the mercy of transgressers. May be they never locked the front door even when they went to bed. It was an ideal place for a wanderer like myself to sojourn on a supermundane trip.

Twelve o'clock and not a stir in the house told me that I was to have my meal soon. Hunger had already set in, but if I could find myself in the atmosphere expressed in the verse, "Stillness reigns over the mountain, none disturbing it," I might just as well go without a meal. Then to paint a picture was a bore, and it would be foolish for me to try to compose a seventeen-syllabled poem as I was already in the poetic atmosphere. I had brought a few books tied to the stool thinking I might read, but I now got so lazy that they were left untouched. Lying flat on the verandah, basking in the spring sun which travels slow, I enjoyed a nap, my bed-sharer being the shadow of cherries. It was indeed a royal luxury. Then thinking is a devil that leads you to hell; moving perilous; if possible, no breathing. How happy and blessed I should be if I were allowed to spend a fortnight thus unmolested, undisturbed, unnoticed like a humble plant rooted deep in the *tatami.*

In a few moments, however, the spell of stillness was broken by footsteps out on the hall. They were coming up the stairs. As they approached, I could plainly tell that they came from two persons. I heard them stop right in front of my room, when one of them without a word to the other went away. The *karakami* softly opened, but alas! it was not *she* that expectation had promised me; she was not the person of the morning, but that self-same damsel of last night. I missed *her* a great deal.

"Sorry we have kept you waiting so long, sir." With this, she respectfully set an individual table before me. No word of apology, however, came from her lips as to the breakfast they had dispensed with. Roast fish with some green vegetable was on the plate. I took off the top of the soup-bowl; lo! and behold l peeping through the transparent fluid there were wee brake-sprouts with shrimps dyed red and white inviting me to take and eat them up quick with my chop-sticks. How could I do such a cruel thing? My eye was indulging in the luxury of the colour-picture in the bowl, when the maid asked if I did not care for the soup. "Yes, I do, but wait," said I. In fact, I thought it a pity to have to eat them.

At a certain dinner table, Turner was happy over the dish of salad served: the fresh colour of the vegetables appealed to his artistic instinct. He said with emotion to his neighbour at the table, "My friend, this is the very colour I use." I remember I have read this little anecdote of the great painter in a certain book. He would have been delighted to see this fresh colour of young fern sprouts set off by the tempting tint of shrimps. Foreign cookery seems to put little importance upon colour: salad or radish is the only treat to the eye. From the view point of nourishment, they may be right, but viewed with the artist's eye, it is certainly an outlandish cuisine. The Japanese table d'hote appears to me far superior in this particular point; look at the *suimono, kuchitori* and *sashimi.* How pleasing they are to the eye! You need not touch them with your chop-sticks; you just look at the bowls and dishes set on an individual table; go home quietly from the restaurant, and you will be amply repaid for the trouble and expense, as your mind's eye shall be gratified to satiety.

"There is a young lady here in the house?" I asked the little waitress as I laid down the *suimono*-bowl.

"Yes, sir."

"What is she?"

"She is the young mistress."

"Have you an elder mistress then?"

"No, sir, she died last year."

"Have you a master?"

"Yes, sir; and she is the daughter of the master."

"Do you mean the young lady?"

"Yes, sir."

"Have you guests?"

"No, sir, none."

"But me?"

"Well—no."

"How does your young mistress spend her days?"

"With her needle-work."

"And then?"

"She plays on the *shamisen.*"

This surprised me not a little. My curiosity was much aroused.

"And what else?" was my next question.

"My young mistress goes to a temple." was her innocent answer. This was another and greater surprise to me. Temple and *shamisen,* what a strange contrast!

"Does she go there to pay homage to the dead?"

"No, she visits it to see the holy priest."

"Is the priest her pupil in *shami?*

"No, sir."

"What business takes her there, I wonder?"

"My lady goes there to see Daitetsu-Sama, the priest."

Sure, he must be the author of the scripts on the hanging tablet. Judging from the rhyming verse, I surmised he was a Zen-priest. The Orategama I found in the closet must be hers, too.

"Who had this room before I came?"

"My young mistress, sir."

"Then this had been her chamber before I came in last night?"

"Well—yes."

"I am very sorry to know that."

"What does she call on Daitetsu-Sama for?"

"I do not know, sir."

"And then?"

"What is it, sir, you want to know?"

"Sure she does many other things?"

"Yes, sir, she does."

"What are they, I wonder?"

"I do not know, sir."

The meal was over with a pause in the conversation. As the maid took away the plates, she opened the *karakami,* when whom should my eye catch but the woman with her hair dressed in ginko-leaf style leaning on the opposite upstairs railing and looking down resting her chin on the palm of her snow-white hand? Seen through the garden trees of the inner court she looked like a *Kannon* (Goddess of mercy) of the new dispensation with a symbolic willow branch in her hand. In the morning she was restless; now she was calmness itself. This great change may have been brought about, because she was unable to send from her eyes their magical message to me, for they were cast down. Of all the gifts which belong to man, the apple of his eye is the most precious, so say the ancients, and they are right. Indeed, man can hide nothing from his fellow-creatures; his eye will tell all. Two swallow-tail butterflies dance up and down as she, leaning on the balustrade, watches; now they approach; now they separate. The instant the *karakami* of my room opens, she turns her glance from the butterflies and darts it towards me.

Like a poisoned arrow, it comes flying whizzing through the air and hits me on the forehead; blood gushes. The door is softly closed. A bleeding heart within; love murmuring spring without.

Again I lay down on my bed. The following verse soon found its way into my memory:—

Sadder than is the moon's lost light,
  Lost ere the kindling of dawn,
To travellers journeying on,
The shutting of thy fair face from my sight.

Had I been deep in love with her and wished to see her even if my body had been pounded into powder, that glance, that single glance like a lightning flash, would have left in my bleeding heart a life-long yearning, 'She might have been;' and the above verse would have been the natural expression of my deepest sorrow, or perhaps I might have added the following lines: —

Might I look on thee in death,
  With bliss I would yield my breath.

Fortunately there existed no such thing as fiery love, or devoted love on my part. Being far above it, I felt no agony whatever even if I had wished, yet the phantasm arising from the event which had just happened was to be fully expressed in the few lines I had quoted. Indeed, there was no such burning passion between her and me as depicted in the poem, yet it would be of some interest to apply our case to that represented in the lines, or it might be somethеing agreeable to try to explain the meaning of the verse by placing ourselves in the scene painted there. At least, part of the situation described in the poem was realized in us, who, led by an invisible cord of destiny, were thus brought together. However, there was not much agony attached to it, as the thread of Fate was so very fine. Moreover, it was no ordinary cord. It was a fabric very delicately woven by a rainbow across the sky; it was a textile spun by haze which trails over hill and valley; it was a spider's web which sparkles with diamond dewdrops. You can brush them all away with one sweep if you so wish, yet how beautiful they are while you look on! Should this cord grow so big and thick as a well-rope while we watch! No, reader, there is no such danger! I am a painter, and she is not a virgin.

No knock heralded her entrance and the *karakami* opened. I looked towards the threshold where stood the woman, partner in the same destiny, holding in her hands a tray with a celadon plate on it.

"Are you still in bed, my dear sir? You must have been startled last night. I disturb you so very often. Ho, ho, ho, ho!" she said with a slightly derisive smile. There was no timidity in her manners; much less was she bashful. She was rather aggressive, anticipating me each time.

"Much obliged to you this morning, miss," I again thanked her. Thrice had I already expressed my sincere gratitude to her and each time had it been done with three words, 'Thank you, miss.'

I tried to get up, she was already at my pillow side. "Don't, my dear sir. We can have a chat just as you lie," she said cheerfully. I thought so, too, and lying flat on my stomach, I held my chin with my two elbow props driven deep in the *tatami.*

"Thinking you must be lonely, I have brought you tea. Will you please let me serve it to you, sir?" She was kindness itself.

"Thank you," came again from my lips as if they knew nothing else to say. How lovely looked the *yōkan* so beautifully arranged on the celadon plate! Of all the cakes, I like *yōkan* best, not necessarily because I have an especial appetite for it, but because of its delicate hue as it receives the sun's ray into its smooth semi-transparent texture. It is a perfect piece of art. Especially the one of greenish colour is agreeable to the eye as if it were a compound of jewel and alabaster. Moreover when it is artistically arranged on a celadon plate, the cake looks so bright and wee that you would wonder if it had not just sprung up to the light from the bottom of the vessel. One would naturally put out his hand to feel it. None of the Western confectioneries gives me such a delightful feeling as our *yōkan.* True, the colour of cream is soft, but a little too heavy. Jelly is a joy; it looks like a precious stone, yet it quivers to the touch and it has not so much calm dignity. A pagoda made of sugar and milk is a monstrous triumph of Occidental cooking!

"Yes, it's beau-ti-ful!"

"Gembei is just back. He bought this down town. This may be palatable to you, sir." The pack-horse man seemed to have staid over night at the castle town. I simply looked on the cake with a nod or two. Who had bought it, or where it had come from, mattered very little to me so long as it was beautiful to look at.

"The celadon is perfect in shape, and the colour is beautiful, too; it well matches the *yōkan.*"

"Pooh!" she said and a slight derisive ripple wavered on her lips. Perhaps she took my remark for a pun. Had I meant it for witticism, she might well have derided me. One who pretends to be a wit often cracks such a dull joke as this.

"Is it China?"

"Don't know, sir," answered my female companion, who seemed to place no importance upon the precious porcelain.

"It is China, it must be," said I, holding it up and looking up at the bottom of the vessel from beneath.

"Do you like these things? We shall be glad to show you lots of them."

"Yes, please."

"Father is awfully fond of curios; he has collected quite a number. He will be delighted to show them to you. We'll invite you to tea sometime."

The invitation to tea scared me not a little. No one of true taste can be so ostentatiously self-conceited as a so-called master of tea-ceremony. The world of poetry is wide and free, yet he builds a fence of exclusiveness around his little citadel. Ceremoniously he proceeds with his tea-bowl in which he stirs up a green bubble. He sips it in a ridiculously obsequious way and declares it just grand. If refined taste were to be found in such trivialities, the barracks in Azabu would be an ideal place to go and find it. Great masters of tea ceremony must be those who daily call out, "Now, lads. Right face! march!" Business men or trades-people who have had no aesthetic training and know not where to seek genuine taste mechanically learn by heart the manifold rules set up since the time of Rikyu, founder of tea ceremony, and proudly give them out as the 'Way to tea!' They are sham masters, swindlers; a man of true taste shall not be imposed upon by them.

"Is your father's tea service of some school, miss?"

"Yes, sir, but it is of a free school where you need not drink it when you do not wish."

"Then I should like to have it."

"Ho! Ho! Ho! Father is fond of showing his curios to his friends."

"Shall I have to praise them?"

"Well, sir; praise is a sweet to old people, and he will be right glad to have you commend them."

"Yes, he shall be treated provided it be a little."

"Pray be generous, young sir. Be not so parsimonious in your praise."

"Ha! Ha! Ha! By the bye, you lived in town; your speech betrays it."

"Yet I am a country lass by birth."

"Well, the best people are found in the country."

"Then I might be proud."

"But you were in Tokyo, were you not?"

"Yes; and in Kyoto, too. Being a bird of passage, I have been in several places."

"Which do you like best, here or there?"

"It does not make any difference to me."

"No anxious thought can disturb you in such a quiet place, I am sure."

"Dear sir, whether you become optimistic or otherwise altogether depends upon the mental attitude you assume. You get tired of the country of fleas and move into that of mosquitoes; the emigration will benefit you very little."

"How will it do if you go to a country free from fleas and mosquitoes? "

"If there be any such place under the sun, please let me have it; pray let me have it right now." She was imperious in her demand.

"Yes, you shall have it if you want it so much."

So saying, I took out my sketch-book and drew in lines a woman on horse-back admiring a wild cherry in full bloom. It was a mere attempt at psychological delineation, a poor picture drawn in no time. Perception was paramount in the drawing.

"Come, miss, please get into this. Neither fleas nor mosquitoes will disturb you here." I put the sketch right under the nose of the enchantress, who I thought would either blush or be at a loss, but not be pained, judging from her defying appearance. I waited and watched.

"What a close, uncomfortable world it is! It has width only. Do you like to live in such a place? You are a crab." She acquitted herself with a dashing stroke.

"Aha! Ha!" I laughed aloud. The nightingale in the hedge stopped her "hohō-hokekyō" in the midst of her song at the sudden outburst of my merriment, and away she flew to a tree far beyond. We paused and listened a while, but her song thus abruptly interrupted would not so easily come to her lips again.

"You saw Gembei at the mountain pass yesterday, didn't you?"

"Well, yes—."

"You visited the pagoda dedicated to the virgin of Nagara on your way here?"

"Yes—."

"Autumn comes with its dew drops,
 They sojourn on the arundo leaves;
Short-lived sojourners they are;
 I feel as if I were they."

My companion recited the poem straight on without giving any explanation or tune. I know not why.

"That poem I heard recited at the teahouse."

"You learned it from the old woman there. She once served in our family, before I got marri—." She stopped short and looked into my face, anxious to know if the remark had cast a cloud upon my features, but I pretended not to have noticed it at all.

"It was while I was a young girl that I told her the story of the Nagara maiden every time she called. The poem at first proved to be too hard a nut to crack, but by repeated pounding she at last mastered not only the poem, but everything else."

"That explains all. I wondered how she could have learned such a long story with such a poem. Is it not a very sad story?"

"Is it, my dear sir? Had I been she, I would never have composed such a poem. I would by no means have thrown myself into the water. It was waste of life. Don't you think so?"

"Yes, I do. But what would you have done under the circumstances? "

"It is simplicity itself, my dear sir. I would have made the Sasada lad and the Sasabe lad both my paramours."

"Both, you mean?"

"O yes."

"You are very ambitious."

"It's no ambition, but a proper thing to do."

"Then of course you need not go to either the country of fleas or of mosquitoes, you can stay right on where you are."

"Yes, I can stay right on here without leading a wretched crab life."

'Hohō-hokekyō' came with redoubled force from the nightingale. The bird had long flown from our imagination, and her sudden loud note startled us both. Once her throat was set right, her songs would, it seems, flow out melodiously and spontaneously. With her head over heels and puffing out her little throat as large as she possibly could, she would sing so loud as though her lips would burst. 'Hohō-hokekyō! Hohō-hokekyō!'

The notes came one after another in rapid succession.

"That is a song spontaneous and genuine," she explained, and I was her obedient pupil.

## V

"I beg your pardon, sir. Sure you come from Tokyō, too?

"How do you know?"

"'How do I know,' you ask? One glance is enough. First, your dialect tells."

"What part of Tokyō do you locate me?"

"Well—Tokyō is such a big place. Certain it is that you are not of down town, but up town. Is it Kojimachi? No? Then Koishikawa? or it may be Ushigome or Yotsuya."

"Well, you are not wide of the mark. I wonder how you could guess."

"Appearance is treacherous, but I am a Yedoite, too."

"That explains all. I wondered how dashingly gallant you looked."

"O no! no! You flatter. Nothing could be so wretched as the lord of creation when he is driven into such a miserable hovel."

"How have you drifted to such an out-of-the-way place? "

"You are right there, sir. Yes, it came off just as you say. I drifted here, a ruined man in the last stage of poverty."

"Have you been the boss of a barber shop all your life?"

"No, sir, I am a simple artisan of the trade and not boss. My home? Matsunagachō, Kanda, was where my home stood. It is such a small untidy place just like the forehead of your Tom-cat. It may have escaped your notice when you passed. There you remember is Ryukan Bridge. You don't know that either? It is a well-known bridge in Tokyo."

"A little more lather, please. It smarts awfully."

"Does it, sir? I am given to over-cleanliness. Nothing

satisfies me until I have given you a close shave by digging into each of the pores with my blade. Barbers of today do not shave, but simply smooth away your face with their razors. A little more patience and I'm done."

"Patient I have long been like Job. I pray you would use a little more hot water or soap."

"Can't you behave a little better, sir? I'm sure it won't hurt more than you can bear. Really your cheeks are at fault; they have grown so hairy."

The barber who had digged his fingers deep into my cheek to stretch the skin reluctantly let go his hold, took a little thin cake of red soap from the shelf, soaked it in the water a second and went with it all over my countenance. Never did I have such an experience before. And the water he put the soap in was suspected to have been drawn several days ago and to be already stale. The discovery was anything but pleasant.

So long as it was a barber's shop, quite proper it was for me to sit before the mirror, but I would have given up the privilege long ago. A mirror ceases to be one unless it be smoothly even, so that it can give a faithful reflection of your countenance. If one hangs up a poor distorted looking-glass and tells you to sit before it, he, like a poor photographer, will be unable to escape the blame that he has deliberately planned to hurt the sitter's self-respect. Perhaps it is one of the means of discipline to drive away your vanity, yet I should think it no virtue in you to affect indifference when your face is represented there far below its actual value. The mirror before which I was compelled to sit was surely meant to be a contumely to distort my face. Turn to the right and your nose would dilate all over the area of your face; turn to the left and your mouth would open so wide as to reach to the roots of your ears; put back your head a little and a flat head of an ugly toad would come out to greet you there; make a little bow and there would come forth an enormous forehead like that of a man begotten after the God of Good Fortune. While you sit before the glass, you will have to play the part of many a monster. True I have no pretension whatever to an undue share of beauty in my features, yet the mirror itself, I should think, can not go with impunity so long as the sun's rays freely penetrate the parts where the silvered-paper has gone, not to speak of its non-artistic shape and colouring. A contemptible man calls you bad names. They alone won't be so hard to bear, but when you are told to make home with him, you are a doomed man.

Moreover he was no ordinary sort of a barber. When I looked into his shop, he sat with crossed legs sending clouds of smoke from his long pipe up to the festoons of miniature flags suspended from the ceiling in commemoration of the Anglo-Japanese Alliance. Time seemed to hang very heavy on his hands. Once I went in and committed my head to his charge I was much startled to see how dashingly bold he, all of a sudden, had become. He seemed to think that the ownership of the head was his own while shaving it, and I began to doubt if it belonged to me at all. So mercilessly cruel he was in dealing with it. Even if it had been nailed firm upon my shoulders, it could never have stood long.

In using his razor, he observed none of the civilized methods. When he applied his blade to my cheek, it produced a certain disagreeable grating sound. In driving his razor along the temples, he gave a shock to the artery. When he began to rake, and rip and tug at my chin, I was greatly scared by a fearful sound *gorigori* as when one walks on frosted ground. And he was fully satisfied at the thought that he was the finest barber in all Japan.

Lastly he was drunk. Every time he addressed me with "Sir," I had to inhale a certain dreadful smell. Frequently would he gasp out upon my nose a poisonous gas, which made me wonder if he was not decaying inwardly. If things went on in this way nobody could tell when and where his blade would go; the barber himself seemed to have no definite plans to go by, and how could I know where he might drive his razor next? I would wedge in no complaints at a little injury inflicted upon my face as I, from my free will, had committed it to his charge, yet what I feared most was a sudden change of mind which might drive him to the cutting off of my windpipe.

"A poor barber will soap you well before he shaves, yet you are as hairy as an ass and it can't be helped," so saying, he tossed the cake up to the shelf, but the unruly soap rolled down to the ground against its master's will.

"Sir, you seem a stranger to this place, how long have you been here?"

"I have been here only a few days."

"And where are you staying?"

"At Shioda's."

"Are you? I thought you were. My guess was right. In

fact, I myself came here looking to the old landlord for succour. I knew him while in Tokyō; being neighbours, we soon became very well acquainted. He is such a good kind soul, ever ready to answer pity's call. His wife died last year, and the old widower dispels his loneliness with his abundant stock of old curios. They say he has lots of precious articles, and if sold, they will bring him a fortune."

"His daughter is such a beauty! "

"Be on your guard, sir!"

"How?"

"Begging your pardon, my dear sir, don't you know she is a divorced woman?"

"Indeed! "

"That's too simple a word to deal with the case. A faithful wife would never have left her husband. Her husband's bank failed, and she came home on the ground she could no longer live in comfort. It's a shame! While her old father is alive, it will be all right with her, but when the worst comes upon the old gentleman, she will be left quite helpless."

"You don't say so!"

"Of course she will, and she is not on good terms with the master of the head house."

"Is hers then a branch-house?"

"Yes, it is. The head-house stands on a hill and commands a very fine view. You must visit it sometime."

"Pray lather it once more; it begins to smart."

"How can you be so sensitive? The fault lies entirely in your cheeks; they are so hairy and the hair is as stiff as that of a hedgehog. Shaving once every three days is a necessity. If I can not give you satisfaction, nobody under the sun can."

"I'll do as you advise, or rather I would come every day."

"Are you going to stay there some time? It's risky; don't do that. It's no use. A fool will be entrapped by such a reckless strumpet, who will lick him to the bone."

"How can it be, I wonder?"

"True, sir, she is pretty, yet she is a lunatic."

"How can you say that?"

"Why, sir, the villagers one and all will tell you that."

"They must be wrong."

"Well, but there is proof, undeniable proof. Don't be enticed by that Siren. Be on your guard, please."

"Don't be alarmed, my dear barber, I'm perfectly safe, but what is your proof? I should like to know."

"It is a strange story. Smoke away at your pipe and be at home, please, and you shall be treated with it. Will you not have a shampoo?"

"No, thank you."

"Let me then rub off your dandruff."

So saying, the barber without any more ado planted his ten dirty finger nails upon my skull and mercilessly began a fierce up and down movement. The nails, thus buried deep in the roots of my black locks, were driven back and forth with the speed of a hurricane. They were rightly to be likened to an enormous rake of a monster giant, with which he raked and levelled everything in his way as he strode through an uninhabited region. I do not know how many hundred thousand hairs grow on my head, but I feared that his nails, after having pulled up the locks by the root, would go deeper down through the inflamed swollen skin, down to the skull and then to the brain destroying every obstacle lying before them. Such was my barber's madcap fingering exercise upon my pate.

"How do you like this, sir? Sure it has lulled you to a sweet nap."

"You are awfully good!"

"Well, nobody can stand this sleepy influence, sir; everybody is delighted with it."

"I thought my head would come off its trunk."

"Do you feel so dull, sir? The fault lies entirely in the weather. It's spring that makes everybody so dull and sleepy. Have a puff, please; you must be very lonely, alone in the inn. The *ennui* will kill you. Do come and have a chat whenever you will. We are both Yedoites and naturally our talks go over the same ground. She comes out to wait on you, does she, that miss? It is a pity that she has not the least bit of decency in her."

"My dear barber, can I remind you that your talk stopped short where your young lady had done something, and my dandruff was rubbed off and my head had a hair-breadth escape from being pulled up?"

"Yes, so it was. Empty-headed as I am, it's too bad of me that a well started story should have no ending. There that monk fell deep in love with—."

"Which monk do you mean?"

"The young priest of the Kankai Temple, of course."

"Monk, or no monk, you have not introduced one yet."

"Indeed? I'm such a hasty soul! Begging your pardon, sir, he was a young priest whose constitution neither fasting nor praying could humble and whose countenance was expressive of carnal appetite. The fellow, sir, fell over head and ears in love with our belle and at last sent her a love-letter. No, wait! He wooed. No, it was an amorous letter, to be sure it was. Well—it's getting funny. Things have got all mixed up in my brain. Ugh! Yes, it's as it is. Then, that one was struck dumb—."

"But who was astonished, my dear friend?"

"The woman, sir."

"Am I to understand then that the woman who received the letter was dumb-founded?"

"No, that wasn't it. Had she been at a loss what to do on the receipt of the letter, she would have been a lovable creature, but she was just the opposite."

"Then which was which?"

"The one that made love to her."

"But nobody wooed her, you remember."

"By Jove! I'm wrong as wrong can be. The one who had received the letter."

"Then sure it was the woman."

"No, it was the man."

"If a man, he could be nobody else but the priest himself."

"Yes, that monk."

"But how was the young priest astonished?"

"Why, sir, he and the old priest, the abbot, were chanting a sutra in their morning service, when the woman rushed into the sanctuary— Sure none but a lunatic could have done that!"

"And what did she do?"

"'If I am so dear to you,' she exclaimed, 'let me lie down and be your companion in a bed made right beneath Buddha.' And she hugged the bewildered priest hard to her breast."

"You don't say so!"

"To Taian, the young priest, it was a thunder-bolt. He had sent a mad woman a love letter and all he could reap was the shameful scene. So ashamed was the poor monk that that very night he disappeared from the temple and killed himself."

"You say he killed himself?"

"I imagine he did; no sane man could go on living in such disgrace, you know."

"Can you be so sure of that?"

"Well, no! His partner being a mad woman, he would have played a fool if he had put an end to his life. May be he still lives."

"What an absorbingly interesting story!"

"Interesting, or not interesting, she was, and is the laughing stock of all the villagers, yet the woman, deranged as she is, takes no notice of the jeers and sneers she is exposed to and goes in and out among the village people as calmly as the Swan on the pond. You, sir, are perfectly safe as you seem quite solid, but such being your woman to deal with, you had better view her from a safe distance, or what will come nobody can predict!"

"I'll take warning, ha! ha! ha!"

Having its birth far on the billowy sea, the sultry spring breeze idly came over the beach and was drowsily playing with our barber's shop-curtain; a swallow making a slanting dive under the curtain cast a spirit-like shadow upon the mirror. An old man of some sixty winters was seen squatting down beneath the eaves of his little cottage. He was quietly opening shell-fish; as he opened the shell with his little knife, it clicked and down went red meat into the basket. A flash went the shell from his trembling hand across the gossamer two feet in width to join its comrades. Oyster shells, clam shells, conch shells and what not piling up formed a veritable pyramid by the willow-tree which stood on the bank of a sandy brook. Unfortunate ones fell to the bottom of the stream and were buried deep under ground, where the light of the world never visits. New shells stepping on the heads of old ones soon formed a heap right below the weeping willow. The old man went on with his monotonous work unremittingly, never asking why, and the monotony was broken only when he cast the empty shells over beyond the gossamer. His basket seemed to have no bottom to hold its contents; his spring day seemed tranquil and mild to an eternity.

A lukewarm breeze coming through the meshes of the nets visits the villagers who are dead to its strong fish odour. The giant Vulcan melting innumerable dull swords in his enormous cauldron pours the molten ore upon the sea. In describing the colour of the sea seen through the squares of the nets, the imagery is true to life.

No harmony seemed to exist between our barber and the surroundings he was in. Had he been such a strong, fiery character as to give one an impression that he could resist the natural influences around him, I, wedged in

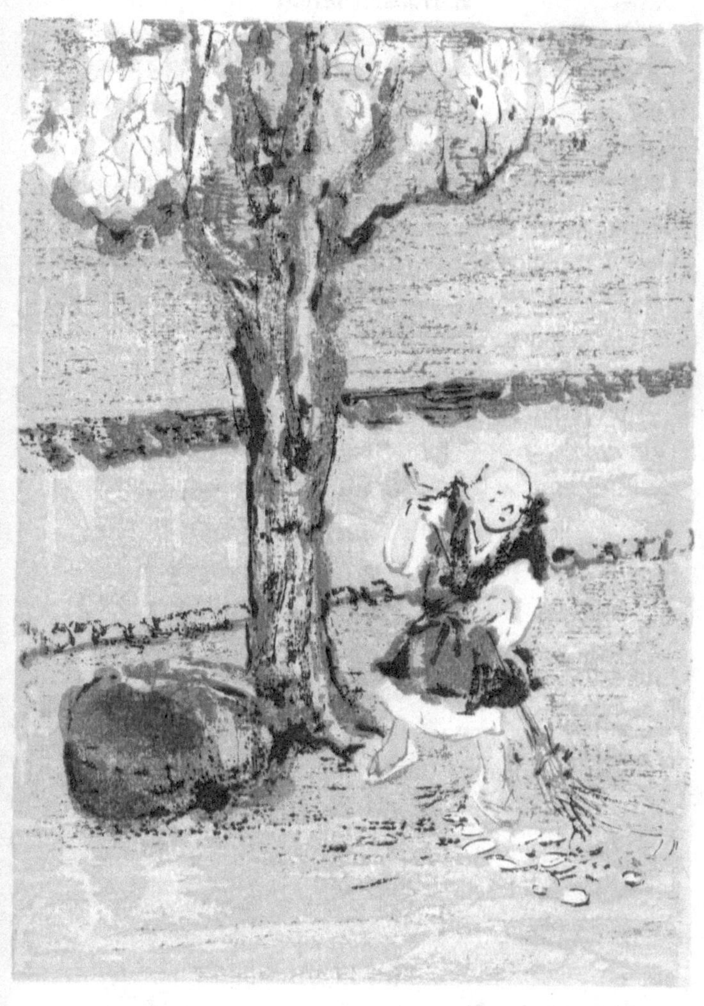

between the two, should have felt out of place, as they say, "A square chisel to make a round hole." Fortunately he was not so great a man, with all the pride he took in his birth right, as a Yedoite; with all his oaths and swearing he shot at you, our barber could not but bow down in humiliation before the all pervading harmonious, congenial spirit of spring. The harder he tried to strike a discordant note upon the harp of Nature, the more he felt his weakness and helplessness until he tottered to her breast, and there embraced he skipped and danced in the vernal sunshine like a happy innocent child.

Inconsistency is a phenomenon found only when things or persons equal in size and strength, or in constitution and will-power, can not get along together any more than water with fire. The moment one perceives in the other superiority far beyond his reach, his fighting spirit begins to slacken until at last it is absorbed by the greater force to be part of, and serve it. Thus, the talented serve the great; the ignorant the talented, and the beasts of burden the ignorant. Now our barber is acting his part as the crack-actor in the broad-farce with a back-ground got up by spring herself. His garrulous sharp tongue should have jarred the universal harmony of spring, but the fact was just the opposite; he was now assiduously trying to help increase the congenial feeling of the balmy spring. I was glad to be acquainted with such an easy-going fellow at a mountain hamlet in the month of flowers. It was an unexpected treat. This simple big talker was a figure that well harmonized with the spring day, a symbol of the piping time of peace.

Thus viewed, our hero becomes a good subject for a picture or a poem. I tarried there in his shop much longer than I had expected, and our conversation was drifting from one topic to another, when in came a little round head from under the curtain.

"Pray, can I have my head shaved?"

The priestling was dressed in a simple cotton *kimono* tied round with a girdle of the same stuff; the gown he had on over his clothes was of the roughest kind of cloth like a mosquito net. He looked quite innocent; still there lurked mischief in the corners of his eyes.

"Sure, Ryōnen-San, you got a scolding the other day from your old master, the abbot? You tarried a little too long on your way home."

"No, barber, I got praise."

"'A nice boy thou art to have been gone so long on thy errand, catching fish on the way'; did thy master commend thee like that perhaps?"

"Young as thou art, Ryōnen," my master said, "thou art really a good boy to have spent so much time on thy errand."

"Yes, indeed! That's how you've got so many bumps on your head. I do not like to shave such a knotty head as yours. It takes so much time; I'll oblige you to-day, but mind! only to-day. Next time you come, come with your head remoulded."

"Should I have to do that, a much better barber shall have the honor."

"Ha! Ha! Ha! His head is uneven, yet his tongue is smooth."

"And a poor artisan, yet a powerful drunkard!"

"You sneaking bastard, how dare you insult m—?"

"I am not to blame, my dear barber. That's what my old master says. Don't be so much excited over a trifle. Age should be more discreet."

"Pshaw! Shame on me! What do you think, my dear sir!"

"Well—?"

"These bonzes living high up a long flight of stone-steps are free from the cares of the world and can amply afford to be clever at speech. Even such a chick of a priest talks big.—Put back your head a little, or you'll smart. Are you ready? Blood will startle you."

"It smarts; be more sympathetic, please."

"If you cannot stand this test, you will never be a priest."

"Begging your pardon, Mr. Barber, I'm one already."

"But you are not a full fledged one. By the bye, how did that young monk Taian kill himself, my dear little holiness?"

"But he is still alive."

"Alive! You don't say so! He ought to have died."

"Taian-San is now at Taibai Temple, Rikuzen Province. Penitent of his past sins, he has entered into a life of fasting and praying. When he comes out of the monastery in a few years he will be a sanctified priest. It is a matter for congratulation."

"Congratulation? True he is a priest and a layman's code will not do, yet I doubt if it is lawful for a clergyman to run away from his home in the darkness of night.

You can not be too cautious of women. A woman is a stumbling-block to a young man. —That reminds me of that mad woman, does she still call on your old master?"

"I never heard of a woman branded mad."

"What a dull-headed monk you are! Does she visit or not?"

"No mad woman comes, but Shioda's daughter does."

"However clever your master abbot may be in his invocations, I'm afraid he won't be able to bind up her shattered nerves. Certain it is that the curse of the husband whom she has deserted haunts her day and night."

"My old master highly commends her saying she is a great woman, a heroine."

"Up the stone-steps, topsy-turvydom reigns. No matter what your master says, she is a confirmed mad woman.— It's shaven nice and clean. Go home right away and get a good scolding."

"No, I'll take much more time and obtain fine praise instead."

"Do as you will, you retorting chatterbox."

"Pooh! You cleaning stick!"

"What?"—

The fresh-green head dived and was out of the curtain. The spring breeze tarrying on the knotted head a second passed on wondering what it had been.

## VI

In the gathering twilight, I sit at my desk. All the *shōji* and *karakami* are wide open.

It is rather a large establishment for a few people to keep. My room being far away by several flights of winding stairs from the quarters where the people of the house behave themselves like decent folks is so quiet that I can indulge in meditation without being molested in the least. It is still quieter today. The master, the daughter, and the domestics seem to have evacuated the house and gone, leaving me all alone before I knew it. However, they can not have gone to an ordinary place. The country of haze or of clouds is where they have gone, or to the region where the clouds and the water spontaneously meet, and amidst the languid dull influence of the bewitched sea the boatman forgets to steer his boat, which, drifting on and on, finds itself in a zone where it can hardly tell the clouds from the water, and while gazing around in utter bewilderment the sail loses itself in the clouds and the water; to such a far place they must have gone; or they have all of a sudden melted into the spring itself, and their bodies now turned into the smallest particles of ether imaginable defy the most powerful microscope to see and find even the faintest trail of them if it could; or they have transformed themselves into skylarks, who, after singing out the day till the yellow tint of *nanohana* grows ablaze in the westering sun, fly to where a purple haze hangs thick over the evening sky; or they have transmigrated into horseflies, which, after performing their duty to make the long day longer with their droning buzzing have got into the sweet bells of camellia flowers to gather honey, but before they get heavy with the sweet juice, the petals fall and they with them. The poor insects now safe from the greedy sparrows under cover of the bells may be enjoying a tranquil sleep enlivened by sweet pleasant dreams. At any rate, it is so very quiet.

The spring breeze passes through an empty house; it comes and goes neither because it is invited nor because it is offended at the rebuff it has met; it comes and goes as fair God wills. As I sit with my chin on my palm, my mind is as unoccupied and vacant as the room itself, and it will come and blow through it, though I invite it not.

The fear that the earth might give way comes from the thought that our feet are on it; the terror that lightning might strike our pates and temples is caused by our consciousness of having heavens above us; the bitterness of the transitory world is felt, as it urges you with 'Be a man and fight it out'; living in the world bounded both on the east and west, you have to walk on the rope of interests; to him actual love is an enemy; wealth he sees is dust. The reputation he grasps, or the honour he grapples, is the honey with a sting left by the deceitful bee. What you call happiness comes from the possession of a thing; so soon as you possess it, it ceases to be pleasure, but becomes pain full of stings. Here is a poet or a painter, who, soaring high above this world of relativity, breathes in the purest air to satiety; he dines in haze; he drinks dewdrops; he discerns purple, he discriminates crimson, until he is content to die. He is not satisfied with sticking to one object, but assimilation is what he aspires to do. Once he has got into the thing itself, he becomes so free and omnipresent as air, so that he can find no place under the sun large enough to admit him. Then anxiety or worry can find no room in his heart to nestle, but the balmy breeze coming through the green leaves will stroke his broken sedgehat as it goes. However, I do not wish to paint out such a land of holies and scare away those poor worldlings by crying, "You wretched souls, you can not approach us," but rather invite those blessed few into the fold by preaching these good tidings.

To be plainer, the poet's or the artist's atmosphere generated by his imagination is the stepping-stone to his own salvation. An old grey-haired sinner whose days are counted groaning under the burden of remorse and regret may review the days gone by and remember with a contented smile that once or twice in his long miserable career a light flashed out of his sinful body, and he, like Saul near the Damascus gate, saw his Lord face to face. If not, his was a dog's life. However, the poet's interest lies in no single object. He will not stick to, or try to assimilate himself to, one thing only. His sympathy goes much further. Sometimes he becomes a solitary flower which blows by the roadside, or a couple of amorous butterflies flirting and dancing in the balmy air, or, like Wordsworth, turns into a host of golden daffodils by the lake, thus enjoying a cool breeze to his heart's content. Absorbed in the indescribable beauty of his surroundings, his heart gets entranced and is unaware where he is, or what it is that has charmed him so. Some will say that he has been visited by the spirit of the universe, or that he has been listening to the enchanting melody of a stringless harp played by an angel. Others will affirm

"No, no! You are all wrong; he has been wandering in a boundless space beyond human knowledge and apprehension, ever enjoying perfect peace under an enchanted bower." They are quite free to say whatever they please. The mood in which I sit alone at my ebony desk is somewhat analogous to one of these states.

Nothing arrests my mind; nothing attracts my eye. I can hardly say I have become assimilated to anything, for there is nothing bright enough in its colouring that it gets on the stage of my perception. Yet I know I do move. True, I do not move in this world, or out of it. Somehow I do get about. Neither flowers, nor birds, nor my fellow-men make me move. I simply move as though in a trance.

If pressed for explanation, I should say my heart is moving with the spring. Every colour, every breeze, any sound, and anything in the first season of the year all blended together will form themselves into holy pills; you dissolve them in the sacred water of Elysium; the liquid thus produced will be brought out into the scorching sun of the "Peach Grotto" to be turned into vaporous essence. The essence, passing through the pores will go into your system and be converted before you know it. Assimilation is ordinarily accompanied by stimulus, and you are pleased with it. Mine differs in that it knows not what it has been blended with. Although I feel no excitement whatever, there creeps into my mind an indefinably vacant pleasurable feeling. The sea lashed by a fresh breeze raises crested breakers whose hollowness gives a shallow discordant sound. The mood in which

I find myself is somewhat similar to the temperament of the great ocean, which reaches from one continent to another with gentle undulating billows that invisibly roll several fathoms deep. In my case, there is not so much vitality and therein lies the true felicity which I esteem most. In the expression of mighty vital power, there creeps at its heels a fear that it might at last come to an end. No such anxiety enters the state of my mind as colourless and tasteless as water, and it is free from the fear that it might lose its vitality any moment. Moreover it is above common place or common sense. I call it 'pale serenity' an indescribable frame of mind free from either care or anxiety. 'Melting into nature,' or 'oneness with the universe' are the favorite terms used by the poet in describing such a state of mind.

How would it do, thought I, if I turned this poetic humour into a picture? However, an ordinary painting would never do. Our so-called picture is the one that represents on canvas the things, whether man or scenery, just as they appear, or just as we see them through our aesthetic eye, and when a flower is painted as such, stream as stream, man as man, people are satisfied. A more conscientious artist will try to paint with fresh colours the rapture he has felt from the scenes unfurled before him. Such an artist would never be satisfied unless his work vividly represented the inspiration with which he had been visited. He boldly announces to the world, "I came, I saw and felt the thing as it had never been before. Tradition and routine handed down and honoured for ages past have no authority over me. Mine is a piece of work born of right, beautiful conceptions perverted by no bigoted views."

These two kinds of artists may differ in the depth of perception of things, or in that one is objective and the other subjective in viewing things, but they agree in that they work upon an external stimulation. There is, however, another sort of artist whose theme for his workmanship is not so distinctly defined. Awakening all your faculties, you try to find out in the physical world what it is, and you will reap only disappointment, for it is neither round nor green, it has neither light nor shade, nor has it an outline even. His is an emotion which comes not from outside, or even if it did, it is nothing that develops itself before your natural eyes, hence no form, no shape. There is, however, something in you, that you can hardly suppress; it is a passion, it is a mood which demands expression in one way or another. How can I make it into a picture, or what form shall I borrow in order to represent it so vividly and graphically that it may be comprehended and appreciated by a connoisseur or a critic?

A thing with little feeling attached to it may suffice the need of the first artist; a thing and feeling emanating from it may satisfy the second; but the one thing needful for the third artist is not to be found in the natural world, but in the artist himself; it is a mood or humour peculiar to him, which will become a picture only when it has found a fit object to illustrate itself, yet it is all but impossible to hunt out such an object, or even if you were successful in your effort, you would be unable to make it represent even a fraction of your poetic exaltation, and the piece you have brought forth will not appeal to the popular mind as such, but rather as a monster. The author himself will hardly think it a reproduction of that scene of nature with which he was so much entranced, and he would be amply repaid if his efforts were crowned with a picture illustrative, even faintly, of the burning passion, by which he was possessed.

Very few, either ancient or modern, have succeeded in this difficult task. The bamboo by Wen-yu-ke, the landscapes by Sesshyū and his followers; later, the portraits by Buson, and the landscape paintings by Ike Taiga are the few representative master-pieces of this school of visionists. Most of the Western painters seem to devote themselves to the study of nature in all her moods, and they seldom try their skill upon the things that exist only in mind apart from matter.

Simplicity, however, being the key-note of our Sesshyū and Buson, the poetic ecstasy they create is too simple and too monotonous to satiate our thirst. Viewed from the angle of artistic skill, I fall far below them, yet that which I wished to make into a picture was a little more complicated and deep, so much so that a sheet of canvas did not seem large enough to contain it all. I took my hands from my cheeks; I folded my arms on the desk and meditated and meditated but all in vain. The colour, the shape and the tone must be all perfect so that I can find my own self in every touch and line of the piece I have brought out. A gipsy woman had kidnapped and carried away the child from its mother. The mother frantic with sorrow had left her home and all and set out on a pilgrimage to recover her lost child. No nook or corner in the sixty-six provinces was left unsearched. The child was in her dreams when she slept. Its image like the "pillar of cloud" ever guided her in her daily wanderings. One day the poor mother wandered into a great city and stood at a crowded cross-road when, like a lightning flash, she saw and ran and pressed her child to her bosom with a cry of joy, "Here you are!" The scene just described well illustrates the attitude in which I intend to paint my picture, but it is very hard work. Could I bring forth this *tone* on the canvas, I would not mind a bit any criticism people may pass upon me, nor should I be sorry if they said it was no more a picture than a bat a bird. Nay, let it be an ox or a horse, or be it neither the one nor the other, be it nothing, I shall be quite satisfied as long as the distribution of colours, the straight or curved lines, or the general tone of the picture reveals some of the passion or hallucination with which I have painted it. The harder I tried, the farther the phantom went. The sketch-book was laid on the desk and I thought and thought until my eyes seemed to pierce the book, but no good idea would come.

The pencil was put aside. "Am I not wrong," thought I, "to try to turn such an abstract theme, however attractive it may be to me, into a picture?" Human heart is the same all over the world, and many fascinated by a similar perception of the beautiful must have attempted to transform it, in one way or another, into some tangible form which promises permanency. What can it have been?

"Music?" suggested a still small voice. "Yes, music must be nature's voice born of such necessity and at such a time. Regret avails nothing, yet I can not but be sorry that I have had very little training along that line. Ignorance is bliss somewhere else, I admit.

Now that the first and the second plans have both failed me, how about the third? Will not Poetry help me in giving expression to my thought? "The development of time is an element indispensable to true poetry," says Lessing, "And poetry and painting differ in their essential qualities." If he be right, the passion I wish to express may not be rendered into verse. Time may have some share in the ecstasy I feel, but the events that take place one after another in the course of time will have nothing to do with it. One comes and goes, followed by another and another, but I find no joy in the changing scenes. Mine is the joy which comes from a certain thing permanently fixed in a certain place. So long as it is there fixed and permanent it may justly be transcribed into a poem in ordinary words independent of any changing scenes of time. The exaltation may be rendered into a pictorial or a poetical composition with a distribution of proper objects in space, but where can we get these objects in order to depict this *motif* wide as the universe, vague as fog? Once this problem is solved, I am sure we can get a good poem despite Lessing's argument to the contrary. Then we need not trouble ourselves about Homer or Virgil. Let me repeat it here. If poetry is a fit vessel to convey a certain mood, it will surely be able to describe it in words, when the necessary conditions for painting are provided also for verse, although time's changing scenes will have very little to do with it.

Setting argument aside, let me proceed with the theme in hand. A closer investigation will perhaps reveal my ignorance, for I have forgotten almost all what "Laocoon" insists upon. A picture having been denied me by the Muse, I took up my pencil to write a poem. The pencil was on the sketch-book; I rocked myself to and fro to shake out a good idea, but in vain. Irritability got hold of me, and not a single line came out of the sharp end of my pencil. I wished to call up the name of a friend; come it would up to the throat, but no further. I gave it up for lost, and it would go back complacently to the snug corner where it had been nestling. The experience was exactly like unto this.

In preparing an arrow-root gruel, you stir it up with your chop-sticks. At first you do not feel it at all, but as you go on stirring, you begin to feel the weight of your hand increase until you can move it no longer. At last the sticky substance will come out of the pot as you pull off your sticks, though you invite it not. Composing a poem is somewhat like it.

On the open page was my pencil which had begun to move little by little. Thirty minutes had hardly passed before I gleaned the following:—

> The spring is in March,
>    My sorrow is long as the fragrant grass;
> The flowers fall tranquil on the empty garden,
>    A solitary harp awaits its player;
> The spider reigns in his imperial web,
>    A curling smoke lingers about the cottage.

Humming these three couplets of verse over and over again, I thought each of them might be turned into a picture. I wondered why I had preferred versifying to painting. How was it that I found it easier to put it into a poem than into a picture? The most difficult part being over, I thought the rest would be covered very easily, but I wanted to try my pen on that which my paint-brush had denied me. After many a misgiving and doubt I was able to bring forth these verses:—

Alone I sit silent,
    A faint light comes to my soul;
Life is a world of cares,
    Where can we avoid them?
Once I was blest with a day of rest,
    The bliss served only as a remembrancer
        of life-long pains;
Where can we vent our agony?
    There awaits welcome in the land of
        fleecy clouds.

I read the poem over again from the beginning; it was pleasing to my aesthetical sense, yet it fell far below the ecstasy I was entertained with just a moment ago. My interest not abating, I took up my pencil to write one more piece of poetry; involuntarily I looked towards the entrance when what should my eye catch but a pretty figure, a phantom! The *karakami* was half open to the width of three feet. My curiosity now became a passion.

When I turned my eyes towards the door to see it better, the spectre had already gone out of sight behind the

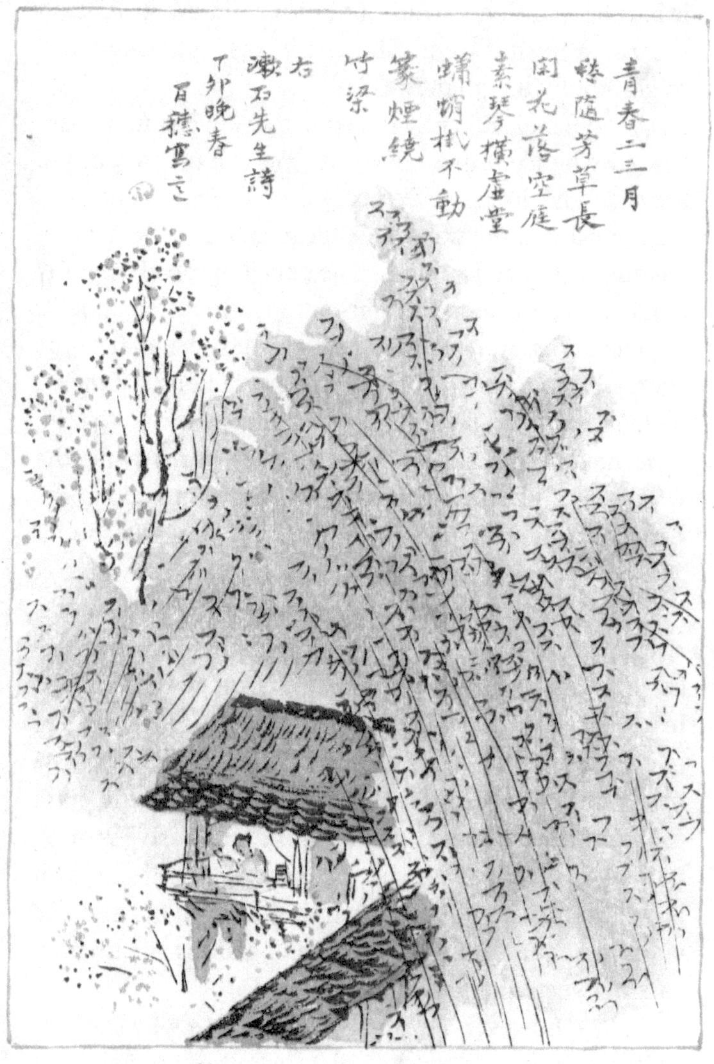

青春二三月
愁隨芳草長
閑花落空庭
素琴横虚堂
蟏蛸掛不動
篆煙繞
竹梁
右
漱石先生詩
丁卯晩春
百穂寫之

sliding paper door. It was easy for me to conjecture that it had been going in and out before I knew it. A flash it came, a flash it went. The poem was laid aside that I might follow the phantom.

A moment had hardly passed before the phantom reappeared whence it had gone out. It was a pretty woman dressed in her long-sleeved fancy *furisode.* The verandah of the opposite storey was where the enchantress was promenading with her airy steps. The pencil dropped from my hand; I held my breath the instant my eye rested upon it.

The sky is overcast with heavy clouds peculiar to the cherry-blossom season; rain is expected any moment; twilight has been gathering force inviting the rain to join. Over beyond the inner court about ten yards wide, the woman in full dress is taking a leisurely walk along the corridor. The dusk of evening is thickening all around. There she comes, there she goes.

Like a sister of charity she moves so quietly that no rustling sound audible even to herself is produced as her long train sweeps along the passage way. She never looks around; her mouth is tightly closed. Distance makes it hard to tell what is the pattern on the skirt of her bright-coloured dress. The space between the plain part and the patterned portion spontaneously forming a fine shading gives the beholder an impression that it is the boundary line between day and night, and the woman in question is indeed walking along the dreamy path between night and day.

It was, however, beyond my conjecture why she was walking up and down the corridor in her long-sleeved garment; how long had she been performing this strange manoeuvre in her strange attire? What motive did she have in so doing? These were mysteries to me. A strange feeling crept over me as I saw her come and go like a phantom. How was it that she thus strangely attired was repeating this miraculous act so decorously and solemnly? If she were complaining of the hasty departure of spring, how could she be so indifferent in her manners? Were she really indifferent to the world about her, how could she be so particular in dressing herself in such a showy magnificent style?

The spring with its serene twilight was lingering about the door of night as if unwilling to go to bed yet. Her gorgeous dress with *obi* of dazzling gold brocade was seen going back and forth through the evening air until it passed away minute by minute into eternal darkness like the bright star that sinks into the depth of the purple sky as the day dawns.

The door of Pluto's nocturnal palace opened to receive our charmer in her flowery dress into its dark chamber, when I thought thus:—

Now while she should be spending the spring eve, every hour of which is as precious as a bushel of gold coins, singing and dancing with a gold screen behind and a silver light before, she is fading away step by step from this beautiful world into the dark one beyond without feeling the least discontentment or making the slightest struggle against her fate. Is it not a pity that she is thus at the mercy of some supernatural power? Through the deepening twilight, I saw her move so lonely, yet there was nothing impatient about her ever keeping up her presence of mind, as she promenaded the same place with a well-balanced gait. If she did not know of the sword hanging over her, her innocence might be the best protector against the imminent danger. If she, being aware of it, could be so calm in mind she was more than human; she must be a weird sister. The dark world being the place whence she came, she might be feeling quite at home in the black surroundings in which she was temporarily placed. If not, how could she be so quiet and peaceful as she lingered on the verge of this world and that? Her long-sleeved ornamental dress with many a pretty pattern was shaded below the waist in one dubious colour—black—the key to the door of the secret chamber of her true character.

Again I thought thus:—

A pretty woman while sleeping a pretty sleep enlivened with so many pleasant dreams is about to breathe her last. Those who nurse and watch her at the head of her sick-bed will be greatly troubled. Were she dying in great pain and agony, not only she, but also her friends watching her day and night might think it a charity to resign her to the cold hand of Death. But the case is just the opposite. She is enjoying a tranquil sleep like a babe. Her purity and innocence should be an ample plea for life, yet Satan is leading her away direct from her sleep to Hades. It is something like being murdered by deception when the victim never dreams of it. If she is destined to die, let her know of the awful event so that she can clasp her hand and say her prayer "Namuamudah" and be ready to give up the ghost. The prayer will not come so readily out of our lips before the sheer fact of death until we have been fully persuaded why she must go. "Ahoy! my sweet love, come back to my bosom; you are still too young and too pretty to be the prey of black Death," would be a more natural voice, as we cry after her whose steps are already half in the other world. It may be that she who is transferred from temporary sleep to ever-lasting repose long before she is aware of it, may think it hard or rather painful to be thus called back, for the fire of carnal passions half extinguished in her will be kindled again. "For mercy's sake, do not call me back; let me go and sleep in peace." Thus she may invoke us, yet we can not help calling after her.

When she appears again at the entrance, I thought, I will call her back to her senses from her fatal sleep. But so soon as she comes in sight, shyness seals my lips and she passes away like a spectre. She shall be fairly caught this time, yet again I let her go free. The moment I am thinking how it is that I can not catch her, she comes and passes on as if she knew not or rather cared not a pin how impatiently and agonizingly I am watching every movement of hers. No feeling of pity or sympathy she seems, as she comes and goes, to entertain for the poor painter, a silent worshipper of hers. "She shall not escape me this time; she shall be caught next time," comes out of my lips; still she is at large. The banks of clouds almost bursting with rain-drops quietly begin to drop them down in fine silvery threads and the gathering dusk hides the woman behind its black curtain.

## VII

It was chilly. A towel in hand, I went down to the bath.

Undressing in the closet, I went down a small flight of steps and found myself in a bath-room about four *tsubo.* Granite quarries being plentiful in the vicinity, the floor of the room was all paved with the beautiful stone; the centre of the floor was dug down to the depth of four feet, where a stone tank as large as that of a *tōfu*-maker's was placed in which the mineral water was brimming over. The water must contain many ingredients as it claims to be a mineral water. It is a comfort to get in there, it is so crystally transparent. Often was I tempted to take it in my mouth, but it had neither smell nor taste that irritated my palate. It claims to have a medical value, but never asking what specific diseases it is good for, I am entirely ignorant of its medicinal virtues. And never have I been bothered about them as I have no special chronic disease to complain of. Yet I could never take a bath in the spring without remembering Pe-le-tien's verse:—

"Smooth and warm is the water of the spring;
There an amorous Venus is busy at her toilet."

At the mention of a hot spring, I am always visited by this pleasurable sensation expressed in the verse. If a hot spring fails to give one this pleasure, I should think it no more a spring than an iron pot a bell, for I entertain no higher ideal about a hot spring than that.

I got into the spring; the hot water came up to my breast. I do not know where it comes from, yet it is ever flowing out of the tank over the brims down to the pavement to keep it comfortably wet. The rays of the spring sun are not strong enough to evaporate the moisture on the stone. You go on the pavement barefoot and your soles feel a delightful warmth. The rain which escapes the alert eye of Night stealthily comes down to the earth to give the flower season its necessary dampness; the particles forming themselves into so many crystalline drops patter down from the eaves to make the quiet night still quieter. The vapour shut in fills every nook and corner, from floor to ceiling of the room and is ever finding a chink or a crevice in the wall or elsewhere to go out and get emancipation from its imprisonment.

Autumnal fog is cool and tranquil; spring haze is mild and delightful; blue smoke rising from the kitchen where the evening meal is being cooked commits its transient form to the boundless bosom of heavens. Each of them, it is true, appeals to our aesthetic fancy, yet the vapour arising from a hot spring in a spring eve softly wraps round the body of the bather until he suspects him to be primitive man in his primitive habit. The vapour is not so thick a screen as to hide one behind it, nor is it so thin and shallow as to convince him that he is the poor fallen angel who has been stripped of the single tissue-like silk gown he wore. You take one layer, another, another and another, yet you can not get at the face you would reach till you find yourself enveloped all around in the warm element. *Saké* makes you tipsy, and we have words to describe it, but I have never heard of a man who has got intoxicated with vapour, and we have no set phrase for it. Even if there be such an expression as 'vapour intoxication,' it would never do for a mist and be a little too strong for a haze, but no other could be more appropriate in describing a man who finds himself in a delightful light fog on a spring eve.

I placed the back of my head on the brim of the tub filled with transparent water. I let my light body drift away where there is very little resistance. Like a jellyfish, it floats together with the soul. Your world will turn into a paradise so soon as you unlock the door of discretion and take off the bar of selfishness. Adaptation is the secret of success in life, and I try to assimulate myself to the hot spring itself. Trust yourself, body and soul to the mercy of the life current and you will be freed from worry and be as happy as the beloved disciple of Christ. Thus viewed, a drowned man might not be so bad, but rather think himself blessed in his novel situation. I remember reading somewhere in Swinburne about a drowned woman who seems happy and cheerful when she is at the bottom of the water. Much troubled I have been about Millais's "Ophelia." How can she have chosen such an unpleasant and comfortless place as the bottom of a brook in order to put an end to her life? Now I understand it all; it may well have appealed to the imagination of the English painter to paint it. Now she is on the water; now she sinks down; now she rises only to sink again; she is simply borne away by the current, like one insensible to her own distress, or as if she were a creature natural to that element. The banks of the stream are profusely sprinkled with daisies, columbines, violets, cowslips and various other wild flowers. Let the colour of the water, the complexion of the maiden whom the current bears away, and the colour of her dress harmonize well and the effect would be just splendid. Were the expression of the drowned virgin peaceful and tranquil with no sorrow whatever, it would be a myth or a fable. Convulsive agony would, of course, spoil the whole atmosphere, yet a calm face of pure innocence indifferent to her environment would be superhuman and interest us little. What kind of face would do, I thought. Millais's "Ophelia" may be a success, yet it can be doubted if the mood in which he painted it was similar to that of mine. Millais is Millais, and I shall play the fool if I try to be somebody else but myself. Can not I, giving a full swing to my imagination, draw a drowned person who is contented and happy wherever he is? Yet the face to my taste would not come.

Here is a eulogy to a drowned person, which I composed while in the bath:—

Wet I shall be when it rains,
  Cold I shall feel when frost comes,
Darkness will shroud me when in the clod;
  Rather let me lie on your back, O wave!
Better still take me down to thy bosom,
                    O spring sea!
  Sure I shall be happy in thy embrace.

Humming this, I was happy in the bath, when *shamisen* music came floating through the vapor. To confess the truth, I am entirely ignorant about this musical instrument, although I profess myself an artist. It disturbs my musical taste very little whether the pitch of the second string gets higher or that of the third grows lower, yet it was a very delightful thing for me to listen to the melody at an irresponsible distance on a still drowsy spring eve with as much sleepy rain, bathing myself body and soul in, the mineral hot spring at a mountain hamlet. The distance made it impossible to tell what she was singing, or what was the accompaniment. Indistinctness often lends a thing charm and it was so with the music. Judging, however, from the quietness of tone, it must be, I thought, a bass accompaniment to some dramatic song often played by a blind minstrel to the Court.

When a boy, I remember there was a wineseller's called Yorozuya beside our gate. The vintner had a pretty daughter Okura-San by name. In the afternoon on quiet spring days, she would practise her *nagauta** accompanied by her own *shamisen.* Then I used to go down into the garden to hear the music which came across the tea plantation of about a dozen *tsubō*. Three pine trees of tolerably big dimensions figured themselves amongst so many nameless plants. The guest-room faced the trees to the east side. The gardener had exercised his skill in planting them in a row so as to add scenic beauty to the garden. It was ever a joy to my boyish mind to look at them. Right beneath the trees, there was an old

---

* A dramatized epic or lyrical song.

ornamental iron lantern turned black with rust. Standing upon an unpretentious red stone, it looked just like an old patriarch of firm conviction brooding over the pedestal. I was very fond of looking at it, too. In front, in the rear and all around, the lantern had a rank growth of grasses, which coming out of the thick lichened clod bloomed to their own delight into so many pretty flowers as if they cared not a pin about the troublesome wind of the sad world. I found in the thicket room enough to get in and I would crouch there for hours together. I looked at the picturesque lantern under the pines; I smelled the fragrance of the wild flowers; I listened to her love-inspiring *nagauta* every day. It was my daily task joyfully repeated.

Her bridal days embellished with everything bright and red having long gone by, Okura-San, now a housewife, must be sitting with a careworn face behind the counter. Is her marriage bed blessed? Does the swallow come back every summer and is she busy building her nest with the mud and dirt she brings with her tiny bill? I can hardly think of the shop alive with the odour of *saké* without remembering that mother bird with her young ones.

I wonder if those pines still stand in the garden without losing their former beauty. The iron lantern must have crumbled into dust by now. Do the herbs remember me who used to crouch in their midst? We were not on speaking terms even then, and there can be no reason why they should remember me after the lapse of so many years; or perhaps they are bold enough to declare, "We do not know you, but we can never forget that sweet voice with which Okura-San daily sang her *Kanjinchō* beginning with "His travelling suit with a string of jingling bells around the collar is wet with dew—."

The sound of the *shamisen* led me some twenty years back to the time when I was an innocent lad. I was absorbed in looking at the panoramic picture which represented a number of my young day scenes unrolled and made to pass before my mind's eye, when the door of the bath-room quietly opened on its hinges.

Thinking somebody was come, I looked towards the entrance without changing my posture in the water. As I had my head laid on the side of the tub farthest from the door, I could have only a slant view of the steps leading down to the bath at the distance of about six yards or so. But nothing came in sight yet when I raised my eyes. Drip, drip, drip, went the raindrops falling from the eaves all along the bath-house. The playing on the *shamisen* had already ceased.

Five minutes had hardly passed before a light step was heard at the top of the steps. One small petroleum lamp hanging from the ceiling was lighting the whole room. It would have been hard to tell one thing from another at such a distance even through transparent air. Harder still, or rather impossible, would it have been to distinguish anything definitely in the room filled with a dense fog of vapour arising from the tank, which, losing its way of exit, was imprisoned, as it were, by a fine drizzling rain without. Until it came down the flight step by step and stood face to face with you in the full glare of light you could hardly tell whether it was a man or a woman.

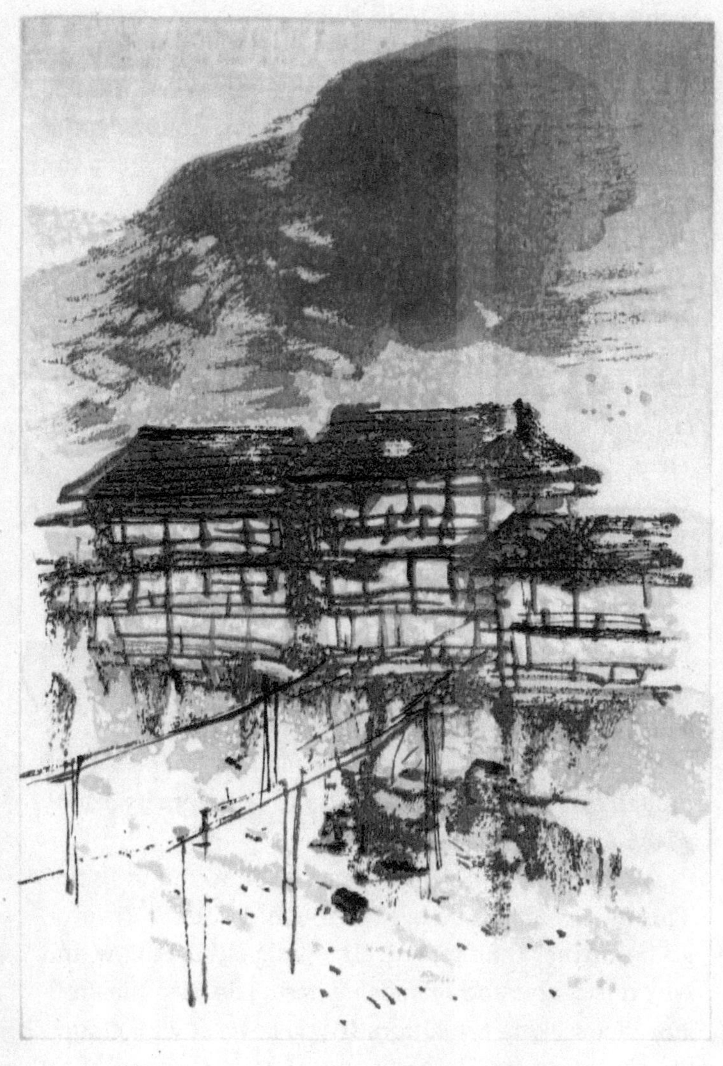

The silhouette takes a step down. The stone floor seems as soft as velvet to its soles. No sound betrays its approach. Yet its outline floats out before me. Being a painter by profession, I have rather a keen conception of human anatomy. The moment I feel the shadow come down the steps, I find a woman and myself alone in the bath-room.

Long before I could make up my mind whether or not to observe her, the woman in her nudity appeared to my full view. The soft ray of the lingering sun coming in turned every particle of vapour into a rosy pink and in the midst of the warm ether I saw the goddess tall and slender, her black hair flowing into a cloud. Then all thoughts of etiquette, decorum, or morals were gone from my head and the sole absorbing ecstasy was that I had at last found a most beautiful subject for my paint-brush.

The sculpture of ancient Greece defies criticism. Every time I saw nude pictures so enthusiastically and elaborately painted by modern French artists as if they were a matter of life or death to them, I wondered, or rather was disgusted, how they could have been so much excited over human flesh as to try to represent its beauty as the one thing needful.

Where is refinement of taste to be found in them? This has troubled me ever so much. I could, however, go no further than to say, "It is vulgar!" Yet how and why it is coarse and offends my taste has been the problem ever seeking a solution. If you cover it with clothes the beauty of the flesh is concealed. If stripped of its covering, it becomes ugly, and the ugliness of exposure is discernible in every touch and line of modern nude pictures and nowhere could elegance of taste be traced in the whole composition. Our contemporary artists seem dissatisfied with the simple representation of naked bodies unless they push out the nudes to the world of propriety and decency. Forgetting that the normal condition of man is maintained by clothes, they try to give all power and authority to nakedness. "Just enough" should be their motto, but they slight the motto and go on and on describing nudity until they drive the audience to satiety and sickness. When an artist has thus abused his technical skill to such an extreme, people begin to doubt his sincerity and blame him as base. The more impatient he gets to make a beautiful thing more beautiful, the less so it grows. "A flow will have an ebb," is a worldly wisdom, but can not we apply it to art, too?

Innocent calmness shows reserve. It is an indispensable element in good painting or in a good style of composition. One of the greatest evils of modern arts is that the so-called current of civilization has turned artists into mere slaves of routine work. The nude picture amply illustrates this. Every town has a covey of belles called *geisha* whose business it is to approach you with smiles and sweet words trying to make profitable merchandise of their flesh. On meeting her sensual customer, the *geisha* will lavish upon him all her charms, either facial or otherwise, to have him secure in her carnal trap. The catalogue annually issued by the Salon is filled with such naked belles as our *geisha*. They never let you forget even a second that they are undressed, and by twitching every nerve and muscle show you that they are ready to be embraced and kissed any moment.

No atom of impurity is discernible in the beautiful figure so charmingly revealed before me. How could I be so wicked and prosaic as to pull her down to the sordid world by comparing her to a mortal stripped of her clothes? You would not be far from the truth if you imagined her a goddess riding on a purple cloud long before she knew she was naked and sewed fig leaves together to make herself an apron. There was neither consciousness of shame nor of guilt about the apparition. It was so very natural.

A dense fog arising from the tub fills up every nook and corner of the room and still goes on and on rising. The ghastly lamp shedding a half-transparent light to dispel the darkness of the spring eve transforms itself, together with the vapour, into a glimmering rainbow bridging east to west. In the midst of which a snow white figure with light black hair waving down to the sloping shoulders dimly reveals itself. Behold how it looks!

Two curves gracefully approaching the snow-white neck force it to make a slight bow; each coming down the sloping shoulder draws a rich round curve along the elbow until at last it discharges itself into five fingers. Right under the soft protuberant breasts, the flesh-wave is down and placid, but towards the abdomen it again swells out in a sweet undulation till it is lost behind. Before it is out, it branches into two fleshy limbs, which are bent a little to keep up the balance. The knee then harmoniously uniting the opposing forces of the thigh and the shin lets them undulate down to the heel, where the flat foot taking all the responsibility of the complicated turmoil of machinery upon the sole finishes up the whole structure. The world has nothing so complicated and yet so symmetrical in composition; nothing can be so natural, so soft and so agreeable to our sense of beauty.

And yet the image is not exposed to our view as our modern nude pictures. A light mist which mystifies everything is the back ground in which our image is unrolled in all her beauty. Only half of the scale is shown amidst all inky black; thus the painter leaves the rest of the imposing dragon to the imagination of those who look at the picture. Viewed from the aesthetic point of view, it has atmosphere, warmth and weird tone indispensable to good painting. The dragon whose thirty-six scales are one by one elaborately and minutely painted excites our laughter. A heavenly ether purifies nakedness even and gives the beholder a sense of divineness as he admires it through the mist. When this beautiful visitor revealed itself before me, I imagined it to be Luna, goddess of the moon, who, having made her escape from the Capital of Honeysuckles, was surrounded by her pursuer, the seven-coloured rainbow, and was at a loss where to flee.

Nearer and whiter the figure comes. One step more and the goddess would have been a fallen angel. Like the bushy tail of the Sacred Tortoise, her black flowing hair flutters a moment and the white figure cutting through the vapour runs up the steps. The treble ho! ho! ho! escape from her rosy lips as she runs along the long corridor until it dies away in the distance. I duck and stand up in the tub. The startled water comes up to my breast in so many fine ripples. The water runs over the tub with a murmur.

## VIII

I was a guest at a tea party. A priest, Daitetsu by name, prior of the Kankai Temple, and a layman, a lad just about of age, were my fellow guests.

The host's room stood at the farthest end of the long corridor which running to the right extremity of my room made a sharp curve to the left. It was a moderate-sized room about six mats with a large ebony table in the centre thus making the room uncomfortably smaller. At the invitation to be seated, I took a seat. It was not an ordinary cushion, but a patterned straw mat probably of Chinese make. The mat had a fantastic cottage and a few weeping willows woven in the hexagon hemmed in by borders dyed iron blue with indigo. Its corners were ornamented with tawny-yellow rings with many fanciful figures of vines. It may be doubted if it is ever used in the parlour over in China, but thus used as a cushion it was quite to my taste. The characteristic trait of Indian chintz or a Persian rug is simplicity almost approaching foolishness, wherein lies an inestimable value peculiar to its own. The straw mat on which I sat pleased me not a little as the same trait pervaded it all. Not only the mat, but also every article produced in China either ornamental or otherwise has a similar peculiarity. No other people than a simple-minded, easy-going nation could have manufactured such things. As we look them over, they will take us into a land of innocents. That is the very thing I value most. Our fellow country men make articles of fine arts with the attitude of pick-pockets. The things manufactured by Western people are large or small as the occasion demands, but they are never free from worldliness. Thus musing, I took my seat on the mat, while my fellow guest, the lad, sat on the other half.

The priest sat on the tiger's coat whose tail stretched far beyond where I sat. His head was under the old man who was bald. All the hair of his head seemed to have gone over to his cheeks and chin, where it grew into white whiskers and beard like a jungle. Our old host ceremoniously set tea cups, each on a zinc saucer on the table.

"I wanted to serve tea to-day since we have been patronized by a guest," the host said turning to the priest.

"Thanks for the invitation. I have been a stranger to you so long and been thinking to call in a day or two," answered the prior, who looked nearly sixty with a round face exactly like the physiognomy of Dharma painted in a running hand. He seemed to be on friendly terms with our host.

"This gentleman is your guest?" The old man nodded and went on draining into each of the cups a few precious drops of greenish amber from the little tea pot of vermilion clay. Sweet flavour came floating.

"You must be lonely in such a retired place in the mountains," said the priest addressing me politely.

"Well—," I answered meaning to be very ambiguous. Had I told him I was lonely, it would have been a lie. If I had said I was not, it would have needed a long explanation.

"No, your reverence," said the host, "the young gentleman is a painter and is here to paint. He is ever so busy with his brush and palette."

"I beg your pardon; it is very nice. You are of the Chinese school, too?" said the priest.

"No, indeed!" I answered fearing he might not understand if I said I was of the European school.

"Well, he is a painter of the Western school now very much in vogue," added the old man, taking up the conversation like a good host.

"Yes, it is Western painting such as Kyūichi-San does, I suppose? By-the-bye, your painting was just fine. It was a treat to my old eye. I had never seen one before, Kyūichi-San!" said the priest.

"No, your grace, it was poor, wretched stuff," corrected the young man, who had not said a word till now.

"Did you ask our prior to see something you had painted, my stupid chick?" inquired the old man of the youth.

That they were closely related might be easily conjectured from the words and manner of the old host.

"No, sir," answered the young man rather embarrassed, "I did not ask our reverence to see it, but he stealthily came upon me while I was busy taking a sketch at the Mirror Pond."

"H'm! Is that it? Come, gentlemen, tea is ready; help yourselves please."

Thus saying, our host set the cups before each one of us. A few drops were the contents in the large vessel. It had on a pale ground certain tawny-yellow pictures or patterns with diabolical visages or some such things painted or rather scribbled all over by a careless hand.

"It's Mokubei," the old man simply remarked.

"Splendid!" I let the praise out of my lips.

The famous potter had many followers; spurious imitations are a legion," continued the old man. "The base, please, his signature dyed there, you see?"

Taking it up, I held it towards the *shōji* to see it better. The shadow of a pot of a broad-leaved orchid sat comfortably upon the paper-door. I bent my head, looked up from underneath, and the small character *moku* (木) was easily made out. The inscribed name of a maker is of very little moment to the experienced eye of a connoisseur, but an amateur seems to be very curious about it. Without setting it down, I took it up to my lips. Choice tea steeped in goodly lukewarm water gives a sweet fragrant dew-like fluid, which you relish, taking it drop by drop on the tip of your palate; it is a pleasure exclusively accorded the privileged few of elegant taste. People in general are inclined to think that tea is to be drunk, but they are wrong. Put a drop on your tongue, and the precious liquid disperses itself and nothing save sweet flavour remains to go down the throat to the stomach. The vulgar will use their teeth in tasting the beverage, but it is too light and too precious. As to *gyokuro* it is a perfect jewel as delicate and costly as diamond dew, too soft and mellow to allow you to smack your lips. It is such a delicious drink. Some complain that they can hardly sleep after they have taken it. "Better be awake all night than not to take it!" say I to them.

A cake-tray of greenish cut stone which the old host had brought out was the next curio to attract our attention. It was a wonder how the carver had hewn and chiselled with so much skill and taste a big block of stone into such a thin, transparent vessel! Holding it up to the light of day, I wondered if the rays of the spring sun getting into it had been shut up and could ever find their way out. Keep it empty and it will look all the nicer.

"Our visitor seems a great admirer of celadon porcelain and I have got out some of my little collection to show him."

"Which one?" asked the priest. "Well, that cake-salver? I like it, too. By-the-bye, young sir, will not oil painting do for the paper sliding door? If it will, can I not ask you the favour to try it on our *karakami*?"

I shall be glad to oblige him, thought I, but it is doubtful if it will ever please the priest. After all my trouble and pains-taking it would never do to be dashed away with, "Western paintings no good!"

"My art will not do for the *karakami,* I'm afraid, your reverence."

"Won't it, sir? Indeed, such a picture as Kyuichi-San was drawing the other day is too bright and gay."

"Mine is no painting, your reverence; it is only a naughty boy's daubing." The young man was humility itself.

"Where is the pond you just mentioned?" I asked the youth in order to make sure.

"It is a little lake, serene and beautiful among the mountains just behind the Kankai Temple. I was taking a sketch that I might kill the *ennui* I was in; I had studied painting a little, while at school."

"Where is the temple?" I pursued.

"It is the temple I live in, sir. It's a beautiful place commanding the sea. Favour us with a call while you are here. It is not far; it is a few *chō* from here, you can just see from over the corridor the stone-steps leading up to the tabernacle."

"Won't it disturb you if I call?"

"No, indeed! You are welcome any time. The old gentleman's daughter, O-Nami-San is our frequent caller. I don't see her about here to-day; can she be unwell, my kind host?"

"No, your reverence, she may be out; Kyuichi, did you not see her over at your place when you left home?"

"No, indeed I didn't, uncle."

"Then she must be taking a solitary walk. Ha! Ha! Ha! She is such a good walker. The other day I was at Tonami on ecclesiastical business; on my way home, I was coming near the Mirror Bridge, when whom should I meet but O-Nami-San with her skirts tucked up and straw slippers on! And she took me aback with, 'Where have you been, my slow legged tortoise?' "But where on earth have you been in such an outlandish fashion?" I retorted.

"'I have been to gather parsley and if you want the herb, you shall have some,' so saying, she filled my sleeve pockets with the grass, mud and all, with no further ado. Aha! Ha!"

"I'm so very sorry—" said the old man biting his lips with a bitter smile. "Gentlemen, I wanted to show this to you," continued the host, thus turning the subject to curios again.

The old damask sack the old man so cautiously brought down from the sandalwood book-shelf seemed to contain some thing heavy.

"Haven't I shown you this before, my dear abbot?"

"What on earth is it?"

"An Ink-slab!"

"Which one, I wonder?"

"The one Sanyō is said to have prized most."

"No, I haven't seen it yet."

"The one with another top by Shunsui.*"

"No, not yet. Might I be favoured with a look?"

The old man carefully opened the damask sack and there peeped out a corner of a square stone of dark red hue.

"What a charming tone of colour! A Tankei, I wonder?"

"Yes, and it has nine beautiful *eyes.*"

"Nine?" The abbot was admiration itself.

"This is the top by Shunsui," so saying, the old man showed us a thin block of wood lined with satin. A Chinese poem of four lines, each consisting of seven characters, autographs of the savant, were engraved on the surface.

---

* Shunsui, father to the famous historian, Sanyō.

"Yes, Shunsui was a prolific writer, yet Kyōhei, his brother, was a better hand at penmanship."

"Indeed?" Our host looked dissatisfied at the frank remark of the priest.

"Sanyō is the poorest in autographs; his talent seems to have been in the way. Worldliness is the pervading trait of the characters he has written; they are not to my taste."

"Ha! Ha! Ha! Knowing that you are no friend of Sanyō's I've hung another scroll of autographs penned by a different scholar. I hope it will please your reverence."

"Have you?" And the abbot turned round to see.

The hard wood floor of the alcove even with the *tatami* had been given a thorough elbow polish and it shone bright like a mirror. A magnolia branch with buds and flowers had been artistically arranged in an old bronze vase coated with verdigris. A large hanging scroll with Sorai's autographs was on the alcove wall. The mounter had exhausted his skill and taste in the making of it. The hems were of exquisite textile of old gold brocade with dark lustre. The paper on which the great scholar had penned the characters having got old harmonized well with the margins around it, even if the autographs were not good. The brocade when it was new, fresh from the loom, had surely had no such transcendent loveliness, but now that the bright colouring had gone and the gold thread sunk, there was brought forth to the surface in the place of its gorgeousness its genuine lustre hitherto hidden, thus giving the whole structure such a sweet tone of perfect serenity.

The creamy white end projecting out from each side of the scroll axis was nicely set off by the dark yellow colour of the alcove wall, and the magnolia flowers in the vase softly floated like a white-robed spirit on the foreground, giving the alcove and its surroundings a touch of quietness approaching sadness.

"It's Sorai?" said the priest as he gave a glance at the scroll.

"Sorai may not so please you, my dear abbot, but he is better, I thought, than Sanyō."

"O yes! he is far better. The characters penned by scholars of the Kyōho period have a certain commanding dignity even if they were poor in penmanship."

"'If Kōtaku were the best penman in Japan, I should be glad to be placed side by side with the poorest autographers of China,' was that not what Sorai said, your reverence?"

"I do not know, but the letters he penned do not seem to justify his proud statement. Wa! Ha! Ha! "

"By the bye, who was your writing master?"

"I? A Zen-priest is not much of a scholar and he generally writes a poor hand."

"Yet, sure you had some master to study?"

"Well, I studied Kōsen a little when I was a young monk. That is all; yet I shall be bold enough to write any time I am asked. Wa! Ha! Ha! While I think of it, won't you please treat us with a look at your slab?" the abbot demanded.

At last the damask sack was off. All the eyes of the company were focussed on the uncovered treasure.

Although the stone was two inches thick, double an ordinary slab, it was a moderate-sized one six inches by four. It had a top of well-polished pine bark with its finny patterns still on. Two Chinese characters hard to make out were painted in vermilion lacquer.

"This top," said the old man. "This top is a rarity, though it is simply pine-bark as you see."

The eyes of the host were turned towards me as if expecting admiration from me. Being a stranger to the history of the top, I could not but frankly express a painter's view that it was a little bit vulgar.

The old man held up his hands in utter amazement.

"Yes, a pine bark top itself as you say may show the lack of taste," he pleaded " but this is what Sanyō, while at Hiroshima, took off the bark of the pine tree in his garden and carved it himself."

Still I could not be dissuaded from the conviction that he was a prosaic, matter-of-fact man.

"If Sanyō himself had carved it, he might have done it a little more like an amateur," I frankly remarked. "A great deal better it would have been, had the fins been left as they stood without giving them so much polish."

"Wa! Ha! Ha!" roared the priest in approbation of what I had stated.

"Yes, the top seems a little bit too vulgar, as the young gentleman says."

The nephew felt very sorry for his uncle and turned his sympathetic eyes towards the old gentleman who, much displeased, took off the top. Behold the prodigy of an ink-slab!

What strikes one most wonderful about the workmanship of the stone is the unsurpassed skill of the carver. His chisel has left out the centre of the stone in the size and shape of your watch, and it represents the back of a spider, whose eight crooked legs reach out in all directions, each having an eye at its extremity. The remaining eye enthrones itself in the centre of the back shining bright and brilliant like a refulgent gem of a soft yellowish hue. Leaving the back, legs, and margins in bold relief, the rest of the stone is scooped into a pool one inch deep. The trench-like pond, however, can not be an ink-reservoir, for a pint of water will not be enough to fill it up. In all probability, one tiny drop of water is spilt on the spider's back from the tiny water-jug by means of ever so tiny a silver-spoon. Then a precious India ink-stick will stir up the fluid well on the stone ready to be used. If not, it would be an ink-slab only in name, and have no practical value whatever. It would be a mere article of stationary curiosity.

"Please see the complexion and eyes of the slab, gentlemen," said the old man as if the saliva would run out of his mouth. Indeed the longer we look, the sweeter it grows, until we are tempted to breathe a breath upon the cold lustrous surface which immediately turns into a purple cloud. The most wonderful thing about the stone is the tone of the eyes or rather the harmonious mingling of colours at the boundary where the light yellow of the eyes imperceptibly melting away into the dark purple of the ground around makes your eyes colour-blind. An illustration will help you a little in forming an idea of the stone. It can be likened to a dark-purple *yōkan* set with kidney beans which you can look through. Even one or two eyes in a slab are precious, but when it has nine eyes regularly set apart at the same distance it must be a unique one naturally taken for an artificial stone kneaded by a potter. The wide world can not have such another!

"Wonderful!" said I, "It is delightful to look at it, but sweeter still it is to take and feel it." And I handed it over to my young companion.

"It is a pearl before swine," said the old man with a laugh. The poor Kyuichi, a little offended, said that he was not the least interested in such bric-a-brac. Probably thinking it impious for him to be looking at the thing, the value of which he could not understand, he returned it to me. Once more I took it up, stroked it deliberately from top to bottom and respectfully returned it to the priest, who after admiring it on the palm of his hand a good while, still unsatisfied, began to rub the back of the spider mercilessly with the sleeve of his black cotton gown until at last it shone out into dark brilliancy. The priest was in ecstasy.

"I am immensely charmed by this tone of dark lustre, my old friend. Did you ever use this slab?"

"No, your reverence. Not wishing to use it save on a rare occasion, it has not yet been used since I bought it."

"I imagined as much. Such a beauty is a rarity even over in China, don't you think so, my old host?"

"Well, Yes!"

"I have been wanting such a stone so badly. Can not I ask you to get me one when you are over in China, Kyuichi-San?"

"Yes, certainly, your grace, but I am afraid I shall be killed before I have come by your slab."

"Indeed! Kyuichi-San, such a misfortune may fall on you and I should be very sorry to ask you the favour. By the way, when do you set out for the front?"

"In a few days, your reverence."

"See him off at Yoshida, do, my old friend."

"Ordinarily old age will excuse me, but I am afraid I may be unable to see him again if fate wills it so, and I am thinking to go with him that far."

"You need not, uncle."

The young man was a nephew to the old host. A certain facial likeness was perceptible in both.

"Don't decline the kindness of your uncle, young man. The river-boat is such a convenience, my old friend."

"Yes, the mountain path is much shorter, but it is a hard job; the boat takes much longer, but is far easier."

The youth this time kept still, not seeming averse to the proposition.

"Are you going over to China?"

I simply asked the young man.

"Yes, yes!" he answered.

This interjectional answer was not at all satisfactory, yet I was not so curious as to ask any further. The shadow of the orchid on the *shōji* had changed its position a little.

"Well, sir. The War—," explained our host for his bashful nephew. "He served some time as volunteer and has been summoned this time."

I understood from what the old man had said that the lad was to go to the front in Manchuria in a few days. I was wrong to imagine that nothing worldly would come and disturb the peaceful serenity of the dreamy mountain hamlet, the very home of fair Poesy and Spring Genius, where birds sing, flowers come and go, and hot springs eternally bubble out. Mountains and seas seem to be no barrier before the sweeping march of the actual world, and the solitary village whose inhabitants are mostly descendants of the refugees of the Taira family, has fallen a victim to the invasion. Before long, millions of men would lie dead to feed the hungry wolves of the boundless hyperborean plains and the young soldier who sits beside me would probably be one of those whose blood coming out of their arteries would dye the wild flowers all crimson. Who can tell if the long sword he wears around his waist may not be the passage-way through which his young blood will gush out? And the poor painter who, thinking all worldly things valueless, simply dreams on and on is the companion of the young knight. They can hear the beating of each other's heart; so close together they sit. In that throbbing, one can already hear the oncoming high tide of devotion that will roll over the ocean-like wilderness stretching out for thousands of miles. Destiny has thus brought us two into the same room, and why? His lips are forever closed.

## IX

"Are you at it again?" says the woman to me, when I, getting back to my room, was reading from a book I had untied from the three-legged stool.

"Won't you come in? And welcome!" say I to the woman.

In she came unceremoniously; she seemed perfectly at home. Her pretty white neck was challengingly set off by her dark neckband. I was immensely charmed by the contrast as she sat before me.

"Sure, it is a foreign book with many difficult things in?"

"No, not so hard a book."

"Then what is written there, I wonder?"

"Well! I hardly know myself."

"And you are hard at it; Ho! Ho! Ho!"

"No, I do not study it, but opening it on the desk at random, I simply go on reading."

"Does it interest you, though?"

"Yes, it does."

"How?"

"Why, it is the best way of reading a novel."

"You are as odd as can be."

"Yes, you are right; I am a little bit eccentric."

"Why is it wrong to read from the beginning?"

"Were you to read it from the very beginning, you would have to go through it, don't you see?"

"Strange logic, I should think. I don't see why it is wrong to go on to the end."

"Of course, not. I myself would do so if I were to read only the plot."

"What else have I to read in a novel, if not the plot? Is there anything else, I wonder?"

"Test her, she is not so bright," I seemed to say to myself.

"You like a novel, miss?"

"I?" and she paused a moment before she added that she hardly knew.

From her ambiguous statement, I surmised that she was indifferent to a novel.

"You mean you do not know whether you like it or not, don't you, miss?"

"I mean to say it matters little to me whether or not I read a novel."

It was plain that she saw no good reason why a novel should be at all.

"If you really mean what you say, then it matters not a bit whether you begin reading it from the first page or take up the last, or reading any page at random. I fail to see why it seems strange to you."

"But you and I are different."

"At what point?" and I looked into the eyes of the woman that I might catch her at this particular point; no wink of her pupils, however, betrayed her; she was as unmovable as a statue.

"Ho! Ho! Ho! don't you see?"

"Yet, novels were your constant companion in your young days, I am sure."

I changed my tactics of regular front attack and came upon her from the rear.

"I hope I am still young, you cruel man!"

No sooner did the falcon leave the hand of the falconer than it watched for a chance to fly off.

"Be on your guard, man!" I say to myself.

"Since you can say such a thing to a man, you are no longer a young maiden." The bird was with difficulty held back by an invisible cord.

"Your crow's foot tells plainly that you have been no exception to the hard grips of Time, and you are still interested in love intrigues, love's coquettish ill-humour, and pimples; you should have been wiser by now."

"Yes, miss, I am, and death only can put an end to the passion."

"Indeed, that accounts for your being a painter!"

"You are right there, dear lady. Being a painter, I am freed from the necessity of reading a novel from beginning to end, but find brimming pleasure in whatever place my eye rests. Your conversation also attracts me and I shall be glad to have your company every hour of the day while I stay here, or far better and nicer would it be if I fell in love with you. Our love would not, however, end in our being man and wife. So long as marriage is the goal of love, the same will be with your novel reading; you'll have to go through it from the very beginning to the end."

"Then must I understand that wicked love is what you painters aim at?"

"No, not exactly. Supermundane love is what I am driving at, and so is it with my way of novel-reading, and the plot matters very little with me. It is something like drawing lots. Opening it at random, I go on reading with pleasure."

"Indeed, it sounds charming. Won't you please oblige me by telling me a little? I am very anxious to know how things develop in there."

"A tell-tale method will spoil all. Even a painting will be of no value whatever if turned into a story."

"Ho! Ho! Ho! then please to read."

"In English?"

"No, in Japanese."

"It would be hard to read English in Japanese."

I thought, however, it would be fun, and began reading the book line after line in Japanese as she requested. Were there any such thing as supermundane reading, mine would be it, and my charming auditress was peculiar to an extreme.

"A breath of love is wafted from the woman; it comes from her voice, her eyes, from the pores of her skin. She goes to the bow, her lover helping her. She to see Venice in the glorious sunset? He to send a thrilling sensation to all his blood tubes? "

"Remember I am a visionary and I may not be exact in my reading; I may skip over some places.

"Agreed, you may add, too, if convenient."

"The two lovers lean over the side of the boat. The blue ribbon fondled by an evening breeze is the only boundary line between the two. They together bid adieu to the eternal city of the sea. Like a second sunset, the Doge's Palace is fading in a faint pink line—

"What is Doge, I wonder?"

"Be not so curious, miss. It's the name of a man who once ruled Venice. I do not know how long his reign lasted. His palace still stands to tell her past glories."

"And who are those lovers, I should like to know?"

"They are unknown even to me, and therein lies brimming interest. It is not my business to inquire into their relation hitherto. Like you and me, they find themselves together. That enthrals my imagination."

"Does it, really? They are on board a vessel?"

"Whether they are on board a vessel or on a hill top, it matters little; it is enough that they are as they are. Don't be so inquisitive, or you'll be playing the part of a detective."

"Ho! Ho! then I shall not be."

"Popular novels have all been invented by detectives, hence no poetry, no thrill."

"Well, I've got so impatient to hear the rest of your supermundane reading. Please, go on."

"Venice goes down and down until a faint line is left just above the horizon. By and by, the line is cut into several dots. Columns stand here and there against the opaline sky. At last the bell-tower that soars highest sinks. 'It has gone at last!' says the woman. She feels as free as the wind which blows in the air, yet when she thinks that she has to return to the city now behind the horizon, her heart fails her. The lovers direct their eyes towards the dark bay; more stars, the softly undulating sea brews no bubble. Stillness reigns. He holds her hand, a veritable bow string whose arrow is just off."

"They seem not to be much above us mortals," observes my auditress.

"Nevertheless, we can be cool, yet I have no objection to my omitting some parts if it is agreeable to you."

"No, sir, don't, please. I am perfectly safe."

"I am by far safer, miss. —Well, wait a minute—let me see—it's getting a little harder to translate—I beg your pardon—to read, I mean."

"You may leave out some if hard to read."

"Well, I shall be free in my reading, my dear miss.—'This single night,' says the girl. 'Why, this night only?' asks her lover. 'It is heartless of you to limit it to a single night, why cannot we say endless nights?' "

"Which is which? Does she say, or he?"

"Of course, the latter, my dear miss. The girl does not wish to go back to Venice, it seems, and her lover is trying to comfort her. To the memory of him who now lies on deck, at dead of night, with his head on the rigging, comes that moment, a veritable drop of seething blood—the moment in which he held firm her hand, comes back like a great wave. He looks up into the black night and makes up his mind to save her from the thraldom of loveless marriage. His eyes are closed."

"And how about the woman?"

"Like a stray sheep, she seems not to know where she is. Like a sparrow in the talons of an eagle, she is being borne away through the air. An unfathomable pit of mysteries! I can not go on reading, it hardly makes sense."

"A bottomless pit of mysteries? and no verb there?"

"A verb will spoil the poetry, let it stand as it is!"

"Ay?"

All of a sudden, the trees all around us shook with a rumbling sound. Our eyes met. The camellia flower in a miniature vase on the desk shivered. Earthquake! With a stifled scream, she came and leaned against me at the desk. Indecency was innocent in this case and our bodies touched. A pheasant much alarmed started off with a sharp flap out of the bamboo thicket near by.

"A pheasant!" I exclaim, looking out of the window.

"Where?" and she drew so suggestively close to me that our lips were brought to a kissing distance. Her breath coming through her small nostrils was felt by the sensitive tips of my mustache.

"We are above mortals, you remember?" says she in a grave tone as she sits up straight.

"Of course!" say I like a philosopher.

The startled water in the cavity of the rock was swinging dull. As the whole element was set in motion at the shaking of the foundation of the earth, there were ruffled up a few irregular curves—ripples—on its surface, but no gap was made. If there be such a phrase as 'all round move' it may be most properly applied to describe the phenomenon. The shadow of a mountain cherry tree which had been resting upon the stagnant water now took life and began to cut fantastic shapes, now a giant bending his huge body as if lifting some heavy tripod; now a pigmy twisting his shriveled features as if coveting laughter, yet ever returning to its original form, a cherry tree.

"It's a delight," exclaimed I—

"It's pretty, it evolves. It's a lesson showing us how to move."

"You mean," cried my lady, "that it is safe if one acts as the shadow of the cherry tree does?"

"Yes, but no mortal can, while sticking to this world."

"Ho! Ho! again your hobby—supermundane!"

"You can hardly say, miss, you are not of our creed, or how about your bridal robe yesterday?"

Hardly had I said this before the siren coquettishly asked if she might not be rewarded with a nice present.

"Why?"

"You wished to see me in my bridal dress and I obliged you yesterday, that is all."

"Did I?"

"A certain painter coming up the pass stopped at the tea-house at the top and asked the old woman, the keeper, if he might not be favoured with a look at me in my bride's costume."

Before I could make up my mind what answer to make, she discharged at me a second arrow—

"Faithfulness on the part of the flower will never tell at all upon the faithless butterfly!"

The arrow-head was venomed with irony and bitter resentment. My position once shaken was hard to regain its footing and our heroine would not give me a chance to get a start of her.

"Then it was your kindness, too, that prompted the bath-room incident last evening?"

With difficulty, I stepped a pace ahead of her.

The enchantress was mute.

"Much obliged, my dear miss; what would you have in return?"

My vantage-ground was, however, of little avail, for she looked absorbed in the contemplation of Daitetsu's calligraphic writings on the tablet over the lintel. Presently she mumbled, 'The bamboo-shadow sweepeth the steps; no dirt ariseth.'

Abruptly turning round toward me, she said as if recollecting herself.

"What was it you said?"

It was such a loud voice as I had never suspected of her being capable of. 'Two can play at the game,' my fair friend, I seemed to say to myself.

"I met that bonze a little while ago, miss." I answered in an all-round way like the water in the pond shaken by an earthquake.

"Was it the abbot of Kankai Temple, who is big and stout?"

"Yes, and it was he who asked me to paint his *karakami* in oil colours. Lack of common sense seems to be a characteristic trait of a Zen priest."

"That is how he has got so big and fat."

"And I made one more acquaintance, a young man.

"Kyūichi must be the man."

"Yes, that is the name of the lad."

"You have found quite a number of friends here."

"No, miss, I know no other person. By the way, Kyūichi-San seems to be a young man of few words."

"Well, he was shy; he is yet a child."

"You don't say so! I should not be surprised, if he is just about your age."

"Ho! Ho! Ho! do you think so? He is my cousin, who is here to take leave of us, as he is bound for the front in a few days."

"Does he stay here in the house?"

"No, he is stopping at my elder brother's."

"Then he was invited out here to tea?"

"Hot water with nothing in it is to his liking, and it would have been much kinder of my father not to have invited him to tea. His legs must have ached in sitting on the *tatami* so long. I would have sent him home if I had been there during the service."

"Where could you have been then? The priest was curious to know. 'Taking a solitary walk again,' he muttered."

"Well, I had been at Mirror Pond."

"Mirror Pond! I wish I could go there, too."

"You can go any time."

"Is it a good place to paint?"

"It is an ideal place to throw oneself into."

"It will be some time before I can do that."

"But I may, before very long. Who knows?"

At her bold remark which was more than a joke, I looked up into her face. She was firm as a statue.

"Do paint me floating on the water, not in agonizing but peaceful death—beautiful as a sleeping babe. Pray do."

"Ay?"

"You are astonished, you are amazed!"

She arose like a flash. Three steps and she was out of the chamber. A pretty smile played on her shell-like lips as she looked at me over her shoulder. Like a phantom, she passed away and I was left alone—a hapless lover with a faint hope, 'she can not fade.'

## X

Here I am at Mirror Pond. Behind the Kankai Temple, there runs a path threading the cedars and leading down to the valley. Before it goes up the hill yonder it branches out to form the natural circumference of the pond. A rank growth of the broad-leaved dwarf bamboo is found all around the pool. In certain places, the bamboo grows very thick overlapping one another from both sides, and nobody can walk among the leaves without disturbing the stillness. The water of the pond is seen through the trees, but where its top or its bottom lies is not to be known until one makes the circuit. Actual step measurement shows that it is a comparatively small pond not being more than three *chō* in circumference. It is so irregular in shape, however, that we find many a huge rock fresh from Nature's hand lying here and there along the coast; the height of the border line varies much like an undulating wave now up, now down.

Innumerable kinds of vegetation hem the pond all around. The warmth of spring has not yet been sufficiently great for some of the trees to put forth their buds. Where the branches are sparse, however, the sun has sent down his congenial rays upon the young grass just sprouted. Modest violets are sprinkled all over like so many precious gems.

The Japanese violet gives the beholder a sense of sweet sleep, and a Western poet's "like a heaven-sent message" may not be just right to describe our modest flower. With this thought, I stopped. Once stopped, I do not leave the spot until I have got tired of it. Happy is he who finding himself on Nature's peaceful lap can do so. If you did that in Tokyo, you would be run over and killed in an instant by an electric-car, or else a policeman would come and drive you away. Peace loving good citizens are mistaken for beggars in a city like Tokyo, and the municipality is paying high salaries to bosses of pick-pockets, detectives.

Quietly I sat on the soft cushion of green grass not fearing that a complaint would be raised against me if I sat here for several days at a time, and herein lies the goodness of nature. When she wills, there is no mercy or hesitation whatever in her, but she is never frivolous, she is no respecter of persons. Many there are, it is true, who look down upon the Iwasakis or Mitsuis, yet nature alone can look the presumption of a king or an emperor out of countenance. Her virtue is far above the sordid world; absolute equality is the permanent principle upon which her rule is founded. A Lucius, a Lucullus, a Sempronius and men of such ignoble type will never cease to exist in the world to invite a Timon's righteous indignation and wrath. Far better would it be then for one to go and plant fragrant orchids in his garden plot and turn an honest gardener among his sweet innocent friends, the flowers.

The world seems to set high value upon justice and fair play. Be they ever so important and precious, why, put a thousand petty thieves to death, and cultivate full many a gem of garden beauties on the corpses of the dead. Nothing can be more just and fair than flowers.

The line of thought has somewhat degenerated to reasoning as dry as dust. I am not here, thought I, at Mirror Pond in order to initiate myself in a middle school boy's philosophy. My hand went into my pocket. A match was drawn across the side of the box; it certainly sputtered, but no flame was visible. I applied it to the tip of an Asahi and puffed at it. Smoke came out of my nostrils and I was fully satisfied to know that I had puffed. A slender smoke like a raindragon curled up from the little bit of burnt match in the short grass and vanished. I slid down or rather floated down to the water's edge of the pond until I could feel the luke-warm water with the soles of my feet, if I desired. There I stopped and looked into the water.

The pond was rather shallow so far as the eye could reach. Long slender weeds were seen growing at the bottom, leading, as it were, a death-like existence. I do not know of any other epithet to describe their resigned lonesome fate. The arundo on the hill knows how to bend before the wind. The sea weed also knows how to wait until she is embraced by an amorous wave. This water weed destined to live life long at the bottom of everlasting stagnant water has likewise exhausted its toilet arts to be attractive and charming and has waited day and night to be fondled and caressed by some gallant wave, but morning has passed to evening, evening to dawn, yet no ripple has visited it yet. Still it keeps up its virginity as a sacred trust. It is so quiet, it never stirs out of its place of confinement. It can not die if it wishes. Thus it drags on its dull lonely life.

I stood up, walked away, picked up from among the grass two good sized stones and came back. Thinking it a pious act, I threw one of them into the water not far from me. Two bubbles came up only to vanish again. "Vanished" said I to myself. Peeping into the water, my eye caught three long hairs swinging dull, stirred as by the vapour from an infernal oven. The disturbed water came up to hide them in its muddy screen as though the discovery was anything but agreeable. Namuamida Buddha!

I took up the other and threw it as far to the centre as I possibly could. A splash, a faint sound and again great calm on the pond as if nothing had happened. A little discouraged, I gave up the trick. The paint-box and hat were left on the spot and I turned round to the right.

Hardly did I walk twenty paces along a very gentle ascent before I came to the place where big trees interweaving their branches shut out the rays of the sun and I felt cold chill all over. On the opposite bank, in a dark secluded spot, a camellia in full bloom came to view. The leaves of a camellia are of too deep green, so much so that, whether seen by day light or by noon day's dazzling rays, they give the beholder no sense of cheerfulness. Especially the one I am describing looks so solitary and lonely standing all alone in a nook some dozen yards away from the projecting rock. Nobody would have noticed it but for its flowers. Oh, its flowers! So numerous are they that a day's reckoning will not do, but they are so enticingly bright that one is tempted to try his arithmetical powers as soon as his eyes rest upon them. True, they are very singularly bright but they never give you a sense of loveliness. You are vanquished, as it were, by a single blow at seeing them in a blaze, but the next moment a sense of ghastly regret will creep over you. No other flower is so deceitful as the camellia. I can never see one blooming all alone in the recess of a mountain without associating it with an enchantingly pretty woman. You are allured by her pair of black eyes, and before you are aware, a fatal poison is injected into your blood vessels. It is too late when you are awakened to the sense of having been taken in. When I first caught sight of the camellia flower over yonder, I wished I had not seen it. The colour of the flower is not simple crimson, but at the bottom of its gorgeous brightness lies an indescribable tone of sadness. The pear-blossom drooping passively in the rain invites our compassion; the aronia in the cool transcendent light of the moon gives us a sense of loveliness; but the atmosphere the camellia creates around it differs greatly. Its tone is that of a terrible sting, black and venomous, but hiding it in the innermost part of its heart, it affects to put on the gayest appearance imaginable. However, it never condescends to flattery, nor does it try to allure men. Pop it opens; thud it falls; thud it goes, pop it comes; thus year after year, for hundreds of years, it has blushed unseen; and has withered and fallen unmoaned in the cool sequestered recess of a mountain.

Yet a glance, and you are no longer a free man. Once caught, you can not get away from the clutches of its Siren fascination. Its red colour is so unique that it is spontaneously associated with the blood which gushes out of a poor prisoner's body under an executioner's axe. Curiosity drives us to seeing it and soon after we are sorry that we have ever seen it. It is weirdly bright.

A moment had hardly passed before a red cup fell and floated on the water. Nothing else disturbed the all-pervading calm of spring; another moment and another red cup popped into the water. The camellia never scatters itself to the wind; it hardly breaks to pieces when it leaves its stem. It comes down in a heap. You may be deceived and think it a brave flower as you see it come down in such good grace. But look at it more carefully and you will be amazed to find how poisonously heavy the flowers are, as they are piled one upon another. Down comes another red bell. The water of the pond will, thought I, turn red in the course of time. Even now, it appears rather red where the flowers float quietly. Down comes another to join its companions which lie upon the face of the water so calm and so still that one all but wonders if they are not on the great solid earth. Another leaves its stem and comes down. Will it ever go down to the bottom of the pond, I wondered. Year after year, hundreds of them will wither and fall on the water and be completely saturated with the fluid that their crimson colour gradually melting away and decaying will turn to mud and sink to the bottom of the pond. In the course of thousands of years this old pond filled with the faded flowers will have returned to its original dry land. Who knows? Again another big camellia spills its blood from its conical cup on the pond. Like the spirit of the dead, it falls, followed by another, another, and another, until at last the pond is camellia, camellia, camellia, still camellia, and only camellia, and camellia and camellia again!

How would it do if I painted a pretty woman floating on the pond? With this thought, I was back again at the spot where I had left my things. A cigarette was my companion in my absorbed meditation, and what Nami-San of the hotel had jokingly said the day before came swelling like a surge to my memory. My mind shivered just as a deck plank does at the mercy of the waves. That face shall forever lie on the water beneath the camellia tree and myriads of flowers shall forever fall upon it. Can my brush ever paint a picture in which that idea is vividly given? In that Laocoon—Well, let it alone. Could I bring out that conception on canvas, even if I acted against the aesthetic principle, I should be fully satisfied. However, it will be no easy matter for a mortal like me to bring out on paper the intimation of immortality. The first difficulty lies in the face. If I use that face for my model, that expression will never do. Too much grief will spoil the tone of the whole, and yet too much freedom from care will work as much harm to the composition. How would it do if I took entirely another face? This? that? I count one after another on my fingers, but none answers the purpose, and I come round again to Nami-San's face as by far the best, but there is something wanting in it; what it is is unknown to me, and my imagination fails to fill up the vacancy. How will it do if I add jealousy to it? Too much uneasiness accompanies that fatal passion. Hatred? It is too strong. Anger? But it will spoil the harmony of the whole picture. Sorrow? It is too prosaic unless it be a poetic one such as the sorrow that misses the departing spring. After many a fruitless search, I have at last struck upon the right one. Of all man's emotions, pity was that which my mind never dwelt upon. It is an attribute unknown to God, yet it is a most God-like emotion, though of human birth. Not even a shadow of this divine passion is visible in Nami-San's facial expression; that is the *one thing* that is lacking. The moment that feeling flashes out like lightning by a sudden impulse, my picture will have been completed. But can I ever hope to see it on her face? The passions that predominate over all others in her countenance are a scornful smile that puts everybody to naught, and a frowning impatience to conquer and place them all under her petticoat rule. These alone will make only a very poor picture.

A rustling sound of footsteps broke the plan of my picture to pieces just before its completion. I looked up and saw a man in a tight-sleeved coat with a load of fire wood on his back coming through the boundless bamboo thicket over towards the Kankai Temple. I dare say he had been up to the neighbouring forest.

The man, pulling off the kerchief from his head, saluted me with "Fine day, gentleman." The blade of the hatchet stuck in his cloth belt flashed as he made obeisance to me. He was a strong man of forty, well-built, whom I remembered to have seen somewhere before. He approached me as familiarly as if we had known each other a long time.

"Are you a painter, too?" My paint-box was open and was before me.

"Yes, I came here thinking I might paint this pond; it is so very lonely that nobody comes along."

"Well, sir, it being among the mountains—. You were overtaken by a shower at the pass, were you not? You must have had a hard time of it."

"And you were the pack-horse man who passed there then?"

"Ay! ay, sir. I take fuel I gather thus to the castle-town." Gembei had unloaded himself and was placidly sitting upon the faggots. He took out his tobacco pouch; it was so very old that you could hardly tell whether it was of paper or leather. I offered him a match.

"Do you go up and down the pass every day. It must be a hard job."

"No, not at all, sir. Habit is an easy task-master, you see. And I do not do it every day: once every three days or often once every four days."

"I shall beg your pardon even if it is only once every four days."

"Aha! Ha! It being hard for the poor beast, I make it once every four days."

"Is that so? You seem to think the horse a sacred trust, more precious than yourself."

"No, not so much, my good sir."

"By the way, this pond looks very old. How long has it stood here, I wonder?"

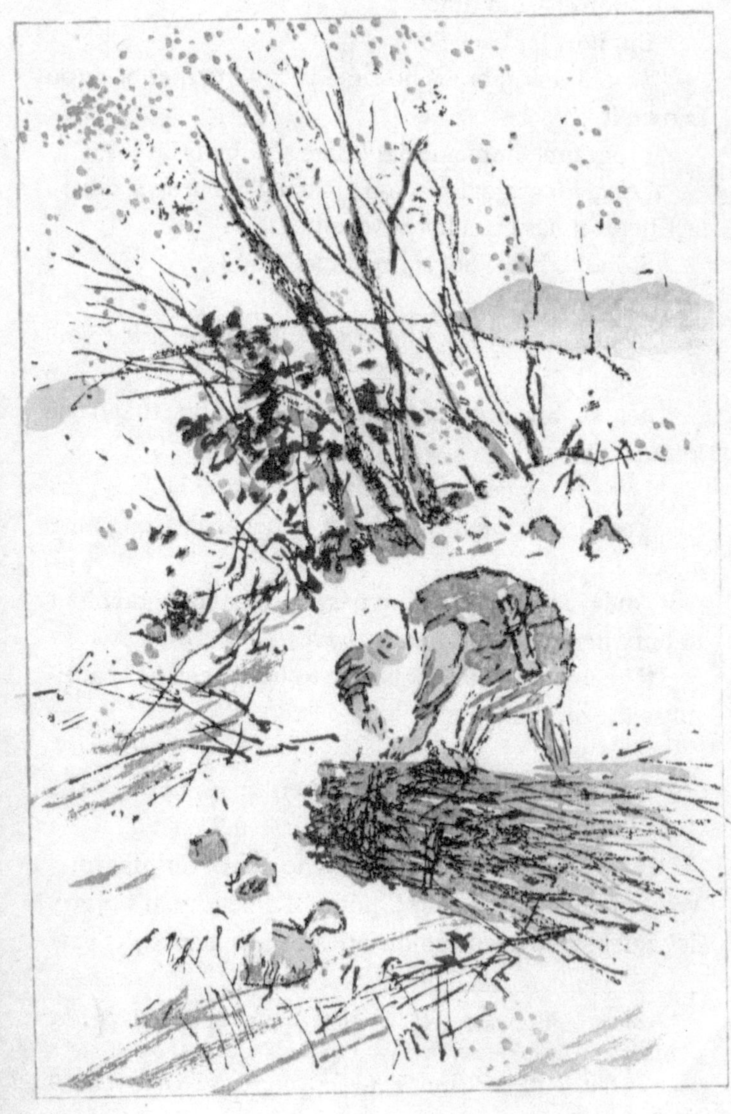

"From very old times."

"But how far back?"

"So old that there is no time in my life that has not known it."

"From time immemorial I dare say then?"

"Long, long ago, Shioda-San's daughter drowned herself here: it has been here ever since."

"Shioda's? that hot spring hotel man?"

"Yes, sir!'

"You don't say so! She is alive and well, don't you know?"

"No, sir. She is not the one. I mean the one that lived long, long ago."

"How many generations back, I wonder? "

"I'm sorry I am not so sure of it, but a very long time ago."

"And how did it come to pass that that daughter had to bury herself in the watery grave?"

"The unfortunate girl is said to have been as beautiful as the present one, sir."

"Yes!"

"One day there came along a certain *boronji.*"

"You mean a *komuso** by your *boronji*?"

"Yes, sir. That mendicant who plays on his flute. While he was staying at Shioda, the headman's pretty daughter fell in love with the minstrel at a glance. As Fate

---

*A *samurai* dispossessed of his estate for some political offence, or dismissed from his service, who travels about in the guise of a begging flute-player. He usually wears a deep rush-hat to conceal his face.

would have it, she would unite with him in marriage; she begged it in tears."

"Wept, did she? Indeed!"

"But the headman would not listen to her petition, saying that a *boronji* should never be his son-in-law, and at last turned the poor piper out."

"The *komuso*?"

"Yes, sir. The poor love-lorn girl followed her strolling lover as far as this pond. Don't you see the spot where a big pine-tree stands? Whence she fell. A splash and—consternation and confusion ensued. Excitement ruled the whole village. She is said to have had a looking-glass with her then; hence Mirror-pond."

"Indeed! then this is no longer a virgin pond."

"It was a very unfortunate event, sir."

"How many generations ago did it take place?"

"I do not know, sir, but sure, hundreds of years have rolled on since then, and (lowering his voice) between you and me, sir—"

"What is it?"

"Dear sir, it has long been known that insanity is hereditary in the Shioda family."

"Indeed!"

"A curse seems to be on the family. The daughter now at home is spoken of as a little deranged."

"No, no, it can not be."

"I hope not, sir, but her mother was a little beside herself."

"Is she still living?"

"No, she died last year."

"Hum!" and I shut my mouth. A slender volume of smoke was curling up from the cigarette ashes I had thrown on the ground. Gembei had gone with his load on his back.

I came here to paint, and my paint box would have been brought in vain, if I had contemplated only such a thing, or heard such idle talk. Days and months would have been spent and yet no picture would have been brought forth. I am in duty-bound today, thought I, to make at least a sketch. Fortunately the landscape over beyond is complete by itself and let me try my brush on that spot, even if it serves only to pacify my artistic conscience.

A perpendicular greenish-black rock about ten feet high coming out of the bottom of the pond soars tapering at the angle where the dark waters meet; on its right, the broad-leaved dwarf bamboo grows thick and close from the top of the cliff down to the waterline. On its crown, a big pine tree three spans in circumference with a huge ivied trunk runs slantingly out more than half its length over the water. The maiden with a looking-glass in her breast must have thrown herself from the top of the rock.

Sitting on the three-legged stool, I looked around and surveyed the things to be painted in my picture. The pine, the bamboo, the rock and the water. I wondered to what extent the water should be taken in. A rock ten feet high will cast a shadow as long. The shadow of the bamboo leaves is so transparently reflected upon the water that you wonder if it were not growing far into the pond despite the water-barrier. As to the pine-tree, it soars very high into the air that the shadow it casts is very long and slender. The canvas of my picture would hardly be large enough to take both in. Rather let me paint the shadow alone; it would be just as interesting. People will be surprised at seeing the picture in which only the water and the shadows it reflects are given. But the surprise it excites will never do unless it be mixed with admiration for its artistic skill. How can I bring forth such an effect? My eyes are intently focussed upon the surface of the pond.

Strange to say, a shadow by itself will suggest you no picture, however closely you may look at it. You will naturally want to compare the real with the unreal, believing the comparison will give you a good picture. Taking my glance from the surface of the water I gradually bring it up and up until it catches the ten foot rock. I turn it back to the top of its shadow on the water and bring it to the point where the water and the rock meet. Like a devout pilgrim on a sacred shrine, I turn up my glance inch by inch, carefully examining and discriminating every effect produced by light and shade and every crease and wrinkle Nature has engraved on it, until at last it all but reaches the tapering point of the perpendicular rock, when helpless as a poor frog in the full glare of a snake, I drop my paint-box on the ground with a bang!

The rays of the sinking sun coming through the green leaves of the tree branches, and the twilight of the latter part of spring which partially paints the rock's crown with its dark colour are the back ground on which comes out in a bold relief a woman's face—the face that beneath the aronia flowers, in my vision in the chamber, in her bridal dress, and in the bath-room, has startled me.

My eyes are nailed to the centre of her pale face; like a goddess, she stands calm at the top of the cliff showing to my full view her graceful tall figure to the best advantage. *That moment!*

Unconsciously I spring up with a start. With a bound, she is already down on the other side of the cliff. As she jumps down, something crimson like a camellia flower flashes out of her sash. The setting sun coming through the tree branches, faintly dyes the trunk of the pine-tree. The dwarf bamboo looks weirdly greener. Another scare!

## XI

The spring twilight of a mountain hamlet suggests poetry and I sauntered out. Going up the stone-steps of the Kankai Temple, I obtained the verse:—

> I look up,
>   The sky is sprinkled with stars,
> I count them one, two, three.

I had neither business to see the priest nor any intention to gossip with him. Like a walker in a dream, I wandered out of the hotel not knowing where to turn my steps, but in a few moments I found myself at the foot of the long stone-case. I had not long stroked the stone-tablet which stood there with "No stimulant (garlic or saké) allowed within the temple grounds" before I was happy and began to ascend the steps.

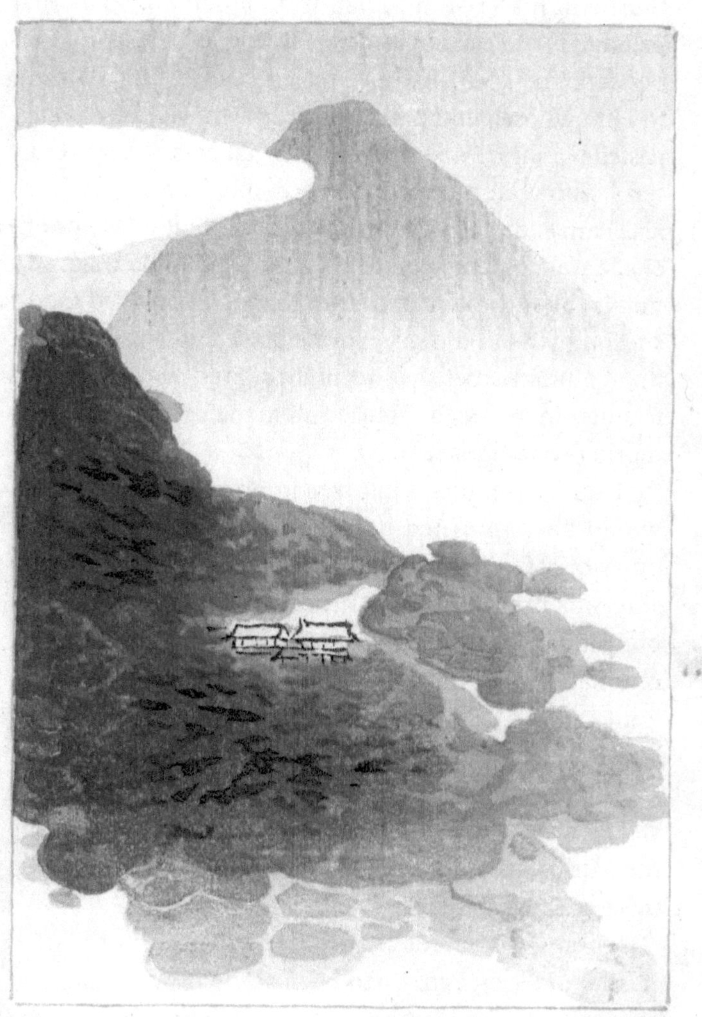

"No other book is written so pleasingly to God," says Sterne in his Tristram Shandy, Gentleman. "The first passage is of course put down by me as best as I possibly can," he goes on "but the rest I prayerfully commit to Him whose pen I am and I put down whatever is suggested by Him. I am unaware of what comes next. True, it is I who write but God is responsible for all I put down and I am entirely free from any responsibility." My promenade was something like this, an irresponsible walk, you might call it. I differ from him in that he invoked God's succour, while I did not. Sterne placed all responsibility upon Him in order that he might be free. Having no god to suffer in my stead, I buried all in the bottom of a murmuring stream that ran by.

I took no pains whatever in going up the steps. I would have returned home, if it had been a labourious work. Going up a step, I looked around; the pleasure was brimming, and I took another step. The second step inspired me with a verse. Silently did I look at my shadow cast on the steps; the angular stones turned it into a fantastic shape with three gradations. My fancy was flattered and I went up. I looked up into the sky; from its deep recess came out little stars rubbing their sleepy eyes. Twinkle! twinkle! all the night. Believing the Muse was at my service, I went up again. Thus step by step, the top was reached at last.

There I recollected the time when I had visited Kamakura long ago. I had been going round, calling at each of the Five Temples; it was, I remember, on the sacred precincts of Engaku-ji that, leisurely going up the stone steps as I was doing there then, I saw a flat-headed priest in a yellow garment who had just come out of the temple-gate. I was ascending and he descending the steps. As he passed, he asked me in a high-pitched voice if I were not visiting the grounds and I answered that I was and paused a moment. "There is nothing to see there," the priest said and went placidly on his way. I was so deeply impressed with the honest simplicity of his remark and felt that I had been outwitted by him. I paused at the top of the steps. My eye followed the priest who, tossing his flat round head, went down until he disappeared among the cedar trees. He never once looked back. How open, independent and fearless the priest was. Indeed, a Zen priest is to my taste. Thus thinking, I entered the gate. Not a single creature seemed to be living there; all was vacancy. The spacious priest's quarters and the chapel as well looked deserted. It cheered me immensely to know that there was such a set of candid people in the world who could treat me with so much ease and frankness; not because I had been initiated into the rudiments of Zen-teaching; I knew nothing of it, yet I was very much captivated with the honest, simple behavior of the flat-headed priest.

This world is a bore; it is poisonously officious. It is filled with many brazen-faced impudent rascals who, having no good reason to be in society, shamelessly expose their large faces to the wind of the world, priding themselves upon the great dimensions of their visages. They set a spy upon you for a decade or more and tell him to count how often you have broken wind. Life is nothing else to them. They will come out obsequiously and tell you how many times you have broken wind without your asking. It would not be unbearable if they came forth and told me to my face that I had violated the law of decorum so many times; I might listen to them for future reference, but they will never do that. They will come after you stealthily like dogs whispering to you of your indecency. Enough! Humbug! Away with your nonsense! These interjections will only serve to provoke another volley from them. If you shut your mouth, they will think that you have been persuaded, and believe therein lies the secret of their successful life. I shall not meddle with other people's affairs; they are perfectly free to think and act as they please, but what I request of them is that they would quietly establish their course of life without disturbing the peace of my mind and it is their obligation to do so. If they say that they cannot carry out their life policy without interfering with ours, I'll simply have to tell them that indecency is my code of life. Then Japan's fate is doomed.

Indeed it is soul-lifting to be thus rambling aimlessly on such a beautiful spring eve. If favoured with pleasure, pleasure is my companion and principle; if not, it should never disturb me in the least. If the Muse honours me with a verse, poetry is my life's guidance; If not, it satisfies me just as much. This way of life bothers none and it is the only true principle of life. To count how often you have broken wind is the policy of personal attack, and the violation of decency by breaking wind is nothing but the principle of self-vindication, and it is the hand of Karma that is leading me up the stone-steps of the Kankai Temple.

The first line of a quatrain:—

> I look up,
> The sky is sprinkled with stars,
> I count them one, two, three.

is just complete, when I find myself at the top of the steps, where the sea like a broad blue sash comes in sight in spring's dim light. I enter the gate. Poetic excitement has gone, and the remaining three lines are left unfinished.

Leading to the monastery, there runs a narrow stone pathway with a hedge of azaleas on the right, and a grave-yard over beyond. The sanctuary itself stands solemn on the left. The tiles of the high roof gave out a peculiar faint light. I looked up to see if the myriad tiles had not each a moon lodged on it. The cooing of doves was heard somewhere; perhaps it came from under the ridge of the roof where the birds had roosted. Imagination conjured up some white spots on the pent roof, which I took to be the dung-hills made by the birds.

Just where the rain-drops fell from the eaves, I observed in the twilight some strange figures standing in a row. They were neither trees nor blades of grass. Were I to speak from what I felt then, they looked just like the horned ogres painted by Iwasa Matabei, who cutting short their incantations, were dancing their elfin dances under the eaves of the temple. Their movement was a model of good manners as they danced about in a row from end to end of the sacred building; their shadows taking up their original steps danced also methodically and to time. Tempted out by the dim light of the night, these supernatural beings, it seemed, came out in a party to the temple grounds to dance, leaving their bells, hammers, subscription lists and all behind them.

Nearer approach disclosed that it was a cactus of an enormous size, some seven or eight feet in height. The stem like a snake-gourd pressed hard so as to form a large ladle with its handle down goes up and up until one wonders if it would ever cease growing. How many more ladles would be added before it comes to an end? Perhaps it would grow like Jonah's gourd so big during the night as to pierce the pent roof and the roof as well. These spoon-like limbs must have come flying from nobody knows where and stuck one by one to the stem. It does not seem that the old ladles giving birth to the young ones have waited patiently until they are as big as they. The limbs are connected with joints so abrupt and singular that one doubts if there be any such plant in any other place, yet it looks altogether innocent and indifferent to the severe criticism passed on it. I have been told that there was once a priest who being asked what Buddha is, answered right away, "The oak in the yard." If asked the same question, I should not hesitate to answer, "A cactus under the moon!"

In my youth, I was a great admirer of Chao-pu-chi whose descriptive style pleased me so much that I soon learned by heart the following passage:—

> "The sky of a September eve was high and the air transparent. The surrounding hills were still as in the days of creation. The moon shone bright.

> The stars were twinkling like precious gems. They looked very near above our heads and we imagined they would talk to us. The windows looked out into a bamboo thicket where the evening breeze, caught and struggling with interlaced branches to get out, produced a soft rustling sound. Here and there in the bush were found some old knotty plums and massive palms which looked like mischievous elf-sprites who were engaged in their frolicsome pranks in the dark. The company were kept awake all night through. No wink of sleep blessed us. Impatiently we waited until the cock crew."

I repeated it from memory and contentedly smiled. There might have been a time and occasion in my life when this cactus would have scared me and driven me back down the hill. I felt the plant all over and found it prickly.

At the extremity of the pavement, you turn to the left, and there you are at the monastery. Before it, stands a large magnolia about a span in circumference. It soars high above the roof of the building, its branches spreading far and near. These limbs are piled one above the other, where the moon sits serene and peaceful. Ordinarily when branches are very thickly intertwined, the sky is not to be seen from below. Much less so when you have flowers on them. How thick, however, the branches of a magnolia may be, they never intercept the light. It is never so proud as to obstruct the view of a man who stands below by shooting out its limbs very close together. Looking up from beneath the tree, the flowers are plainly visible and you can easily tell one from another. Nobody can tell how far up the chain of flowers may be reaching, yet one flower is one flower after all, and the light, blue sky will peep out from between. The flower of a magnolia is not pure white. Snow white suggests cold. Pale white is associated with an artful coquette who practises her eyes upon you. It is never so very white; it is a modest, humble flower always wearing light-yellow. Vacantly did I stand long on the stone passage, admiringly looking up at the clusters of the modest flowers thus hung up in midair. Nothing but flowers! No leaf, no foliage.

"I look up into the sky;
  The sky is alive with magnolias."

is the verse I obtained at the time. Somewhere doves were heard cooing.

I entered the house; it was open to all comers. No burglar seemed to disturb the people here, nor was there a dog to bark.

"Pardon," I called, but no response; all was still. I repeated the call, yet no answer. The doves were cooing.

"I beg your pardon." My voice was much louder this time.

"Oh! Oh!" somebody returned farther away. Never did I have such responsives before when I made a call. Soon a foot-step was heard in the passage, and a paper lantern cast its shadow upon the ornamental screen in the hall. It was Ryōnen, the boy priest.

"Is his holiness in?"

"Yes, he is. What has brought you here?"

"Please tell him that the painter staying at the Hot springs is come."

"The painter? Come in then."

"Before you tell him so?"

"I am responsible, man. Come in." I left my clogs and went in.

"You ought to learn better manners, painter."

"How?"

"Put your clogs in order. See!" And the light of his lantern was on my *geta*.

About five feet high from the earthen floor, I saw pasted in the middle of the blackened pillar a little piece of paper, a quarter of *hanshi* (rice paper) with something written.

'Look well below your legs.' "You can read the letters?"

"Yes, indeed!" and I adjusted my clogs. His holiness's room stands right next to the temple as you turn the passage way at a right angle. My usher opened the paper sliding door carefully, and ceremoniously placing his hands on the door sill, said.

"Your holiness, Mr. Painter from Shioda, if you please." The little priest was politeness itself. I was not a little amused.

"I am very glad; please to come in."

Ryōnen left and I entered. It was a very small room with a fire-place in the middle. An iron kettle was singing over the fire. The head priest had been poring over a book at the opposite side of the fire-place.

"Be seated, please." With this, he took off his spectacles and pushed aside his old volume.

"Ryōnen! Ryō-ō-nen!"

"Ay, ay! sir!"

"Won't you give our guest a cushion to sit on?"

"Ha—a—i" came from Ryōnen far away.

"Very happy to see you. *Ennui* must be killing you."

"The moon is very bright to-night. She has guided me here."

"Yes, it is very bright," and the *shōji* was ajar.

Two stepping stones and one pine tree were all that were found in the small flat yard with a precipice over beyond, whence I could command a view of the sea in a dim moon light. I began to feel much freer. Fishing torches far and near rose and fell. They would at last melt away into the sky and come out so many stars.

"The view is just splendid, your holiness. It is a sin to have the *shōji* closed."

"Yes, but it loses novelty, as I see it every night."

"Does it, I wonder? I would be looking at it without going to bed even."

"You are a painter and I am—."

"You are a painter, too, so long as you are charmed by a thing beautiful, my dear abbot."

"Indeed! You are right. Priest as I am, I can draw an outline picture of Dharma or some such things. Don't you notice the picture hanging on the alcove wall? It is a Dharma painted by my predecessor. Don't you think it pretty good?" A picture of the saint was indeed found on the wall of the small alcove. It was a very indifferent picture to the eye of a connoisseur, yet was perfectly free from worldliness. No attempt was made to hide his poor technique. Nothing could be more innocent than the performance. His predecessor must also have been a man free from worldly cares as the picture itself.

"The simplicity of the picture appeals to me most."

"We are satisfied if our picture is thus represented—if our mood is fairly expressed."

"Far better than a clever picture which flatters popular taste."

"Ha! Ha! Ha! It's very kind of you to encourage us so. By the way, is there a doctor of painting nowadays?"

"No, I haven't heard of it yet."

"Ah! is it? I met a certain doctor the other day."

"Indeed!"

"Is a *hakase* a great man?"

"Well, I should think so."

"It is time, I should presume, for your profession to create a *hakase.* Why not, I wonder?"

"And I see no reason why your own community should not have a doctored priest, too."

"Ha! Ha! I'm fairly caught. Let me see who was it whom I met the other day. His card must be somewhere about here."

"Where did you see him, in Tokyo?"

"No, right here. I have not been in the capital these twenty years. I have been told that they have invented a car driven by electricity, which I have a mind to get in and have a ride."

"It is a dull invention with so much noise."

"Yes? The dogs* in the province of Shu barked at the sun, and the bisons in the province of Wu all panted at seeing the moon, and it may be wise for a country cousin like myself not to meddle with the electric car, for I may get into trouble."

"No anxiety on that head, your holiness, but disappointment!"

"Well—!"

The kettle on the charcoal fire was sending out steam from its spout. The priest took out the tea-set from the tea-shelf and served me a cup.

"Help yourself, please; but ours is not so nice as the beverage served at the old gentleman of Shioda's."

"Just to my taste, your holiness."

"You seem to be travelling all the time; it is to paint, I presume?"

"Yes, I carry my paint-box everywhere I go, but it is not necessarily the case that I paint."

"Ha-ah! Then you paint only for your own amusement."

"Well, you are not very far off, your holiness. I dislike to have them count how often I break wind a day."

Quick-witted as he was, the priest seemed to be not a little at a loss what to make out of the strange phrase.

"What do you mean, my dear painter?"

---

* The sun shone very seldom in the province of Shu and the dogs would bark when it appeared, while the province of Wu was scorchingly hot with a dazzling sun above all through the year and the bisons panted at seeing the moon as it is round and shines like the sun.

"Too long residence in Tokyo results in that."

"How?"

"Ha! Ha! Ha! Counting itself is harmless, but analyzing your fart, they go on examining your anus, even telling you it is triangular or quadratic."

"Then it must be a hygienic process."

"No, your holiness, it is a detective's business."

"Detective? It is police then. What on earth is the use of a police-office or police-force. Is it a thing necessary, I wonder?"

"Well, it has nothing to do with us painters."

"Neither has it anything to do with us. I have never come upon the police."

"I shouldn't be surprised."

"Why, let them do as they please. Coolness is our safe guide. Even police can hardly find fault with you when you have done nothing wrong."

"Yet nobody can put up with the punishment inflicted on one for his indecent manners."

"When I was a stripling, my master used to say, 'Deem not your training is perfected before you can sit quietly in the throng of Nihombashi with your bowels all exposed to view.' Educate yourself in that way and you need be a tourist no longer."

"It won't be hard to do when my life is dedicated to painting."

"Go ahead then. I can see no reason why your life should not be."

"Your holiness, it can hardly be possible while they are trying to cast the mote out of my eye."

"Ha! Ha! There you are! Nami-San, the young lady of Shioda's, where you are staying, had worried over so many things after she was separated from her husband and returned home until at last she came and asked me the Ways of Buddha, and of late she enjoys perfect peace which becomes an enlightened person. Now you see in her a sensible woman."

"Well, I thought she was no ordinary woman."

"Indeed, she is a woman of strong character, sharp and quick. She was at the bottom of the bitter experience the young priest Taian had during his 'retreat' here in our temple—an experience which led him to drink the cup and find the one thing needful; he will be a holy man before long."

The pine-tree casts its graceful shadow upon the quiet yard. The sea in the distance, as if responding or not responding to the light of the sky gives out a faint dim glow in the soft melting atmosphere around. The torches of fishing boats out on the lonely sea are flickering.

"Look at the shadow of the pine."

"Beautiful!"

"Pretty only?"

"Well—."

"It is not only beautiful but it cares not a pin if it blows ever so hard."

I drank the remainder of the tea in the cup; placing it upside down on the saucer, I stood up ready to go home.

"Let me see you off at the gate." "Ryōnen," he called, our guest is going."

As I was coming out of the monastery led by my host and his pupil, I heard the doves cooing.

"Nothing is so lovely as these birds. I clap my hands and they come down flying. Shall I try my skill?"

The moon shines brighter; the night is far advanced; the flowers of the magnolia like little clouds float in mid air. Crack goes the clapping of his hands breaking the death-like silence of the spring night. The sound dies away into the air, but no dove comes down.

"Strange they don't come down," said my host wonderingly.

Ryōnen looked towards me, a mischievous smile lurking in the corners of his eyes. The priest seems to think that the birds can see even at night. Blessed indeed is such a man.

I bade them 'good night' at the gate. The stone-pavement had two shadows cast on it, one large, the other small. They disappeared one after the other, and I looked on.

## XII

"Christ is an artist in the highest sense of the term," says Oscar Wilde, if I remember right. I shall not gainsay it, but the remark made by the British author comes very true in the case of our priest of Kankai Temple; not that he has a nice perception of taste, nor because he is able to read the signs of the time. He is so simple as to be happy with a picture of Dharma which can hardly pass as a picture. He believes there is a *hakase* of painting; he thinks the doves can see at night. For all these drawbacks, I say he has the best qualifications for a true artist. His mind is a bottomless bag; all goes through and nothing remains. It is a wind that cometh and goeth as it listeth; it is pure gold, no dross settles in the crucible. Inject a germ of taste into his brain, and he will be an artist through and through by adapting himself to any circumstances he finds himself in. I can never be one, if I would, while they set a spy upon me in order that he may count how often I have broken wind. True, I can sit at my easel with the palette, but never can be a painter. Thus finding myself in an out-of-the-way village among the mountains and burying, as it were, my body in the serene atmosphere of the departing spring, I can for the first time be a true artist both in mind and soul. Once in that felicitous situation, the world of the beautiful is mine. One need not necessarily draw a sketch or even an outline of a picture, yet he can be a great painter of the first rank. As to technique, he may be inferior to Michael Angelo; or to Raphael as to artistic skill; but with respect to character as a painter, he is a match for any of the stars of the fine arts, both ancient and modern. No picture I have painted since I came here to the Hot Springs, and it may seem as if I had brought my paint-box simply for appearance's sake. People will point at me with an ironical smile and say, "Behold the painter who never paints." Let them sneer at you as much as they please, but do not be discouraged, for you are a painter genuine and noble. It does not necessarily follow that a painter placed in such a condition will or can paint a master-piece, yet it goes without saying that one who will produce a noble picture is the one that has been visited by such an inspiration.

The above is what I felt and thought as I was enjoying a cigarette after I had breakfasted. The sun was far up above the misty air; the shōji was ajar; over beyond, the hills with many trees lay undulating before me. The trees had never looked so bright and green.

One of the most interesting studies on earth is, I believe, the relation of air to object and colour. Shall colour be the principal theme with air subject to it? Shall object be the chief subject upon which air is dependent? or shall air play the principal figure, giving colour and object subordinate parts? A variety of tones is produced according to the mood in which a painter is working, and the tone is determined by the taste of the painter himself. However, it is not to be denied that time and place are two great factors which will modify a painter's natural faculty of perceiving the beautiful. Never have I seen a bright landscape painting by an Englishman.

A bright picture may not appeal to the British taste. Even if it did, what could he do with the dull gray air of his native land? Frederick Goodall is an English painter, yet his tone of colouring entirely differs from that of his fellow-artists, and no wonder. It seems that an English landscape never appealed to his fancy; his favourite theme for his brush was always found in Egypt or Persia, where the air is very clear and transparent. Those who have never seen his works will be greatly surprised to know that an Englishman could give such a bright picture.

Everybody is perfectly free as to his likes or dislikes. But were we to paint a Japanese landscape, we should have to give the air and colour peculiar to the country. Granting that French painting is superior to ours, will it ever do to blindly imitate colour and all and tell you, "Behold this Japanese scenery"? Naturally we will have to see Nature face to face and study every hour of the day the ever-varying colours and forms of atmosphere and clouds with the devotion of a worshipper and when we have come across the colour we have so long been looking for, we shall lose no time in taking out the three-legged stool and putting the hue in our portfolio. Colour ever changes. Once lost, another opportunity will never come. Settled on and above the top of the hill I have just looked up there appears such a sweet tint as is seldom met with in this part of the country. Let me hurry on and make a rough draft of it, for my coming here will have been all in vain, if I missed it.

I open the *karakami* and am out on the verandah. Nami-San is leaning against the shōji of the upstair's room beyond. Her chin is buried deep in her neck-bands, and I can have only a side-view of her face. I am about to salute her, when she drops her left hand and begins to move her right as fast as wind. Like lightning, it flashes, it forks out twice or thrice just about her breast before it goes out with a clicking sound. A white-sheathed dagger is in her left hand; she disappears behind the shōji in a twinkling of time. I go out of the hotel feeling as if I had had a peep into the stage of Kabuki-Theatre from early morning.

Coming out of the gate, you turn to the left and there you find a steep path running along the precipitous side of the hill. Nightingales sing here and there. Orange trees planted in regular rows cover the face of the eminence which gently slopes down to the valley. On your right stand two modest hills whose sides are also covered with delicious fruit-trees. Some years ago I was here once. I forget how long ago it was, but it was towards the close of the year, in the cold month of December. Never had I been favoured with a sight of such a great number of orange trees loaded with so much fruit. On my asking her, if I might buy a branch, the fruit-gatherer said that I could freely help myself to as many as I wanted and welcome, and began to sing a strange air as she gathered the fruit on the tree. In Tokyo, thought I, even the peel of an orange has some value, and you'd have to go to the druggist's to get some for money. At night, reports of guns were constantly heard and I was told that hunters were shooting wild ducks. Happily did I spend the time then without a glimpse of Nami-San.

Were she to act on the stage, Nami-San would no doubt acquit herself nobly as a fine player of female parts. An ordinary actor or actress will put on affectation as soon as he or she appears on the scene. Her home is Nami-San's permanent stage on which she is ever acting and she is unaware that she is playing her dramatic parts. Spontaneity or naturalness is the characteristic trait which pervades all her actions. Such a life of hers may well be called aesthetic. I have learned a good deal from her—many a hint invaluable to my vocation.

Unless we think her performances dramatic, no day would pass without our feeling uneasy. If we were to study her from the same view point as that of an ordinary fiction-monger, with honour and love for the background, we should soon get sick of her, as the stimulus would be too strong. Were there some complicated relations of flesh as often found here below, my pains would be very great as to defy description. As my journey this time was to leave all worldly things behind and be a painter through and through, I must see everything as a work of art—every person as found only in *No,* or play, or poetry. Viewed from this angle, she has never been surpassed by any other in performing the most beautiful things, much superior to those of an actor for she never tries to show off her accomplishments.

Misunderstanding may arise, I am afraid, from the observation I have just made; you will probably condemn me as a dangerous member of society. Hard it is to do good. To be generous and virtuous is by no means easy; integrity of purpose is a rare virtue: to lay down your life for the sake of duty is a loss, yet you dare do such painful things. Why? Simply because there is a joy that surpasses all these painful sacrifices. Painting, poetry or drama is another name for the joyful feeling found deep down in these pains. Once we taste it, our actions become elegant and sublime and we only get anxious to satisfy that pure and noble desire by overcoming all these hardships. Gladly and boldly we go forward, putting aside all physical pains and privations; joyfully we plunge into the tripod to be boiled to death for humanity's sake. If we were to define fine arts from the narrow human point of view they are a crystallization of divine feeling found in the recess of the minds of us educated people, that shows us the way of the righteous instead of the way of the wicked; that teaches us to be a friend of the honest instead of the dishonest; that makes us impatient with ourselves until we have lifted up the weak by putting down the proud. In a word, they are the sun that, driving away all darkness, makes everything shine out a gem.

People often laugh at one whose actions are dramatic. Men of the world seem to think it foolish to pay an unnecessary sacrifice in order that one may satisfy his taste for, the beautiful. They are inclined to deem it unwise and inadvisable to go ahead and do what one's aesthetic conscience dictates without patiently waiting for an opportunity to come in the due course of time. It is well for those who understand the psychology of such an action to smile, but it is unpardonable for those vulgar people who comprehend not what refined taste is to judge and doubt the sincerity of one's motive out of the meanness of their own minds. Once there was a youth who threw himself down into the whirlpool of a cataract fifty feet high. Misao Fujimura willingly laid down his precious life for the sake of the beautiful. This was amply proven by the words he had left engraved on the trunk of a tree that grew over the precipice. Death itself is sublime, but what is hard to comprehend is the motive that drove one to that extremity. But those who fail to find a charm even in sublime death will never be able to make their end sublime even if there be a good reason to do so. This limitation makes them much smaller in respect of character than the unfortunate youth. Shame on them, say I.

It is true I live among men like myself, but being a painter by profession, I think I am more refined than those vulgar people all around me. As a member of society, I stand in a position which requires me to educate others. I believe I can act more beautifully than one who has no poetry, no painting, no aesthetic ideals. In the society of man a pretty action is that either of justice, righteousness or integrity; a model citizen in this world is one who shows these virtues in his actions.

Having thus wandered away from the society of man, I need not at least during my journey go back to it. If I did, my ultramundane trip would come to nothing. I have, so to speak, to strain humanity—the grating grains of sand—through a sieve until at last there remains nothing but beautiful gold dust upon which my eyes shall feast. As a member of human society, I am fully convinced that I am very poorly qualified. Cutting off every thread of personal interest, I am trying hard to become a painter thoroughly, who himself will get about to and fro on the canvas he is working at. Now mountain, stream or person will appear all alike to me and I shall be enabled to observe the acts and actions of Nami-San just as they stand.

Three blocks up and there you see surrounded by orange trees a white-walled mansion over beyond. Soon the road branches out into two. Turning to the left, giving a side glance to the white house, I look back when my eye rests upon a maid with a red petticoat as she comes up the hill. At first I notice her red underskirt; next her brown ankles; then her straw slippers become visible gradually approaching. On her head fall wild cherry-blossoms like pretty snowflakes; on her back she carries a beautiful glassy sea.

The mountain whose east side sloping down formed a plateau, and there I found myself as I came up the steep path. On the north stood a range of dark blue mountains which I thought I had seen from the verandah in the morning. On the south, a grass-plot—a meadow—about a block wide stretched out until it fell off in a precipice beneath which stood the orange plantation I had just passed. Over beyond the little village snugly nestled in the valley, you could feast your eyes on a broad expanse of water, the blue sea.

Many were the roads interweaving with one another so intricately that it was hard to tell which was the main road. All were roads, but none the road. The grayish black earth peeped out here and there from amongst the grass, challenging one to follow the right track if he could. Very irregular and winding were the lanes, but irregularity is a joy.

I wandered about far and near in the grassy plain to find a good spot to set my three legged stool. The scenery which I had looked at from the verandah and thought would make a fine picture would never do on my closer examination, and the hue was rapidly changing. The inspiration to draw had left me while wandering in the meadow grass. If I was not to paint, thought I, any place would do to sit and wheresoever I sat would be my temporary abode. The spring sun sending his congenial rays deep down into the roots of the grass had brewed a fine gossamer-like vapour, and when I sat down I felt as if I had smashed the invisible thread mercilessly.

The sea shone beneath my feet. The spring sun without any single drop of dew to intercept his rays, not only lighted up all the surface of the water, but also imperceptibly going down, down to the bottom of the waves seemed to have illumined the subterranean world, too. It looked very warm. You take up a limner's brush, dip it well in Prussian blue and boldly draw a broad dash—a woman's sash—with shining white dots on it, each dot being a pretty fish of silvery fins. That will give you a faint idea how beautiful the land and the sea were in the genial rays of the spring sun. Under the canopy of heaven lay the boundless expanse of water with many white sails that looked as small as the tips of your fingers in the distance. They were painted ships, so motionless, so serene. They reminded me of those Korean barges, loaded with precious tribute, that had in days gone by come over to this country. Excepting these, the universe was one vast mass of sunshine over both land and sea.

Lazily did I lay myself down in the grass. My hat coming off my forehead tilted back to the rear of the head. Small bushes of wild quince grew here and there undermining the roots of the grass one or two feet around. Just where I lay, there was one as if expecting my caress. The quince is an interesting little plant whose branches are so obstinate that they never bend. One may imagine it must be a straight tree, but it is not. It has short, upright limbs which meeting at certain angles make way for each other to form one perfect whole. The flowers are never of a definite colour; they are neither pink nor white, but they look very innocent with a few soft leaves to embellish or protect the flowers. Of all the flowers on earth, I may justly say, the wild quince is the simplest, and, though it may sound a bit paradoxical to you, it is the most enlightened. People sometimes say, "He lived simple and died simple." Such a man would be born a quince in his second birth. I would be one, too.

When a boy, I remember, I made a pretty pen-rest of quince twigs with flowers and leaves by giving them artistic straightenings and twistings. Placing it on my desk, I put a cheap writing brush on its fork, and was so happy to see the white head of the pen peep out from amongst the flowers and leaves that I went to bed not without many a longing after the rack. Next morning when I awoke, I sprang out of bed and rushed to the desk on which I had left my pen-rest. The flowers had faded and the leaves had died during the night, and the only thing that shone out as before was the white head of the brush. I wondered how those beautiful things could have withered away in a single night. Whenever I recollect that time, I am filled with remorse to think that I am not what I was.

The wild quince my eyes rested upon as soon as I laid myself down was, so to speak, an acquaintance of twenty years' standing. The eye cleaved to the modest plant as if it were the only thing worth seeing. The pleasurable feeling it aroused in me stirred up the Muse from her long nap.

In my grassy lair I meditated and meditated. Every verse I obtained I put down in my portfolio. It was not long before I thought my poem was finished. I read it through from the beginning,—

Once out of the gate, many a thought comes,
  The spring wind blows on my garment,
The fragrant herbs blow on the ruts,
  The deserted road reaches to a misty eternity,
Leaning upon my staff I look around,
  Nature wears her robe of glory,
I hear the nightingale sing,
  I see flower petals fall as snow,
The road leads to a wilderness,
  I write my poem upon the door of an old temple,
My thought goes up to where fleecy clouds float,
  A solitary goose measures the firmament with his wings,
Quiet sadness creeps into my heart,
  In the poetic atmosphere I forget right or wrong,
At thirty, I feel as if old,
  The sun still lingers on,
My soul saunters and is content,
  Leisurely do I look at falling blossoms.

"It's done, it's well done!" I seemed to hear somebody whisper; it may have been a trick of my fancy, but the poem faithfully depicts the feeling I had as I lay looking at the quince, forgetting every worldly tie, and I was quite satisfied, although it had no mention of the plant or the sea. I was happy to hum it from beginning to end, when I was startled by an 'Ahem,' a human cough.

I turned towards the direction whence it came. A man came out from amongst the brushwood that grew towards the prone edge of the mountain. He had on a brown felt hat so old that one wondered if it had ever been new. A pair of sharp eyes darted a fearful glance at me from under the slouched brim. Of what shape they were, nobody could tell, but certain it was that they were staring around to seek something, somebody. He was dressed in indigo blue striped clothes tucked up to the hip. He had on wooden shoes with loose heels. His feet were bare. It was hard to tell who and what he was. Judging from the whiskers, moustache, and beard which grew wild, he must be a tramp-*samurai* or a highway man.

Instead of going down the steep-path as was expected, the man turned round at a sharp angle. Sure I thought he would go back to the place whence he had come, but no; he was coming towards where I lay. One who takes a walk in this plain would be thus walking up and down, but he did not seem to be a mere stroller, nor could I imagine him to be a dweller in the neighbourhood either. He would pause now and again. He would often hang his head, or oftener still would he lift up his head to look around. Sometimes he would seem absorbed in profound meditation, or he would show the posture of a man awaiting someone to come and meet him. I was entirely at a loss how to account for the actions of the stranger.

However my eyes would cleave to this suspicious character. I feared no threat from him, nor had I any intention to make him the subject of my picture, but I could not let him alone. My eye followed him wherever he went, from right to left or from left to right. Amidst this optical manoeuvre the man in question all of a sudden came to a full stop. No sooner had he paused than another came into the range of my vision. Each seemed to have recognized the other; they appeared to be drawing closer. The range of my sight gradually grew smaller and smaller until at last it was focussed into a single point in the centre of the field. The two stood face to face, one with the blue mountain at her back, the other with the blue sea at his.

The man was of course that tramp-*samurai*. His companion? It was a woman: it was Nami-San. The dagger I had seen about her in the morning was immediately associated with her appearance on the scene, and the fear that she might have the blade hidden in her breast was anything but pleasing. Ultramundane as I am, it sent a chill over my whole system.

Both the man and the woman remained long in the same posture. Movement of any kind seemed impossible for them now. They might be speaking, but not a word reached my ears. Pretty soon the man hung his head; the woman turned round towards the mountain; her face was completely hidden from me.

The mountain was alive with the sweet music of nightingales. She might be lending her ears to the songs of the bushwarblers. Long had not passed before the man determinedly held up his head and was about to step away. 'Calm before storm,' I said to myself. The woman with a dexterous motion turned round again towards the sea. Something peeped out of her sash; it must be the dirk. The man in a fit of passion had already moved away a few steps; the woman following him two or three paces. She had on straw-shoes; he paused, I dare say, held back by the invisible message from her eyes. No sooner did he turn round towards her than she thrust her right hand into her sash. "Look out, man! " I was about to call out.

A dagger it was not that she took out, but it was a small package like a pocket-book. She held it out with her pretty white hand. A long ribbon dangled down; the spring breeze was teasing it.

With a step forward, her body a little straightened above the waist, she holds out something purple on the palm of her pretty hand. The posture alone would make a fine picture.

Two inches is the gap that separates two continents, one Nami-San's, the other the tramp's. It is all but bridged over by the purple purse she holds out and the longing attitude of the man. "Union in disunion" may be the very terms to describe such a delicate relation of the two. Hers is the attitude of pulling; his is the posture of being pulled back, but in reality, she is no more pulling than he is being pulled. Their affinity, if it ever existed, is snapped at the end of the purple pocket-book.

While an exquisite harmony is thus kept up in the attitudes of the two, it is also of special interest to the painter to note the contrast between them regarding their faces and clothing.

He was short, thick-set, with a dark bearded face; she was graceful with sloping shoulders, a swan-neck and a clear-cut comely face; he an outlandish tramp with cheap clogs, who unmannerly twisted his body round; she, dressed as she was in everyday coarse silk, looked very charming as she gently straightened her slender body above the waist; he in his shabby old gray hat and blue striped clothes tucked up to the hips; she whose glossy black hair was so well combed as to start gossamer even had on a black satin sash with a crimson crape-holder peeping out of its recess. What a bewitching theme for an artist to exhaust his skill and colours on!

'Heard melodies are sweet, but those unheard are sweeter!' It might have been nice for the man to accept the purse from her, but far nicer would it have been if she had continued pulling and he being pulled thus maintaining the sweet balance between them. No sooner had the purse been found in his hand than the charm went out. No longer did she try to draw; no more did he wish to be drawn. They lived in different worlds. Never before did I imagine what an important factor the psychological phenomenon is in the composition of a good picture!

Right and left they go. There being no more spiritual communion between them, they will make a very poor composition for a painting. The man gives a backward glance once as he is entering the copsewood. The woman never looks back. Sweepingly coming up to where I was, she stood before me.

"Master! master!" she called out twice. I did not dream to be thus found out.

"What do you want of me, lady?" I said and held up my head above the bush. My hat was lying on the grass.

"What have you been doing there, sir?"

"I have been lying here composing a poem."

"A liar you are, sir. Sure you have been a witness to the scene."

"Well—. that scene? Yes, I saw a little."

"Ho! Ho! Ho! You need not have been frugal in that; you could have indulged in it with impunity."

"To confess the truth, miss, I saw more than enough."

"I suspected as much, sir. I say, won't you come out of that den? Come out of that bush, won't you? "

In a moment I was out of the bush as I was told.

"Have you any further business there in the bush?"

"No more, miss, and I am thinking if I may not go home."

"Let me go with you then."

"Eh! Eh!"

Again I was obedient as a slave. I went back to the bush, put on my hat and with the paint-box was walking along together with Nami-San.

"Did you paint?"

"No, I did not."

"You have painted no picture since you came here then?"

"No, miss."

"But you are here expressly to paint, and it will hardly pay if you do not."

"Well, miss, it pays."

"You don't say so! How, I wonder?"

"Why, it amply pays. Whether or not I paint will come to very little in the long run."

"Do you mean it as a pun? Ho! Ho! Ho! You are ever so hopeful."

"Freedom from care is my creed that guided me to this secluded, out-of-the way place, and it will never do if I do not take life easy."

"Place, sir, counts very little. Life won't be worth living wherever we are, if we don't take it easy. As for me, I am neither abashed nor ashamed even if I was caught in such a scene as you just witnessed."

"You need not be, I should think."

"Thanks! But what do you think that man was?"

"To be frank, miss, he did not look very rich."

"Exactly! Ho! Ho! Ho! You seem to be a good fortune-teller; he got so poor as to come here to ask my help; he can no longer live in Japan."

"Where did he come from, I wonder?"

"From the castle-town."

"Did he really come so far, and where is he going?"

"I understand, to Manchuria,"

"What is he going there for?"

"I do not know, sir. He may be going there either to pick up money or death. It is entirely beyond my comprehension."

Here I raised my eyes and looked into her face. A

faint smile upon the corners of her closed lips was fading away. It was a riddle to me.

"He is my husband."

Like a lightning flash it came before I could cover my ears. It was altogether a surprise to me. I did not, of course, expect to hear such a thing from her, nor had she meant, I believe, to go so far as to make a clean breast of that particular point.

"Why, you were taken by surprise, I'm sure." Said the woman.

"Yes, I was, I admit."

"But he is not my husband; he was the one from whom I separated."

"Indeed,——"

"That is all, good sir."

"All right, ma'am. Look, you see a fine white-washed mansion over there amongst the orange-trees in such a pretty place, whose house is that?"

"It's my brother's. Let us just drop in on our way home."

"Have you any business there?"

"Yes, to deliver something I have been asked to."

"Let me go with you then, please."

Instead of going down the steep path to the village below, we turned directly to the right, and going up hill about a block, found ourselves just in front of the gate. We did not enter the gate to the portico, but made right away into the yard. She boldly went before me and I followed. The garden faced the south and some half a dozen fan-palms stood there like giants keeping watch.

Just beneath the mud-fence there stretched an extensive orange-orchard.

Nami-San sat on the edge of the verandah and said,—

"What a beautiful view! Pray look!"

"Yes, it is just splendid!" I answered. Nobody seemed to be within the *shōji*. It was very quiet, and Nami-San apparently forgot to knock. She sat on and on composedly looking down on the fruit-farm. I doubted if she had any business here at all.

Having nothing more to talk about, we remained silent with our eyes fixed on the oranges below. The sun nearing the meridian poured down his warm rays upon the surrounding hills embellished with the fruit-trees whose myriad leaves shone bright as they fluttered in the noon breeze. All at once, a loud "cock-a-doodle-doo" was heard towards the barn-door at the back of the house. It came from the proud chanticleer announcing the time of noon meal.

"It's noon. Time passes so quickly. Wait, I had business here. Kyuichi-San! Kyuichi-San!" She called aloud and stretching her body, she opened the closed *shōji* a little. It was a ten mat room with no article of decoration save a pair of picture scrolls after the Kanō school, which, hanging lonely on the alcove, told the beholder that their spring was a sad one.

"Kyuichi-San!" she called out again. "Aye" at last came from towards the barn; soon foot-steps stopped on the other side of the *karakami*. Hardly was it opened when a dagger in a white scabbard rolled over on the *tatami*.

"It's for you, Kyuichi. Uncle's parting gift." I did not know when her hand had got into her breast until the dirk with some two or three somersaults rolled up to the feet of the startled youth. Flash went the cold blade as it came out an inch from its sheath. It had not been well bound.

## XIII

We took a river boat to see Kyuichi off at Yoshida Station. The passengers were six in all: the young recruit, the old gentleman of Shioda, his daughter Nami-San, her elder brother, and Gembei who took care of the luggage, and myself among the number. I was there just to keep company with them.

However, I would go anywhere in any capacity if invited, even though I did not understand the meaning of the invitation. No scruple whatever was needed in such a supermundane pilgrimage as mine. The boat was something like a raft with low sides and a flat bottom. The old man sat in the middle; Nami-San and I at the stern; her brother and Kyuichi at the bow, while Gembei sat alone apart from the rest in charge of the baggage.

"How do you like war, Kyuichi-San?" was the abrupt question of our heroine.

"I can hardly tell before I go to the front. I expect a hard time of it, but I may sometimes have a change," was the answer of the youth who had never been in war before.

"However hard it may be," said the old man, "it is for the country which gave you birth, Kyuichi."

"Does not the sword your uncle gave you tempt you to fight a bit?" She was again original in her question.

"Yes, a little!" And the young man lightly nodded; the old man held up his grey beard and laughed, while her brother sat silent, affecting not to hear her remark.

"Do you think you, can fight if you are so indifferent, Kyūichi?"

She was not a whit considerate on her part and expectantly put out her white face before the young man who exchanged a glance with her brother.

"You will surely make a brave soldier if you become one, Nami-San," was what her brother said to her.

He had never spoken a word before. It did not seem from the tone that he meant it simply as a joke.

"I? I a soldier? Had it been possible for me to be a soldier, I should have been one and been dead by now. Kyuichi-San, you had better be killed. It is more respectable than to be alive."

"Don't, dear; that's too bold a statement," said the old man, "Come home a happy victorious warrior, and a hearty welcome awaits you. To die is not the only way to serve your country. I expect to live some two or three years more, and we can meet again."

Had you followed up the thread of the old man's words until you came to the end, you would have found it change into tearfulness, but having a stout heart that becomes a man, the old gentleman kept them back. The young man said not a word, and turned aside to look towards the shore.

On the bank there stood a large willow tree. Underneath, a man in a boat was fishing with a rod and line

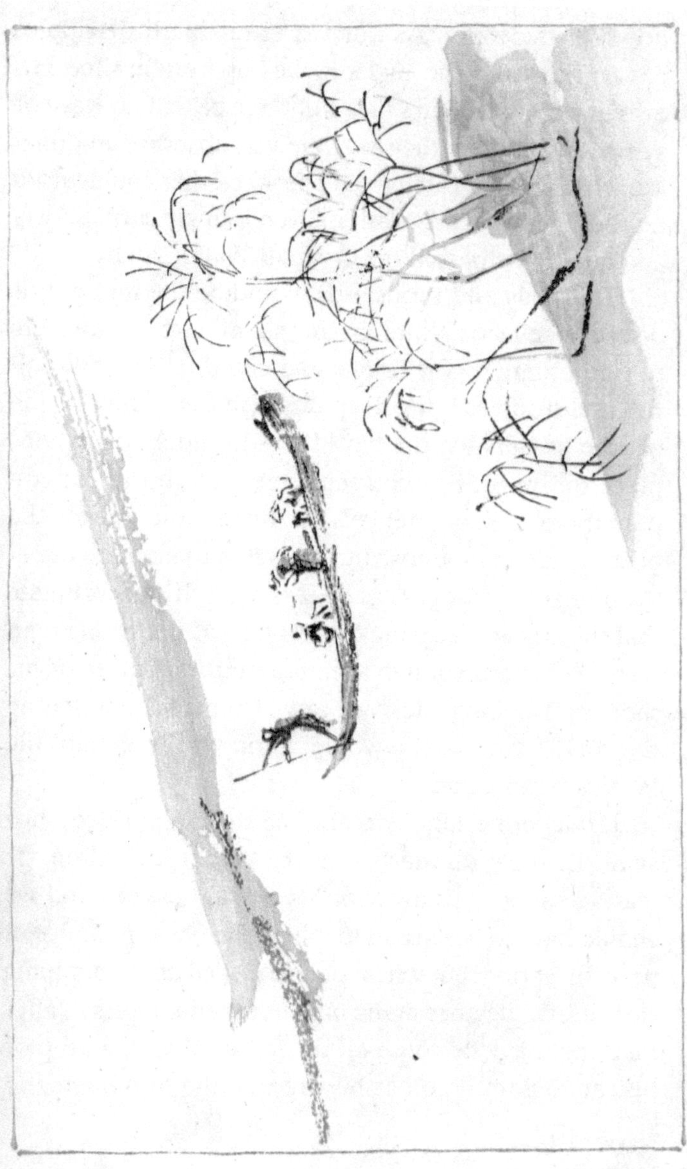

intently watching the gay cork which bobbed up and down in the water. As our vessel raising little ripples passed slowly by, the angler looked up from his line. His eyes and Kyuichi-San's met, but there passed no wave of sympathy between the two: one was absorbed in thinking what his next catch would be; the other could afford no room in his heart to admit even a single carp. Slowly and quietly we passed the Oriental Waltonian by.

Hundreds and thousands would be the number of people who cross Nihombashi in a minute. If you were to stand there by the bridge and could tell the difficulties and troubles lying deep down in the mind of each of the passers-by, the world would indeed be a hard place to live in. But you meet them as strangers: you pass them as such, hence so many candidates for the post of flag-man whose business it is to stop the car at the bridge, or let it pass as he sees right. It was fortunate that the angler on seeing the sad face of the young man was not curious enough to inquire into the cause of his sadness. Looking back, we saw him placidly watching the cork. I dare say he would go on watching until the War came to an end.

It was not a large stream; neither was it deep nor swift. Leaning on the side of the boat, I looked on the water as it bore us away on its placid bosom. And we should have to be carried to where there was no longer a peaceful spring, but where people jostled about bumping their heads together in the pursuit of gain. Destiny, after marking the poor youth on the forehead with a drop of his sanguinary blood as his prey, bound him hand and foot with his ghastly rope and was mercilessly dragging him away, away to the far gloomy North; and it was our fate, too, to be tied, before we knew, to the unfortunate youth on a certain day, a certain month, a certain year; so we had to go with him until the rope of destiny was cut. No sooner was it snapped than he must, willy-nilly, be hauled in up to the foot of the ugly deity, and those of us who were left behind should have petitioned, invoked and struggled to go with the lad all in vain.

The boat glided smoothly on. On each of the shores the horse-tail might be found growing; on the banks there stood many willows with graceful branches; low-thatched cottages with their sooty *shōji* would peep out now and then from amongst the trees. Sometimes a squadron of white ducks would come out stately from the barn-door; quack, quack, they would cry and come bravely out into the middle of the stream.

Peaches seemed to connect the willow-trees on the banks with the gay festoons of their white blossoms. The alternating sounds of the looms interwoven with the cheerful ditties of the weavers reached us coming over the stream. The melody was very pleasing, but what they were singing about was simply a confusion of sounds "*Haai, iyō-ō!*"

"Won't you please oblige me with a picture of myself, master?" says Nami-San. The young soldier and her brother are absorbed in conversation about a soldier's life; the old man has fallen asleep and is nodding.

"Yes, with pleasure," so saying, I open my portfolio and write down this,—

"O spring Breeze,
Why dost thou not untie the satin sash
And confide me with the name of the enviable weaver?"

I show it to her, and she laughs and says, —

"Sir, such an outline sketch won't do. Give me a more detailed one that delineates my character true to life, please."

"That is the very thing, Nami-San, I should most like to do, but the trouble is that your face just as it stands will make only a poor picture."

"What a compliment! Then how can I meet your requirements? Show me how, pray."

"Why, I can make a portrait right now, but there is something missing, and I shall be very sorry to paint before it comes out."

"Something wanting, you say? But it can not be helped as I was born to be homely."

"Ill-favoured as one may be, it can be altered as one wills."

"You don't mean that I can do with mine as I will?"

"That is about it."

"You men think lightly of us women and indulge in making fun at our expense."

"Suspicion, lady, is woman's characteristic trait that makes you talk in that vein."

"Then will you please oblige me by showing different aspects of your own face?"

"No day passes without showing you some; more than enough, I should think."

The woman said no more, but turned her eyes towards the banks where water came up almost to the very brink. From the boat we could easily command a view of the paddy fields all covered with milk-vetch. These fields were a veritable sea of pretty flowers whose pink half dissolved by the previous rains stretched as far as the eye could reach until at last they melted away into the trailing haze over the horizon. Far beyond, we saw a high mountain which, printing its bold outline on the spring sky, was breathing out a light purple cloud half way up.

"Don't you see that mountain? You were amongst us after you had crossed it," so saying, she leaned over the side of the boat and pointed at the dreamy height with her white hand.

"Is it about where the Fairy's Rock stands?"

"Do you see a purple spot just beneath that deep green?"

"Do you mean that shaded spot?"

"Is it a shadow, I wonder? I thought it bald."

"Why, it is hollow; it would appear gray if it were bald."

"Is that so? At any rate, the Fairy's Rock must be just behind it."

"Then we have the "Seven Turnings" a little bit on the left."

"No, sir. The pass is located far away; it is on the height over beyond that one."

"Yes, you are right; but I am not wrong in the direction; it must be where we see a light cloud hanging."

"Yes, I think the bearings are as you say."

The old gentleman who had been dozing over the side of the boat took his elbow off the side and awoke as if startled.

"Not yet, lads?"

Pushing out his chest, pulling his right elbow backward and holding out his left arm straight, the old man went through the same manoeuvre as an archer's giving a long yawn as he did so. " Ho! Ho! Ho!" came from Nami-san.

"I can not get over this habit—," said the old man.

"You seem to be very fond of archery?" I asked with a smile.

"When young," said he, "I could pull the bow almost as full as the waxing moon; even now my strength of pushing has not waned yet," so saying he patted his left shoulder. At the bow war stories were brisk and lively.

Now our boat goes threading her way into a town. Public houses with old fashioned straw curtains over their entrances come in sight, tempting thirsty souls to have a drink with alluring "Sake and Eatables" painted in a bold hand on their sash-doors (*koshi-shōji* *). We see a lumber-yard; we hear the rattling sound of *jinrikishas;* swallows are flitting and twittering with as lithe and rapid a motion as the glancing of shadows. Quack, quack go the ducks. Everything tells of the din and bustle of city life. Leaving the boat, we hasten to the station.

---

* *Koshi-shōji,* a sash door whose lower part consists of boards, the rest being pasted over with thick strong paper.

At last I find myself again amidst the busy world. Busy indeed it is with the train that goes on puffing. Nothing represents the civilization of the twentieth century so well as the railway train. It packs up hundreds of people in the same boxes and passes on with a deafening roar. There is no mercy, no shrift whatever; those poor people in there have to go at the same rate of speed calling at the same stations, and have to thank Giant Puller, Steam, for the trouble and care he has taken of them. People say they get in the train; I say they are packed in. They tell us they travel by rail, but I tell them that they are borne away by the Giant who utterly disregards their individuality. Civilization, after having helped us cultivate our personal character as much as we possibly can, tries to trample it down into annihilation. A civilized man is allotted a land of small dimensions where he is granted perfect freedom whither to lie or to rise. He is not, however, allowed to go a step out of the fence built around the assigned lot. Those who have enjoyed liberty in the enclosure naturally wish to extend their freedom to the outer world, but their wish is not to be granted, so they bite the bars of their iron cage and roar day and night to be set free. Civilization gives each man liberty and encourages him to grow as fierce and strong as a tiger, but she never hesitates to throw him in a dungeon in order to preserve the peace of the world at the top of a volcano. It is not the true peace; it is a peace like that of the zoo in which the tiger lying down on his side stares at the people who have gathered around his iron cage. Once one of the bars came off, the world would be a mass of devastation, a chaos. A second "Reign of Terror" will come upon us. The revolutionary fire has already been kindled and is burning in our individual mind with a terrible fury. Our great Norwegian dramatist Ibsen has given us many an instance of the revolution which is to come. Every time I see the train blindly rushing on carrying so many individuals as if they were human commodities, I can not help comparing those poor unfortunate souls with that iron monster vehicle which pays no attention whatever to the personality of those passengers it carries and crying out a warning, "Danger! danger! Beware!" The modern civilization is full of those forebodings and perils and the train rushing recklessly on like a wild boar is a good example of the danger signals.

While waiting at the tea-house in front of the station with my eyes on the *kusamochi**, I thus reflected on the railway train. As it was of course not to be entered in my portfolio, and I had no need of telling it to others, I sat silent sipping the tea and helping myself to the cake.

Opposite me there sat two country people both in straw sandals: one had on a red blanket, while the other was in light-green drawers with his hands on the carefully knit darns on the knees.

"Then no hope?"

"No, it is hopeless!"

"It would be nice if man had two stomachs like the cow."

---

* *Kusa-mochi,* a cake made of glutinous rice mixed with the boiled leaves of *Yomogi.*

"Yes, everybody will be glad to have two; when one goes wrong, it simply needs to be cut off."

Indigestion seemed to be troubling them. They appeared entirely ignorant of the war clouds which had burst in all their terrible fury over the land of Manchuria; in vain you would have told them of the evils of modern civilization, or of the meaning of revolution. The word itself would have been Greek to them. I dare say they did not know whether they had one or two stomachs. Taking out my hand-book, I sketched them both.

Jangle, jangle went the bell telling the people to get ready. Tickets had already been purchased.

"Let us go," said Nami-San who stood first.

"Well— ," said the old man and followed. The party, passing through the wicket, got on to the platform where the bell was lustily clanging.

With a roar, the train, a long snake of civilization, pulls into the station gliding over the shining rails, sending up black smoke from its mouth, the funnel.

"Parting at last!" says the old man.

"Fare you well, uncle," says Kyuichi and bows.

"Come home borne on the shield," says Nami-San.

"Have you seen to your things yet?" asks her brother.

The carriages halt before us. The doors open one and all. The passengers go in and out. The young man gets in. The old man, Nami-San, her brother and I stand outside on the platform.

One turn of the wheels and the young recruit is no longer a dweller in our world. He will have gone to the world far, far away where thousands and millions busy working amid the choking smell of gun-powder drop down pell-mell by losing their footing on the slippery blood. Bang! bang! goes the cannonading above their heads. Our young soldier who is going to such a place stands silent in the car never taking his eyes from us. The affinity between him who has drawn us out of the mountains and us who have been drawn out by him is going to sever, it is all but snapped; the door and the window are still open; we can still see each other face to face, and the space which lies between him and us is still six feet, yet the last moment will come only too soon.

The guard comes rushing towards us, slamming the doors one after another as he runs; each time he shuts a door the distance between the people who go and those who see them off grows greater; the door of his carriage is also closed, thus placing us in two separate worlds. The old man approaches the window and the young man puts out his face.

"Look out! Step back, please!" says the conductor, and our cruel Giant Puller begins to move: puff, puff goes the engine keeping its own good time. The doors one by one pass on. The lad's face grows smaller and smaller in the distance. The last third class carriage is about to pass us by, when another face comes out of the window.

And whose do you think it was but that hairy face of the tramp-*samurai* with an old shabby grey hat on! He put it out of the window and turned it towards us wistfully, when his eyes and Nami-San's met. Puff, puff went the locomotive, and his face soon went out of sight. Vacantly did she look after the train as it glided on, and in that vacant stare one could see overflowing 'compassion' to which she had been an absolute stranger.

"That's it; that's it, that will make your picture perfect," I said very softly as I patted her on the shoulder. The finishing touch of my mental picture was given at that very moment.

THE END.

# BUNCHŌ

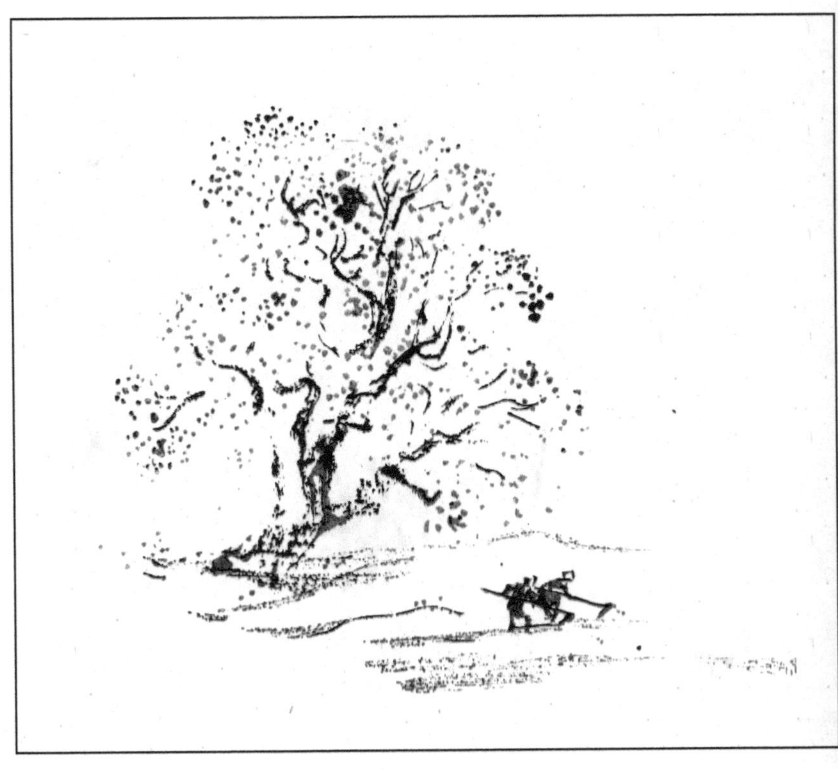

# BUNCHŌ

WE moved to Waseda in October. Alone in the study which was like a cathedral, I had been sitting, my composed face leaning upon my hand, when in came Miyekichi, who said, "Sir, don't you want a pet bird?" "Well, yes, I do, but what bird shall it be?" I asked, to make sure. A *'Bunchō'* (Java sparrow) was his answer.

The bunchō must be a pretty bird, thought I, since it often appears in the novels written by Miyekichi. "Yes, please, get me one." I said, and yet he kept insisting upon my having one, although I repeatedly told him that I would. My chin resting upon the palm of my hand made me a mumbler, and what I meant to say, it seems, made no special sense to him. Miyekichi's sudden silence first awakened me to the idea that he was disgusted at my absent-minded response.

Three minutes had hardly passed before Miyekichi asked me if I would buy a bird cage. At my affirmative answer, "Yes, I will," he, instead of ascertaining if I was in earnest, began a lecture upon bird-cages in general. His explanation was a lengthy, elaborate one, but I am sorry to say that very little of it was retained in my memory. "A good one," he went on, "will cost twenty *yen* or more." This my ear caught and made me say that mine should not be so costly. A derisive smile played on his lips.

"Where are you going to buy?" I asked. "Any bird-fancier's will do, sir," he answered. The reply was quite trite. "How about the cage?" I quickly followed. "Sure enough! the cage . . . . . . Yes, the cage . . . . . . Depend upon me, sir, it can be procured somewhere," he said. This answer of his reminded me of one who tried to seize a cloud. "Nevertheless, you must have a certain place in mind, or how could you . . . . . ." I said, and showed a dissatisfied expression on my face.

Miyekichi was a little puzzled, and putting his hand to his cheek, said that he had heard of a master bird-cage maker somewhere in Komagome, but that he might be dead, for he was said to be very old, This remark of his made me rather pessimistic.

At any rate, thinking it just right to lay responsibility upon the one who first proposes the thing, I asked Miyekichi to take the steps necessary for my keeping a pet bird. He told me then to give him some money, which I of course handed to him. I did not know where he had purchased his pocket-book; it was made of a silk cloth called *Nanako,* which he carried about everywhere he went. It was, so to speak, his breast companion, and it was his confirmed habit to put his or anybody else's money indiscriminately into that pocket-book, and I was satisfied to see him deposit there the five *yen* bill I gave to him.

Thus I handed him the money, the necessary fund to invest in my pet bird, but the bird and the cage were very slow in coming.

In the meantime, the fall had advanced to what is called the "Early winter spring" with its beautiful sunshiny days. Miyekichi's visits were very frequent, yet his talks were generally along the line of the women he was acquainted with; not a single word escaped his lips about the bunchō and his cage. He always went away leaving me in the dark. In the verandah five feet wide, we had so much sunshine coming through the glass doors. If I were to keep a pet bird at all, I thought such warm weather would be the very season in which I could take out the bird-cage into the hall where the little bird would have a sun-bath and sing a sweet song from his little throat.

According to Miyekichi's novels, the bunchō seems to sing 'chiyo,' 'chiyo.' He had taken a fancy to this note, and used it very often in his works. Maybe he had a sweet heart of the name "Chiyo." No word came from his lips about it, nor did I ask. Sunshine every day visited the verandah, and no bunchō was there to sing.

Jack Frost began to visit the roof and the garden every morning, spreading his white winding sheet wherever he went. As for me, I spent every day in my cathedral-like study with my face either calm or disturbed, either resting it on my hand or taking away the hand. The windows of the room were doubly shut. The fire in the brazier was constantly nourished with fresh charcoal. The bunchō affair had altogether left my mind.

It was towards evening one early winter day that the triumphant entry of Miyekichi startled me. It being very cold, I had been warming myself over the brazier with my breast opened to the charcoal fire. Warmer and warmer I got; still I was discontented. Miyekichi's visit brought cheerfulness with it. Hōryū came with him as companion; I felt rather sorry for Hōryū. They each brought a cage, and Miyekichi, as Hōryū's elder had a large box besides. Thus it was one early winter evening that the five *yen* bill I had given Miyekichi was turned into a bunchō, two cages, and a large box.

Miyekichi, very much elated, told me to come out and see. "Hōryū, bring that lamp nearer," he said. However triumphant he might be, the tip of his nose got a little purple with cold.

A beautiful cage it certainly was. The bottom was varnished with genuine lac. Its bamboo bars were thin, polished and dyed ; yet it cost only three *yen.* "Don't you think it cheap, Hōryū?" "Yes, very!" was Hōryū's response. I was not quite sure whether it was reasonable or not, but found that I myself had been calling it cheap. "A good one will cost twenty *yen* or more," Miyekichi said to me; and it was the second time he mentioned twenty *yen.* It was indeed incomparably cheap: three *yen* and twenty *yen* made of course a great difference.

"Sir," he said, "the exposure to the sun will turn the lac from its dark tint to light-vermilion, and the bamboo bars are perfectly safe as they have been well seasoned by a boiling process." He went on, explaining very eloquently. "How safe?" I at last asked. "Just look at the bird, is it not pretty?" he answered.

It was indeed a pretty bird. Placing the cage in the adjoining room, I looked at the feathered inmate from the distance of four feet. It did not move a jot, a mere white spot on the dark ground quite motionless. Nobody would have thought it a bird, had it not crouched itself there very lonely in the cage. It looked ghastly white and shiveringly cold.

"Don't you think he's cold?" I asked. "Yes, hence this box. At night, you'll have to put the cage into this box," he answered. "What is this other cage for?" I continued, and was told that I had sometimes to put the bird into the plainer cage and give him a cold bath. A lot of trouble, I thought, when Miyekichi added that I had also to clean off the little dung piles made by the little bird. He was very exacting in his demands for the bunchō.

In all these things I acquiesced. He then, taking out a package of Italian millet from his pocket, told me that I had to give it to the bird every morning; that even when I did not give him fresh seed I had to blow off the chaff in the seed-box, so that the bird might be spared the trouble of trying to tell a full grain from an empty one; and that a fresh supply of water must be given him every morning. "It would be a splendid cure for a late riser like yourself, sir," said he, who seemed kindness itself to the little bird. Upon my telling him that I would faithfully attend to all those duties, Hōryū, his friend, took out from his pocket seed and water cans and laid them before me carefully and ceremoniously.

Thus everything was ready for me to put to use. It would have been only justice to take good care of the bird. Something in my heart whispered to me, "Can you really do it?" However, I made up my mind to try. If I failed, I thought, somebody in the family would take care of the bird in my stead.

In the meantime, Miyekichi had carefully put the cage into the box: taken it out into the verandah, and went home, telling me that I would find the cage there in the hall. As for me, I turned in into the cold bed made in the middle of my large study. I had a dream in which the bunchō Miyekichi had bought for me played the principal part. It was rather a cold dream, yet deeper sleep made the night just as peaceful and comfortable as other nights.

Next morning when I awoke, the sun was sending in his bright rays through the glass doors. I thought I had to give food to the little bird immediately, but get up I could not, or rather would not; the bed was so warm and delightful, and such excuses as, "Wait a minute," "Pretty soon," were ready to come to my mind until at last it struck eight by the clock. Slowly and deliberately I got up. As I hurried away to the washstand, I slipt out into the cold hall barefooted, and opening the lid of the box I placed the cage in the broad rays of the morning sun. The bunchō was soon blinking his eyes in the dazzling light. I felt sorry, for he might have been brought out into the light much sooner.

The bird had black eyes; around the eyelid he had a fine stripe like a pink silk thread. As he blinked, the round thread would turn into one straight line, and again spring back round. No sooner did I take out the cage from the box than the bird with his white head inclined a little looked at me, and chirped as if to say, "Good morning, sir; I am glad to see you." He had never looked at me before.

The cage is quietly placed on the box. The bird flits and is again on the perch as quick as lightning. Two dark green pieces of wood thrown across at proper distances like bridges are his perches. The feet resting on one of the perches are very delicately shaped with pearl-like nails at the tips of slender light-crimson toes. Taking hold of the perch just right for his little feet, the bird looks like a sprite, with motion as lithe and rapid as the glancing of a shadow. The moment he turns his eyes, his position on the perch changes. Now he inclines his head to the right, now to the left, and bringing it to proper position, he bends a little to the front; lets go his white wings like a flash, and there on the middle of the opposite perch, you find him safely posted like the decentest gentleman in the feathery world. He chirps and curiously looks at you from a safe distance.

On my way back from the bath-room, where I had been for my morning toilet, I stepped into the kitchen, and taking out from the cupboard the millet package Miyekichi had bought and brought to me the night before, I put a fresh supply of seed into the seed-box and filled the can with fresh water and was out again in the verandah.

Miyekichi is a man careful and scrupulous to a fault. He did not go home the previous night until he had explained to me how food was to be given to the bird. He said that careless opening of the cage-door would mean the escape of the bird ; that I must place my left hand just beneath my right one while opening the door, and added that the same process was necessary in taking out the seed-box. He emphasized his explanation by gesture; it was, however, lack of foresight on my part not to have asked him how one could put the seed-can into the cage while both hands were thus employed at one time.

Not knowing how to do it otherwise, I pushed up the wicket of the cage with the back of my right hand, which was still holding the seed box and blocked the opening with my left hand. The bunchō cast me a glance as he turned and chirped. I was quite at a loss what to do with the hand I applied to the exit. I was rather ashamed to know that the bird was very innocent, and not so sly as to watch for a chance of unguardedness on my part. Miyekichi was a bad teacher.

My big sinewy hand went slowly into the cage. Greatly alarmed, the bunchō began to flutter his wings and struggled to keep away from the forked monster very hard and his warm downy feathers fell out of the bars like snow flakes. My big ugly hand made me feel very bad.

No sooner had I safely deposited the seed and water cans between the perches than I withdrew my monster hand. The door of the cage shut with a click. The bird returned to his seat on the perch, where turning his white neck on one side, he looked at me as I stood outside of his cage. Then stretching his neck straight, he gave a glance at the seed and water placed at his feet. I left him there alone and went into the dining-room to have my breakfast.

At the time I am describing, I was writing a novel as my daily task. The time between meals was usually taken up in writing at the desk. When quiet, I could hear the sound of my pen driving over the paper. It was understood that nobody should venture into my cathedral-like study when I was at work. There were, however, mornings, afternoons, and evenings when the loneliness caused by the monotonous sound of my own pen made me feel very sad. Sometimes the sound would cease all of a sudden, or very often it was that I had to stop writing altogether. Then resting the chin on the palm of my hand still holding the pen between the fingers, I would look out through the glass-doors into the yard laid waste by wintry blasts. Getting tired of this, I would give my chin a squeeze. If this magical process failed to bring about the necessary stimulus to inspire me to write something on the paper, I would try to draw out my chin with my thumb and forefinger. It was on one of these occasions that the bunchō in the verandah chirped twice 'chiyo', 'chiyo'!

Laying the pen on the desk, I went quietly out into the hall. There the bird with his white breast so thrust out as all but to fall down from his perch chirped aloud 'chiyo' as he looked at me. Miyekichi would have been very much pleased to hear such a sweet note. He had gone home assuring me that the bird would certainly chirp and sing as he got tame.

Stealthily did I approach and crouch again near the cage. The bunchō changed the position of his plump neck twice or thrice, once to one side, then to the other. Flash went the white lump off the perch; pretty toe-nails were half seen on the brink of the seed-box; so tiny a box that a touch of your small finger would turn it over was perfectly safe and quiet as a temple bell. Nothing indeed could be lighter than the bird. I almost wondered if he was not the spirit of light snow.

Down came the bill of the bird into the midst of the seed-can. He shook his bill right and left, twice or thrice. The millet filled to the edge of the box fell by ones and twos to the bottom of the cage. Up came his bill; a faint sound was audible in his little throat. Down his bill went again into the seed-box; again a faint sound was heard. It was such a tiny magical sound. Quietly listen, and you would hear perfect music coming out of his little throat; it was so harmonious, now quick, now slow. A man as tiny as a violet would produce such a melody if he played scales on an agate *go*-stone with a gold hammer.

The colour of his bill was rouge tinged with a little purple. The rouge thinned into creamy white as it ran down towards the tip of the bill with which the bird picked up the seed. The white was that of an elephant's tusk half transparent. The movement of his bill was very quick when it darted into the seed, and the gems of millet looked very light as they were scattered right and left. The bunchō, bending his lithe body as if he were going to turn a somersault, thrust his sharp bill into the yellow grains and shook his swollen throat so mercilessly hard that nobody could tell how many grains fell off from his little mouth. Yet the seed-box stood undisturbed, as firm and quiet as a mountain. And one and a half inches was the diameter of the box.

Quietly getting back to my study, I was lonesomely driving my pen over the paper. Out in the verandah, the banchō gave his usual chirps; often he sang 'chiyo' 'chiyo'. A wintry blast was raging without.

One day towards evening, I saw him drink water. Taking hold of the edge of the watercan with his slender little feet, he would dip his tiny bill into the can, and with his head upturned a little, he would swallow a precious drop down his little throat. I returned to my study thinking that a can of water would be enough for him at least for ten days if such a little quantity was needed each time. In the evening I put the cage into the box. On going to bed, I looked out through the glass-window. The moon was shining bright and the frost was white on the roof. The bird's box was as quiet and still as death.

I was not a bit kinder to the banchō the following morning than the morning before, for it was past eight when I rose and took out his cage from the box. The bird must have been wide awake long before, yet he did not show even the slightest sign of displeasure at the ill-treatment he received at my hands. No sooner had he been brought out into the broad daylight than he winked his eyes, shrugged his shoulders a little and innocently looked at me.

Long ago, I had known a beautiful young woman, who one day, absorbed in meditation, was leaning on her desk. Stealthily approaching her from behind, I took hold of the end of her purple sash-holder, pulling it up and letting it down, down to her slender neck I gave her a tickling sensation. She indolently looked back, and knit her eyebrows a little. Still there lurked a charming smile both in the corners of her eyes and on her rosy lips. She buried her pretty neck deep down in her sloping shoulders. The bird's glance at me called up in my mind the memory of this young maiden. She is now a married woman. It was two or three days after she had been engaged that I played the trick upon her.

The seed box was pretty full, but there was much chaff. The husks were floating all over the surface of water in the can. The water was soiled and dirty. A fresh supply of seed and water was badly needed. Again my big hand crept into the cage. Although I did this very gently and cautiously, the bunchō was very much terrified and flew about, wildly fluttering his white wings. I felt very sorry for the bird even when a single tiny feather came off from his body. The husks were carefully blown off. The wintry gust took them up on its wing and carried them away I knew not where. The bird was also given fresh water, which, being city-water, was extremely cold.

I spent all that day in hearing the lonely sound of my pen going. At intervals *chiyo, chiyo,* was heard out in the verandah. Perhaps the bird might be chirping his plaintive notes out of loneliness, too. I went out into the hall and there I found him flitting to and fro between the two perches. His movement in the cage was too incessant to let discontent creep into his little heart. He looked very happy.

Night came, and I put the cage into the box. Awaking next morning, I saw the frost was sharp without. The bird might have awaked long ago; I was still in bed. I felt too lazy to put out my hand even to reach the papers at my pillow side. Yet I was smoking away at a cigarette. This done, thought I, I would get up and take out the poor bird from the box. I had been intently watching the direction the smoke was going, when I noticed in the midst of the smoke the face of the young maiden who, once shrugging her shoulders almost indiscernibly, knit her eyebrows with a smile in her tender eyes. I sprang out of bed, sat on it, put on my *haori* over my night-gown, went out into the verandah, opened the box and took the bird out into the light of day. The bunchō chirped twice as he was coming out.

According to Miyekichi, a bunchō, if well treated, will get so tame as to give a chirp at seeing you. His pet bird would sing *chiyo, chiyo,* every time he came near its cage. Moreover, the bird would pick food from his finger tips. I wished my bird had been as tame as to take food from my hand.

The next morning I again was lazy. No vision of the maiden haunted me that morning. It was not until after I had finished my morning toilet and taken my breakfast that, a little alarmed, I ran out into the verandah. The cage was already on the box. The bunchō was merrily flitting to and fro between the perches. Often he would stretch out his neck and look out of the bars with his head a little upturned. He looked very innocent. The young woman upon whom I once played a trick with her sash-holder was the owner of a graceful figure with a beautiful neck. She had also a habit of looking at you with her head slightly turned to one side. Plenty of seed was still in the seed-box; enough water was in the water-can; the bird looked quite contented. I retired into my study greatly satisfied.

In the afternoon, I went again out into the verandah; I had intended to read a book while walking up and down the corridor five or six feet long. It was my regular exercise after meals. To my surprise, however, seven-tenths of the seed was already gone and the water much soiled. The book was thrown aside in the passage, and soon the bird was having a fresh supply of seed and water.

The following day again found me a late riser. I did not go out into the verandah until I had washed my face and had my morning meal. When back in my study, I just peeped out into the corridor to see if the cage had already been out as it was the day before, and was pleased to see it there nice and clean with a fresh supply of seed and water. Greatly satisfied, I was going back into my study, when the bunchō gave two chirps in succession. Again I peeped, but this time the bird was silent. He was wonderingly looking at the heavy frost out in the yard through the glass-door. At last I was back and sat at my desk.

As usual, a rustling sound from my pen was audible in my study. The novel I had been writing made good progress, and my finger tips were cold. The *Sakura*-charcoal I had in the morning banked up carefully in the Chinese brazier was already white ashes, and the iron kettle on the *Satsuma* trivet had long before ceased to sing. The basket was empty; I clapped, but nobody in the kitchen responded. I stood up, opened the door, and there I found the bunchō motionless like a statue on the perch. It was unusual. Closer observation revealed to me that he had only one leg. Setting down the charcoal basket in the passage, I stooped and looked closely into the cage. Still he had only one leg. Calmly resting his whole body upon one leg so delicately formed, the bird stood perfectly still in the cage. No chirp! No song!

I thought it strange. Miyekichi who had given me so detailed an account about the bunchō seemed to have left out this important fact. Returning with the basket refilled with charcoal, I looked again and found him still standing on one leg. I stood on the cold verandah and watched the bird pretty long, but he would not stir a bit. Silently and quietly did I stand and watch until his round eyes dwindled into two slender lines. Thinking that he must be sleepy, I was about to enter my study. Hardly had I taken a step before he opened his eyes, and with it came the missing leg out of his snow white breast. I closed the door and fed the fire in the brazier with more coal.

Busier and busier I got with the novel I was working at. Morning after morning I rose late. Ever since somebody in the family had taken care of the bird, I began to feel my responsibility towards the bird much alleviated. When he was forgotten by my family, I myself took care of the bird. I gave him seed and water, put his cage into and out of the box. When busy, I called in my folks and he was properly attended to. Thus I became step by step a mere idle listener to his sweet melody.

However, every time I was out in the verandah I would pause before the cage and watch the bird. The narrow limits of his cage did not seem to cause him any discomfort; the little room between the two perches was his domain in which he could get about as freely as he wished, unmolested, undisturbed. On a fine day, the bird, bathing in the sun which came through the glass, would sing and chirp as though he would burst his little throat. But he did not seem to specially entertain me with his sweet songs at seeing my face. Miyekichi had told me that he would.

Nor would he take grain from my hand. When he was in a happy mood, I sometimes put in my forefinger with some bread crumbs on its tip from between the bars, but the bird turned away from it. A bolder attempt, and he, terrified at my big ugly finger, would fly about the cage wildly flapping his white wings. After several attempts, I was sorry for the bird and made up my mind to stop the trick. It is doubtful if anybody in the world we now live in could do this. A St. Francis [or a Hiawatha] might do it. Miyekichi was not so conscientiously true when he told me.

One day, as I was as usual driving my pen over the paper writing something sad and melancholy, my ear caught a certain strange sound; it was a soft rustling sound coming from the verandah. A woman, thought I, might be approaching me, her long skirt trailing behind; yet the rustling it made was of no ordinary kind of an ordinary woman. It came so distinctly and constantly. A doll-queen, moving with her long crimson deep-folded skirt sweeping over the dolls' platform, might make such a delicate sound. The analogy would be very appropriate. Putting aside the novel I had been working at, pen in hand, I went out to the corridor to see where the sound came from. The bunchō was having a bath.

The water in the can was just full and fresh. Putting his light feet into the water right up to his downy breast, the bird often spread his white wings right and left. Stooping a little, he would press his little breast to the bosom of the water and give a thorough shake to his whole body. Now he comes up to the edge of the can; then down he goes again with a splash. The can was one and a half inches in diameter. He plunged into the can, but his head, tail and back were all out of the water. His feet and breast were the only parts he could bathe, yet the bird was happy and contented.

The plainer cage was brought out and soon the bird was in it. I went to the bath room and fetching water in the watering pot, I gave him a shower bath. Hardly had the water in the pot been all poured out before many precious gems of watery hue were rolling down from his white wings. The bird's eyes went winking on perfectly contented.

Years ago, the woman upon whom I had played a trick with her purple sash-holder was busy sewing in the parlour. I amused myself by throwing the rays of the spring sun on her face from upstairs by means of a pocket-mirror. She lifted her cheeks a little reddened, and shading her forehead with her plump hand winked and blinked, not knowing what else to do. The bird and the maiden must have been in the same frame of mind.

As the days went by, the bird sang better and oftener. Oftener was he forgotten, though. Sometimes his seed-box was full of husks; often the bottom of his cage was dirty with dung piles. One night, getting home very late after attending a dinner party, I found that the winter moon was pouring in her rays through the windows and the broad verandah was faintly lighted. In the dim light, the bird's cage stood alone and solitary on the box. The silhouette cast by the bird on a perch in the corner of the cage was so unsubstantial that it looked just like a fairy. Turning up the cape of my cloak I immediately put away the cage in the box.

The following day, the bunchō gave us lively music as usual. However, the first neglect led to a second. He was often forgotten at night, and it was not seldom that his cage was left alone on the box in the cold night air. One night I was busy writing, the rustling sound from my pen only disturbing the stillness around, when my attentive ear caught a sound out in the corridor; something had tumbled down; still I did not spring upon my feet. I just kept on writing the novel which needed prompt completion. You start out greatly alarmed and are often disgusted at finding there is nothing serious, and it is a very annoying experience, you know. Not but that my mind was not disturbed by that sound out in the verandah, but I gave it a deaf ear and sat on. It was past twelve o'clock that I went to bed that night. Going out to wash my hands, out of uneasiness I looked into the hall to see if every thing was right there. Behold! the cage was down from the box; it lay on its side. The seed box and the water can were upside down. The seed covered the corridor all over; the perches were off and the poor bunchō was holding the bars with all his little might. I made up my mind with an oath that the cat should never come into the verandah again.

Next morning the benchō did not sing. The seed-box was full to the brim; the water can was sparkling with fresh water, but the bird did not get about. He stood long on one leg, perfectly still on his perch. After the noon meal I sat at my desk thinking that I should write to Miyekichi. Three lines had not been finished before the benchō chirped twice. I stopped my pen. The bird again gave two notes. On coming out, I was very much pleased to find that the bird had been helping himself to the seed and water. The letter to Miyekichi was discontinued and went to the waste-paper basket in pieces.

In the morning the bird was again silent. He was not on the perch; he was down with his breast pressed on the bottom of his cage. His breast appeared a little swollen and the downy feathers slightly disturbed like ripples. In the letter from Miyekichi that morning, I was requested to meet him at a certain place on "*that affair.*" As I was to be there by ten o'clock, I set out from home without taking care of the bird. Meeting Miyekichi, I found that the business could not be settled satisfactorily in a short time. We took our luncheon together; we were again together at supper. I was not able to come home until the following day's meeting had all been arranged. It was about nine when I got home that night. The bird had altogether been out of my mind. I was very tired, went to bed and slept soundly till morning.

No sooner had I waked next morning than "*that affair*" came to my mind. "The maiden in question might contentedly go as bride to that family, but her future would be blighted if she married that young man," I reasoned to myself. "The girl yet very young might think she should marry any fellow she was told to, but would it be just for her guardians to let her commit such an irretrievable mistake? Once married, it would be very hard to get free. Alas! So many in the world contentedly go to ruin and misery!" Thus musing, I finished my toilet, breakfasted and went out to settle "*that business.*"

It was not till three in the afternoon that I returned home. Putting my cloak on the peg in the entrance, I was hurrying to my study through the passage-way and naturally went out into the verandah. There the cage stood on the box, but the bird lay dead at the bottom of it. His stiff legs now set orderly together were stretched at a right angle with his body. I stood still by the cage and gave a steady glance at the poor bird, whose pale eyelids hid the eyes closed in everlasting sleep.

The box was full of husks and little seed in it. The poor bird had no grains to pick. The water can was so dried up that its bottom shone in the light. The sinking sun coming through the glass cast his sombre rays aslant upon the cage. The lac on the bottom of the cage had already begun to turn, as Miyekichi had said, from its dark hue into vermilion.

I looked at the bottom by the light of the winter sun. I looked at the seed box which stood lonely. I looked at the two perches thrown across like bridges with no passengers. I gazed long and steadily at my poor pet bird, now stiff and motionless. I stooped, held the cage with both hands and carried it into my study. I set it down in the middle of the ten mat room. Reverentially sitting before the cage, I opened the door, put in my big hand and touched the bird. Warmth had already gone from his little body.

Withdrawing my hand from the cage, I opened it. There he lay quietly on the palm of my hand. I gazed long at the poor bird which lay dead in my open hand. Slowly and sadly I laid him down on my cushion. Hard clapping of my hands followed.

A sixteen year old maid appeared at the door, asking me what she should do. Her hands were respectfully put together at the door sill. The bird on the cushion was immediately shot at her like a bullet. The maid hung her head and remained silent. I told her that the bird was dead as she had forgotten to take care of him. I stared hard into her face, but she returned not a word.

I turned and sat again at my desk. I wrote a card to Miyekichi, which ran as follows:

> "Dear Miyekichi,
> They forgot to give the bunchō food and he is dead. Putting one into a cage without his consent, they failed to perform a simple duty as to care. Don't you think it cruel?"

I told the maid to take and post the card immediately, adding that she might also take away the bird. She asked me where she should take it. I swore at her that she might take it away anywhere she pleased. The terrified maid carried it away to the kitchen.

In a little while, the children in the back yard were clamouring that they were going to bury the bunchō. They seemed to be very much excited. The gardener who was at work in the garden was asking, "My dear miss, won't this place do?" As for me, I remained in my study writing. But the writing made very little progress.

Next morning I had a slight headache and did not get up till ten. While in the lavatory, I looked out into the back yard. My eye rested upon a small piece of wood set up at a place about where the gardener was the day before. The board stood beside a Dutch rush bush. It was much smaller than the bush. Putting on my garden clogs, I approached the spot where the board stood, my clogs printing their soles on the hoar frost in the shade. On the board were found these words,

> Here does the bunchō lie,
> Our dear pet birdie.

with a note below, "Don't step on the mound!" The writing was that of Fude-ko, my eldest girl.

In the afternoon, an answer was received from Miyekichi, in which he simply said that he was sorry for the bird, but he found no fault whatever with my family.

THE END.

# About the Text

This publication reprints the English texts of *Kusamakura* and "Bunchō" from the 1927 Tokyo edition published by Iwanami-Shoten, translated with a preface and introductory essay by Umeji Sasaki. That work is now in the public domain.

The spelling and punctuation of that edition have been preserved. The inconsistent uses of accented "ō" and "ū" have not been regularized. The following emendations, listed by page and line number, have been made. Those marked with an asterisk (*) were listed in the Errata to the original 1927 edition.

| | From | | To |
|---|---|---|---|
| 33.19 | on | > | an |
| 35.15 | kōsen | > | Kōsen |
| 42.13 | assertain | > | ascertain |
| 44.28* | *swake* | > | *awake* |
| 62.17 | colletced | > | collected |
| 69.10* | pretenstion | > | pretension |
| 71.20 | helpless.' | > | helpless." |
| 74.20 | Jove!" | > | Jove! |
| 75.15 | know," | > | know." |
| 79.17 | way; | > | way'; |
| 89.6* | lighting | > | lightning |
| 89.8 | your | > | you |
| 102.23 | *tsubō* | > | *tsubō*. |
| 107.14 | sinceriy | > | sincerity |
| 107.30 | *geisha* | > | *geisha*. |
| 108.25* | as | > | at |
| 112.25-26 | embarrassed," I | > | embarrassed, "I |
| 115.14-15 | call?" "No, | > | call?" ¶"No, |
| 115.18-19 | host?" "No, | > | host?" ¶"No, |
| 119.23 | Wa! | > | "Wa! |

| | From | | To |
|---|---|---|---|
| 121.29-30 | host?" "Well | > | Host?" ¶"Well, |
| 125.26* | dont | > | don't |
| 128.28* | babble | > | bubble |
| 129.4 | you. | > | you." |
| 129.17* | trynig | > | trying |
| 132.1 | enchantless | > | enchantress |
| 132.29 | kyūichi-San | > | Kyūichi-San |
| 135.29* | orchid | > | orchids |
| 137.25* | two | > | too |
| 139.5 | excutioner's | > | executioner's |
| 140.17 | Laocon | > | Laocoon |
| 156.1* | that | > | and |
| 162.27 | "Ryōnen, | > | "Ryōnen," |
| 162.28 | our | > | "our |
| 168.25 | puttting | > | putting |
| 171.3* | glassy | > | glassy |
| 173.13* | very | > | so |
| 173.19* | night. | > | night, |
| 173.27* | years | > | years' |
| 174.12 | nightingle | > | nightingale |
| 190.17 | lively | > | lively. |

# Notes

iii KUSAMAKURA ] 草枕 is literally "Grass Pillow", a Japanese expression for a journey or being "on the road."

iii UMEJI SASAKI ] (1873–1929) was a teacher and translator in Japan.

iii HIRAFUKU HYAKUSUI ] (1877–1933) Japanese artist and illustrator

v Zōshigaya cemetery ] In Tokyo, established in 1874.

vi E. W. Clement ] Ernest Wilson Clement (1860–1941) wrote *A Handbook of Modern Japan* (Chicago, 1903), *A Short History of Japan* (Chicago, 1915), and other works.

xiii Kaizō ] A general interest magazine, published 1919-1955

xiv Dr. Nitobe ... Bushidō ] Nitobe Inazō (1862–1933), *Bushido: The Soul of Japan* (New York, 1899)

xx *Bungakuhakase* ] Doctor of Literature

7 *natane* ] *Brassica napus,* known in English as rapeseed or canola.

11 Chrysanthemums ... Nan-Shan ] From Chinese poet Tao Yuan Ming (356–427), in "Drinking Wine" 喝酒 .

12 Alone I sit ... nightly visit.] From Chinese poet Wang-wei (699–761), "Lodge in the Bamboo" (Zhú Lǐ Guǎn 竹里館),

12 "Hototogisu" ] Novel by Kenjirō Tokutomi, serialized 1898–1899, and a best-seller book in 1900; known in English as *Nami-Ko* or *The Cuckoo.*

12 "Konjikiyasha ] Novel by Ozaki Kōyō, serialized in 1897; known in English as *The Golden Demon*.

12 "Grotto of Peaches" ] From a fable written by Tao Yuanming in 421 CE about a hidden land whose people live in harmony with nature, unknown and unaware of the outside world.

14 "Seven Cavaliers' Flight" ] *Shichiki ochi* 七騎落, a traditional Noh drama.

14 "River Sumida" ] *Sumidagawa*, Noh drama by Kanze Motomasa (1394?–1432).

17 'Change ] The stock exchange or financial market.

18 shōji ] A room divider made of translucent material on a lattice frame.

18 one *sho* dry measure ] Roughly equivalent to half a U.S. gallon, or 1.8 liters.

19 "Takasago" ... Hōshō ] *Takasago* is a classic Noh drama about an elderly couple who maintain their relationship despite distance; Hōshō is one of the five schools of Noh performance.

20 *tatami* ] Soft mats used as flooring, normally 3 feet by 6 feet.

22 Rosetsu ] Nagasawa Rosetsu (1754–1799)

24 "Less than a ri ... twenty-eight chō ] One ri is approximately 2.5 miles or 4 kilometers; there are 36 chō in 1 ri.

24 The War ] The Russo-Japanese War 1904–1905

27 *shimadamage* ] A traditional formal hairstyle for women, gathered in a bun at the crown of the head with a small portion pointing outward.

28 Ophelia's face painted by Millais ] John Everett Millais's painting "Ophelia" (1851–1852) depicts the drowned Ophelia from Shakespeare's *Hamlet*.

32 ten *sen* ] One-tenth of a yen.

33 about six mats in size ] Tatami mats were normally 3 feet by 6 feet, so the room would have measured 9 × 12 feet.

35 "London Charivari." ] *Punch, or The London Charivari* was a British humor magazine.

35 Kōsen of the Ōbaku sect ] Renowned calligrapher Kosen Shoton (1633-95; Chinese name, Gaoquan Xingdun) was a Zen Buddhist monk who emigrated from China to Japan. Ōbaku was one of the Japanese schools of Zen Buddhism

35 Ingen, Sokuhi and Mokuan ] Ingen Ryūki (1592–1673), Sokuhi Nyoitsu (1616–1671), and Mokuan Shōtō (1611–1684) were Chinese Zen Buddhist monks and calligraphers who emigrated to Japan and were known as the "Three Brushes of Ōbaku."

35 Jyakuchū ] Itō Jakuchū (1716–1800), famous painter of the Edo period.

36 Mukōjima ] Area along the Sumida River in Tokyo.

36 Tai-hui ] Ta-hui Tsung-kao or Dahui Zonggao (大慧宗杲) (1089-1163) was a Chinese monk belonging to the Lin-chi school of Zen Buddhism.

39 aronia ] *Aronia melanocarpa*, also known as Black Chokeberry, has clusters of showy white flowers.

41 the beam in your eyes ] Matthew 7:3—"And why behold thou the mote that is in thy brother's eye, but consider not the beam that is in thine own eye?"

41 the railway train ... Turner painted ] "Rain, Steam and Speed—The Great Western Railway" (1844) by J.M.W. Turner (1775–1851).

41 Ōkyo ] Maruyama Ōkyo (1733–1795) painted the ghost of his deceased lover, the geisha Oyuki, who appeared to him in a dream.

# Notes

41–42 Salvator Rosa ] 1615–1673; Italian Baroque painter.

45 Morpheus ] Greek god of dreams.

48 Unkei ] c. 1150–1223; Japanese sculptor of the Kei School

48 Hokusai ] Katsushika Hokusai, 1760–1849; painter and printmaker

50 *yūzen* crape ] A type of Japanese crepe fabric with colorful traditional patterns used in kimono and other garments.

50 Orategama by Hakuin ] *The Embossed Tea Kettle*, a letter collection, by Hakuin Ekaku (1686–1769), an influential teacher in Zen Buddhism.

50 Isemonogatari ] *The Tales of Ise,* a collection of poems and narratives dating from the Heian era (9th to 12th century)

54 *karakami* ] sliding door made of decorative paper

55 brake-sprouts ] *warabi,* the bracken fern; *Pteridium aquilinum.*

56 *suimono, kuchitori* and *sashimi* ] Suimono is a clear soup with tofu and vegetables; kuchitori are colorful appetizers; sashimi is raw fish or meat with decorative presentation.

57 *shamisen* ] A three-stringed traditional Japanese musical instrument.

58 Kannon (Goddess of mercy) ] In Japanese Buddhism.

59 Sadder than ... from my sight. ] From George Meredith, "The Story of Bhanavar the Beautiful" in *The Shaving of Shagpat* (1856)

60 celadon ] Pottery glazed with a pale jade green color

61 *yōkan* ] Jellied dessert made from azuki bean paste, sugar, and agar-agar.

62 the barracks in Azabu ] District in Tokyo where the Imperial Army was stationed.

63 Rikyū ] Sen no Rikyū (1522–1591), Japanese tea master, influential in aspects of the tea ceremony.

67 Yedoite ] Yedo, or Edo, was re-named Tokyo in 1868.

69 God of Good Fortune ] Fukurokuju, who is usually portrayed as bald with an elongated forehead.

69 Anglo-Japanese Alliance ] Military pact signed in 1902 between the Empire of Japan and the United Kingdom with the main object of opposing Russian expansion. It remained in force until 1924.

80 bonzes ] Buddhist priests

84 sedgehat ] *Sugegasa*, a type of conical hat traditionally made from sedge grass.

84 Saul near the Damascus gate ] In Acts, chapter 9

85 Elysium ] Afterlife realm of the blessed, heroic, and fortunate in Greek mythology.

85 "Peach Grotto" ] See note to page 12.

88 Wen-yu-ke ] Wen Tong 文同, courtesy name Yuke, (1019–1079), artist of ink bamboo painting.

88 Sesshyū ] Sesshū Tōyō (雪舟 等楊; 1420–1506), Zen monk and master of Japanese ink painting.

88 Buson ] Yosa Buson (1716–1784) Japanese poet and painter.

88 Ike Taiga ] Ike no Taiga (池大雅; 1723–1776), Japanese painter and calligrapher.

89 the "pillar of cloud" ] That guided the Israelites in the wilderness, Exodus 13:21.

90 Lessing ] German philosopher and art critic Gotthold Ephraim Lessing (1729–1781). His *Laokoön oder Über die Grenzen der Malerei und Poesie* (1767)—"Laocoön: or the Limits of Poetry and Painting"—was published in English translations by William Ross (London, 1836), Ellen Frothingham (Boston, 1904), and Sir Robert Phillimore (London, 1905).

94 *furisode* ] Literally "swinging sleeves," a style of kimono distinguishable by its long sleeves; formerly worn only by unmarried women.

95 *obi* ] Belt or sash worn around the waist of the kimono.

95 Pluto's nocturnal palace ] Pluto was ruler of the Underworld in Greek mythology.

96 "Namuamudah" ] "Homage to Amida Buddha"

97 *tsubo* ] The area of two tatami mats, side-by-side, forming a square of roughly six feet; four tsubo would be 12 feet by 12 feet.

98 Pe-le-tien's ] Possibly Pei Di (b. 714), Tang-era poet.

100 Swinburne ] Charles Algernon Swinburne (1837–1909), perhaps referring to the poem "The Triumph of Time" (1866).

104 *Kanjinchō* ] 勧進帳, "The Subscription List" is a kabuki dance-drama by Namiki Gohei III, based on the Noh play Ataka.

107 catalogue annually issued by the Salon ] The *Catalogue Illustré du Salon* contained listings of the annual art exhibition administered by the Société des Artistes Français in Paris.

108 fig leaves ... apron ] In Genesis 3:7.

109 bushy tail of the Sacred Tortoise ] The minogame or mythical turtle is conventionally depicted with a long wide hairy tail.

113 Mokubei ] Aoki Mokubei (1767-1833) was a renowned Japanese potter and painter.

113 *gyokuro* ] Literally "jade dew," a type of shade-grown green tea from Japan.

116 Ink-slab ] An inkstone

116 Sanyō ] Rai San'yō (1780–1832), Confucianist philosopher, historian, artist and poet of the later Edo period.

116 Tankei ] 1173–1256, sculptor of the Kei school; son of Unkei.

117 Sorai's autographs ] Ogyū Sorai (1666-1728), Confucian scholar, philosopher, and calligrapher in the cursive script style (sōsho) during the Edo period.

118 Kyōho period ] 1716–1736

118 Kōtaku ] Hosoi Kōtaku (1658–1736), Confucian scholar, calligrapher and seal carver in early Edo period Japan.

121 *yōkan* ] See note to p. 61.

123 Taira family ] Clan of imperial descendants founded in Heian period (8th century); opposed and defeated by the Minamoto clan in the Heiji Rebellion (1160).

132 'The bamboo-shadow sweepeth the steps ; no dirt ariseth.' ] A traditional Zen koan, or verse for meditation; sometimes attributed to Kyōgen Chikan (Xiangyan Zhixian), c. 820–898; included in the *Kaian Kokugo* of Hakuin Ekaku (1686–1769). The second part is: "Moonlight penetrates the depths of the pool, But no trace is left in the water."

135 Iwasakis or Mitsuis ] Iwasaki Yatarō (1835–1885), Japanesee industrialist, founder of Mitsubishi; and Mitsui Takatoshi (1622–1694), founder of the Mitsui family, the richest in Japan.

135 Lucius, a Lucullus, a Sempronius ... Timon's ] In William Shakespeare's *Timon of Athens,* Lucius, Lucullus, and Sempronius are Timon's friends whom he has entertained generously and lavishly, accumulating large debts. When Timon seeks their help, they refuse, leaving him embittered and misanthropic.

136 arundo ] Genus of tall hardy grasses.

139 Siren ] In Greek mythology, human-like females with alluring voices that tempt men to destruction.

153 Iwasa Matabei ] (1578–1650), painter, illustrator, and printmaker

154 Jonah's gourd ] In Jonah, chapter 4.

154 Chao-pu-chi ] Chao Buzhi (1053-1110), Chinese poet known for a specific type of lyric poetry called "Ci".

159 *hakase* ] Doctorate

161 Nihombashi ] central district in Tokyo

161 to cast the mote out of my eye ] See note to page 41.

163 Christ ... Oscar Wilde ] In "De Profundis," a letter Wilde (1854–1900) wrote in 1897 during his imprisonment in Reading Gaol; it was published in part in 1905 by journalist Robert Ross.

164 wind ... listeth ] John 3:8, "The wind bloweth where it listeth."

165 Frederick Goodall ] 1822–1904, English painter who visited Egypt in 1858 and 1870.

169 Misao Fujimura ] (1886–1903) Student whose death became a national issue. He carved a suicide poem into a tree before jumping off 300-foot Kegon Falls.

182 Kanō school ] Dominant style of Japanese painting from late 15th through mid-19th centuries, founded by Kanō Masanobu (1434–1530).

186 Waltonian ] Alluding to Izaak Walton's *The Complete Angler; Or, Contemplative Man's Recreation*, first published in 1653 and often reprinted.

187 horse-tail ] *Equisetum*, a genus of vascular plants that reproduce by spores.

199 Waseda ] Residential area in northwestern Tokyo; Sōseki moved there in 1907.

199 Miyekichi ] Suzuki Miekichi (1882–1936) attended the Imperial University of Tokyo and, at Sōseki's suggestion, published *Chidori* in the magazine *Hototogisu*. He published a collection of short stories, *Chiyogami*, in 1907.

200 Komagome ] Neighborhood in north Tokyo.

208 *go*-stone ] A small game piece used in the board game Go.

211 *haori* ] Traditional jacket worn over a kimono.

212 *Sakura*-charcoal ] From cherry-blossom trees, sakura.

212 *Satsuma* trivet ] Satsuma ware is a type of Japanese pottery originally from Satsuma Province in Kyūshū.

*Some artistic works mentioned in the text are presented in the online Appendix at*

**https://digitalcommons.unl.edu/zeabook/168**

Paul Royster
Lincoln, Nebraska
July 6, 2025

## Appendix

Art or Artists mentioned in the text

- The Mountain Witch, by Nagasawa Rosetsu (1754-1799)
- Ophelia (1851-1852), by John Everett Millais (1829-1896)
- Calligraphy, by Kosen Shoton / Gaoquan Xingdun (1633-1695)
- Crane, by Itō Jakuchū (1716-1800)
- Rain, Steam and Speed—The Great Western Railway (1844), by J.M.W. Turner (1775-1851).
- The Ghost of Oyuki," by Maruyama Ōkyo (1733-1795)
- Landscape with Armed Men, by Salvator Rosa (1615-1673)
- Oliver Cromwell, by Samuel Cooper (1609-1672)
- Kongō Rikishi (1203), by Unkei and Kaikei at the Nandai-mon, Tōdai-ji temple complex, Nara, Japan
- Hokusai manga (1812)
- Bamboo, by Wen Tong (Yuke) (1019-1079). National Palace Museum, Taipei
- Winter Landscape, Sesshū Tōyō (1420-1506). Tokyo National Museum
- Fukurokuju, God of Good Fortune, by Tachibana Morikuni (1679-1748)
- Matsuo Bashō. By Yosa Buson (1716-1784)

- Landscapes in Summer and Winter, by Ike no Taiga (1723–1776). Metropolitan Museum of Art
- Urashima Taro with Minogame, by Nagayama Koen (1765-1849)
- Tea bowl, by Aoki Mokubei (1767-1833)
- Calligraphy, by Rai San'yō (1780–1832)
- Calligraphy, by Ogyū Sorai (1666-1728)
- Calligraphy, by Hosoi Kōtaku (1658–1736)
- The Finding of Moses (1885), by Frederick Goodall (1822–1904)
- Two works by Utagawa Kuniyoshi (1797–1861) depicting the creations of Iwasa Matabei (1578–1650) coming alive:
    - Iwasa Matabei in Tosa & Akamatsu Totamaru in Chikuzen (1852)
    - Miraculous Paintings by Ukiyo Matabei (1853)
- Kanō School, two hanging scrolls:
    - Zhou Maoshu Appreciating Lotuses, by Kanō Masanobu (1434–1530)
    - Spring Landscape (1672), by Kano Tan'yu (1602–1674)

These works are presented in color online at:

**https://digitalcommons.unl.edu/zeabook/168**

www.ingramcontent.com/pod-product-compliance
Lightning Source LLC
LaVergne TN
LVHW091125080826
845145LV00008B/2042